This book is for my Nana, Sheila, and Granny, Hilary.

Love you both x

# PART I

Dustin,

I'm sorry. There's no way to make you understand how sorry, so I can only hope that, in time, you will.

For weeks I've been asking myself where it all went wrong, but now I see that it was only ever going to end like this. You deserve so much better, you and Zara, and I hope you find it.

When she's old enough, I hope you'll explain things to Zara. Explain to her that I love her and this was all for the best.

I'm so sorry.

Willow

# Chapter 1

# Dustin

I read the letter again. As if reading it for the fifth time will somehow change what's written, will force the words into an order I can make sense of. But they are still the same.

The pounding in my ears is so strong that I am only vaguely aware of Zara screaming from the living room. I should go to her. Instead I lightly place the note down, smoothing it out with my fingers, reading it again.

It's a joke. A sick kind of prank. I put salt in her tea, she covered our bedroom in tinfoil, I woke her up by pouring confetti on her, it's what we do. It's our thing.

And now she's taken it to the next level – albeit an inappropriately extreme, off-the-scale level. Any moment now she's going to jump out of the cupboard, or out from under the bed. Maybe not those exact spots, because I've checked them four times already, but maybe from some secret hideaway I haven't discovered yet. Then she'll spray silly string in my face, jump into my arms and tell me, 'I got you good, D-bag.'

And I might be annoyed but only for a second because I'd have to give it to her, she really did get me good. Mostly I'll be so relieved I'll just hug her close and breathe her in and she'll laugh and say I'm such an idiot for thinking she would ever leave me. Because she would never leave me.

✦

As soon as I stepped through the front door, I knew something was wrong. Zara was screaming, and yet the flat felt weirdly still.

'Wills?'

Without taking off my shoes or coat, I dashed into the living room. There was Zara, sitting purple-faced and trembling in her playpen. She had even dropped her knitted blanket, neglecting it in her distress. She stopped screaming as soon as she saw me and I whisked her up into a hug. Where the hell was Willow? There was no way she'd leave Zara alone in the flat. She had to be here.

'Where's Mummy?' I asked. 'Is she here?'

But Zara just nuzzled into my shoulder and said nothing. She doesn't say all that much at the best of times, but she can definitely say 'Mama' and 'here', neither of which she uttered then.

'I'll be right back,' I said, kissing Zara on the forehead and setting her down. She needed changing, but she could hang on five minutes.

'Willow?'

After briefly checking all the rooms in the flat I started again, but searching properly this time. If this was some sort of joke and Willow was hiding, I'd find her. It was harsh of her to leave Zara crying like that, but then Willow takes pranks seriously. The living room: I checked under the sofa, through the coat rack, in the toy box. The kitchen: through the cupboards, in the pantry, under the table, even – though I knew it was crazy – in the fridge and the oven. After all, Willow was good.

Then our daughter's room, behind the army of soft toys in the corner, under her crib, in her wardrobe. Only as I was leaving did I glance at the mantelpiece and that's when I noticed it. The Disneyland Fund Box, the tin we've been putting coins and small notes into for months, was gone.

'Willow?' I could hear the fear in my voice.

Our bedroom: there, on our bed, was her ring. The slender silver ring, twisted into an infinity sign, that she has worn every single day for the last two years. I rustled through the drawers of the bedside tables, looked inside the wardrobe. Some of her clothes were gone. Some, but not all. Her jewellery box was gone too and all of its contents, other than that one ring on the bed. The one I gave her. Nice touch, Willow. She knew how to really make me panic.

Finally, I went to the bathroom.

Behind the door, the shower curtain, then in the cupboards, the first aid kit, the medicine cabinet. Then I saw the letter, stuck in front of the mirror. She'd often leave me notes – little Post-its whilst I was in the shower getting ready for work. But this was different. This letter wasn't the 'I love you, have a good day, D-bag', not the 'Missing you already', not the sugar sachet, stuck to the paper, with the words 'you make my life sweeter'. Not that she'd left me any of those for a while, thinking about it.

No, I could see straight away this was different. I am still staring at the letter as I now fumble in my coat pocket for my phone. Hands shaking, I call her.

Straight to voicemail.

Call again.

Straight to voicemail.

It's not even ringing.

I can feel my breath catching in the back of my throat.

It's just a joke, Dustin, there'll be some explanation. I call

Georgia. She's Willow's cousin and her best friend. If anybody knows where Willow is, she will.

She answers on the sixth ring.

'Dustin, still alive, are you?' she says coldly.

That is Georgia all over. It hasn't been *that* long since I last called. Anyway, I don't have time for this right now.

'Gee, have you seen Willow?'

There's a pause.

'What do you mean?'

'I've just got back to the flat and she's not here. Some of her stuff has gone, and Zara was on her own. And she's left me this weird note.'

I know I'm gabbling, and I can hear in my own voice how close I am to tears.

'Dustin, is this some sort of joke? Because if it is, it's not funny ...'

My heart sinks. So she hasn't seen her.

'No, I'm being serious. Fuck, Gee, do you think something has happened to her?'

Again there's silence. I can hear Georgia breathing heavily down the phone.

'I'll call you back, Dustin. I'll try and get hold of her. In the meantime, don't, don't panic, yeah?'

I hang up and wander back into the living room. Zara is no longer wailing, she's asleep. How long has she has been on her own for? How long would she have been on her own if I'd said yes to the pub with the boys after work? The thought makes me feel sick.

I look back at the note, clutched in my fists, trying to breathe through the panic pounding in my chest and to block out the words in my head.

*It's not a prank, Dustin. She's gone.*

Because that makes no sense at all.

# Chapter 2

# Dustin

'We aren't the sort of couple to argue,' I say firmly, staring at the two police officers now sitting on my sofa. 'We don't argue, we never argue, we always agree on everything, we are really happy, like, really happy.' My leg is bumping up and down, bouncing Zara as she moodily sits on my lap. 'My friends thought it was weird, actually, how happy we were, but why was it? We never found anything to argue about.'

One policeman looks from me, to his notepad, to his colleague and I know I sound like I'm protesting too much. She nods gently at him.

So far, they have tried to suggest that Willow actually wrote the letter. That she wanted to leave, that it was her decision. Yes, it was in her handwriting, but someone must have forced her to write it. That must have been it. I came to that conclusion after Georgia called back to say she couldn't get hold of Willow either. Why wouldn't she answer the phone, unless something, or *someone*, was stopping her from doing so?

And OK, there is no sign of forced entry, but maybe the front door was unlocked. Maybe Willow was just opening the door and they ran up behind her. How could they believe she actually decided to take off and leave me, leave her child?

Even though she's quiet now, I can't stop thinking about how I found Zara all alone. Her nappy full, eyes red, cheeks hot. Suddenly I realise I haven't changed the nappy yet. The last few hours have been a complete fog. After Georgia called back I tried everyone I could think of. Naomi and my other friends from the office – not that Willow was ever friends with them, as such, but they might have seen her. And then all of our New Haw friends, one by one. Nobody had heard from Willow.

I hope the policemen can't notice the smell. I hope they don't start making assumptions about my capabilities as a parent. I know they're already judging Willow, even they don't know anything about her. They don't know how happy we were, and what a good mum she was. I know it sounds clichéd, and Georgia especially would roll her eyes at hearing me say this, but for us it was love at first sight, and that feeling never went away. We were special, we still are.

'How old is Willow?'

'She's recently turned twenty. She's a year younger than me. We met in New Haw, when Willow moved down there for college.' I'm giving them more information than they strictly need, trying to fill the silences. I know they're thinking Willow is young to be a mum, I can see the judgement in their eyes. But I'm hoping that the smallest detail might be useful, might be a clue as to Willow's whereabouts.

The policewoman, who introduced herself as Nancy, looks down at Zara. They can smell her nappy, I'm sure of it. I can.

'And how old is your daughter?'

'Fifteen months ... but I don't see how that's relevant,' I reply sharply.

They're going to ask why she's such a quiet baby, aren't

they? They're going to say that's something to do with our parenting: trauma or neglect or something. People always say how quiet Zara is and how surprising it is given I rarely shut up. But she's fine, she's just taking her time. The doctor said it's fine and it is.

'We're just getting an idea of you and your family.'

'This is about Willow, you need to be looking for her,' I say a little bit too loudly. 'Why are you in here chatting to me, instead of out looking for her? She's in trouble, someone could be hurting her!'

My breathing is really shallow. Willow used to get panic attacks and I wonder now if this is how she used to feel, like no matter how hard she tried she couldn't force enough oxygen into her lungs. I feel like I'm choking on the emotion of it all. Why are we wasting time? Every second we spend here could be spent getting us closer to Willow.

'We understand that this is a horrible situation—'

'It's not a "situation". It's a ... an abduction or something!'

'Dustin, it's important you remain calm and don't jump to conclusions.'

I'm squeezing Zara so tightly, I feel her start to squirm in my grip, but I can't bring myself to let go. 'I can't. I can't ...' I try to say something useful, to make them take this seriously, but words don't come. 'I don't know what to do.'

'You don't need to do anything just now. We will report her as a missing person, but we have to let you know that as she's over eighteen and not vulnerable ...'

'But—'

'And if, once we've looked at the evidence, it seems likely she left of her own accord—'

'But she didn't!'

'*If* she did leave of her own accord ... well, there isn't a lot we can do, as she is an adult. Especially, as I said, since she doesn't have a history of mental illness and isn't a danger to herself or others.'

No. This isn't how it's supposed to go. They are supposed to help. If they knew Willow like I did, if they knew what our life was, they would never think she *wanted* to leave.

'But for now, you can help us, by giving as much detail as possible.'

I swallow, shuffling Zara closer to me. 'I want us to be looking for her,' I mumble quietly.

'This will help as well, Dustin,' Nancy says. 'Did Willow seem sad? Did she open up to you about anything at all? Was there anything out of the ordinary when you saw her before work this morning?'

I shake my head.

'And she didn't take anything with her? Apart from the clothes missing from her wardrobe and those you've described her as wearing when you left the house this morning?' She looks down at her notes. 'Black leggings, an oversized grey jumper, Adidas socks and red puma trainers?'

I nod my head, then something occurs to me. 'She must have also been wearing her necklace, I'm guessing. She didn't leave it behind, at least. She took the jewellery box she keeps it in.'

'Could you describe it?'

'She always wears it. It's a silver chain with a small angel pendant.'

Nancy notes it down.

'And . . . ' I hesitate. 'There's some money missing too.'

Both officers exchange glances, and it doesn't take a genius to work out what they are thinking. 'It was just a money box, we were saving for our trip to Disneyland. It was Willow's idea, and it was in such an obvious place,' I say quickly.

They both look at me and nod, but fail to write anything down on their notepads.

'And you're sure she doesn't have any family that she could have gone to? Not even a distant relative?' Nancy asks.

'She has a cousin, Georgia, but, like I said, I've already spoken to her and she said she hasn't seen her. Otherwise it's like I told you – it's just us.'

'Friends?'

'We're friends with all the same people. But they haven't heard anything. I've already told you this. Do you think I didn't try calling everyone I knew when I was waiting for you guys?'

'Is that how you met – mutual friends?'

Why is she asking me that? Why does that even matter? 'We met about three years ago, in a pub ...'

Thinking about that night now makes me choke up again. I look back at the two people sitting opposite me, feeling my stomach sinking further and further. I swallow. 'I ... I just want her home.'

They look at each other, before turning back towards me. Nancy's voice is gentle. 'Do you have family, Dustin?'

I nod slowly.

'Maybe it would be a good idea to stay with them tonight?'

I'm shaking my head so vigorously, I know it must look ridiculous, childish. 'No, no, I'm not in touch with my family. I haven't been back home in a long time.'

'Dustin, we believe it's best you go somewhere you aren't alone, where you can get support.'

'I've got friends here. My work friends.'

'Will they be able to help you with Zara?'

'Well ...'

I think about staying at Danny's house. Danny, who sees girl after girl and goes out drinking more nights of the week than he should. I think about being there with Zara when he gets up for work, still drunk the next day. Or Naomi's, sleeping on her tiny, lumpy sofa, Zara's crib crammed into her cramped little living room. God, no.

Besides, I can't leave our flat – what if Willow comes back? I have to stay. I think about asking one of them to stay over, to keep me sane as I pace back and forth waiting powerlessly for Willow to return. I sigh. What would they be able to do or say? It's not like they'd be able to help really.

'I need to stay here in case Willow comes back.'

I can tell by their faces they think I'm being difficult, but I don't care. If I ever had a right to be difficult, it's now.

Nancy places a hand on my arm. 'If there's anyone at all you can stay with tonight, who can give you a bit of help with Zara, we really want you to get in touch with them. Besides, Willow has your number, I'm sure she will call when she's on her way back.'

# Chapter 3

# Willow

Then – July 2017

I know I am dangerously close to a panic attack. It has been brewing for hours, and now I can feel it rising to the surface. I get up from the bed and go to the bathroom, wash my hands, then come back and sit down again. My breath is already really shallow, and I can feel my heart start to race. It's not getting better, so I go and wash my hands again – really scrubbing at them, soap under the nails – as they didn't feel clean enough the first time anyway. Just as I come back into the bedroom, my phone pings.

> OMG, me and Mum have just been chatting the whole journey home, about how many plans we have now you've moved to Surrey! So happy you're so close 😊

I stare at the text a little bit too long, before turning my phone off. Gee and her mum – Auntie Jayne – have just left. They spent the whole day unpacking boxes, moving boxes, doing whatever they could to help. Auntie Jayne even made an extra trip to Brighton and back in her car, which saved us getting a moving van. Everyone seemed in a good mood, even Gran who has been fidgety and quiet since the night she announced we were moving. And the positive atmosphere didn't seem forced either, though that was mostly down to Auntie Jayne and Georgia. Georgia is the sort of person whose good mood is infectious: bubbly, positive, impossibly outgoing in a way I can't begin to emulate. I will never understand how she can chat to people so easily, laugh with people she's only just met. Or how she can toss her hair over her shoulder in a way which seems completely natural. Somehow Georgia just does everything so naturally in life, it's like she was born to exist perfectly in this world. Whereas I constantly feel out of place, misshapen, a square peg in a round hole.

Around five o'clock, after we had finished most of the unpacking, we ordered pizza – two large ham and pineapples between us – from a takeaway Georgia recommended down the road. Gran and Auntie Jayne sat on the sofa, whilst Georgia and I were cross-legged on the floor, because the armchairs Gran ordered haven't arrived yet.

After they left, Gran and I washed up the plates in an uneasy silence. I knew she was waiting for me to say how actually it was OK here, how it would be fun having my cousin and only friend down the road, and how thinking about it I didn't miss Brighton at all. But I didn't say any of that, and she clearly didn't want to ask me outright. So after we finished I made an excuse about needing to do some more unpacking and came upstairs.

Our new home is a place called New Haw, and yes, it's OK, albeit tiny. There's a train station in the next village, technically within walking distance but still, and there are one or two pubs, a little shop, and a prettyish park. Put it this way, it's no Brighton.

Now, as I'm counting to ten to try and get my breathing under control, and barely making it to five, I scramble for my backpack, and rifle through it until I find my purse. I unzip the small pouch and take out the silver necklace concealed inside. Fumbling clumsily with the clasp at the back of my neck, I eventually manage to fasten it. I don't have a bedroom mirror yet, so I go back in the bathroom. Avoiding my own reflection, I stare at the necklace instead. It is really beautiful: a delicate pendant in the shape of an angel, attached to a thin gentle silver chain. I slowly run my thumb over it, and gradually a sense of comfort seems to seep through my skin. Finally, I feel like I'm taking in oxygen again. I run my hands under the tap, grab my backpack from the bedroom, and go into the living room.

Gran is sitting there, knitting, probably waiting for me to join her, as I usually do. She smiles at me, that smile that makes my heart swell, but still I can't bring myself to return it. 'You joining me?' she says, nodding her head towards the knitting basket. It's positioned right next to the sofa, exactly as it was in Brighton. Except this isn't Brighton.

I shake my head.

Gran has been trying so hard, I know she has, but she can't think that's going to make up for it. For the way she just announced our sudden departure from our home and all that was familiar.

'I want to go home, Gran.'

Gran sighs. 'Willow, please, not this again. You know that I wanted to be near Auntie Jayne for when she has her hip operation.'

I clench my teeth. If she wants to convince herself that's the reason we suddenly upped and left the city I've been living in for the last seventeen years, fine, but she won't be able to convince me.

'Don't lie to me, Gran.'

'Willow.' Gran's voice is calm, but stern, and I know not to push it.

But I'm angry. No, I'm furious. And I don't know what to do with this anger, because Gran and I never argue. I walk into the kitchen, grab the bottle of wine Auntie Jayne brought over from the fridge, and chuck it into my bag. When I go back into the living room, my chest is pumping, my cheeks heated. Guilt over the wine is already seeping in. 'I'm going to Georgia's, Gran.' Gran starts to stand up. 'I just need space,' I say firmly.

'But Willow—'

'I'll be home safe, but I don't want to be here right now.'

'Well, shall I call Auntie Jayne—'

'No! Just leave it for once, Gran.'

She pauses, then sits down again. 'OK,' she says quietly.

I don't say anything else. I leave the house, slamming the door. But halfway down the street, I feel my stomach sink. Gran had looked so small somehow. Because however much she screwed up, however much she doesn't understand, we both know why she insisted on leaving Brighton. She thinks she's protecting me. Shit.

I stop, get out my phone, and text her.

Love you.

I press send, and all dread has gone away. I swig from the bottle and head right, in the exact opposite direction of Georgia's house.

# Chapter 4

# Dustin

> Hi, Mum. I know this is weird, and it's been a while. But I really need to come home.

Nineteen words after two years, and I decide to do it over Facebook messenger. I would have texted her, if I hadn't deleted her number. I could have tried the home phone, which I still know off by heart, but apparently I'm too cowardly for that.

I didn't think my mum would see the message initially – we aren't even friends on Facebook. I had to find her through Alicia's page first. I was considering messaging Alicia in the first place, but I knew that would make everything weirder. It had to be Mum.

But by the time I awoke, groggy and disorientated, to Zara's cries the next morning, her message was there waiting for me.

It was brief.

> Get the next train.

I didn't tell her why, and she didn't ask. That was all that was said, and yes of course it's weird, and confusing, but the last twenty-four hours have been a lot of that.

It was Georgia who persuaded me to message Mum in the end. After the police left and I had wrestled an exhausted and over-wrought Zara into a clean nappy and pyjamas, I didn't know what to do with myself. I called Willow again. And again. I kept calling her until my battery died and as I was waiting for it to recharge, I realised I had to give up. So as soon as it flashed back to life, I called Georgia. It was so late, almost three-in-the-morning late, but Georgia answered immediately and I felt a pang of guilt. I should have thought about how worried she'd be. She's Willow's cousin, after all. Before I had even told her about the police's suggestion, she said quietly: 'You should come home, Dustin.'

She had a lot of reasons. *You'll be back in Surrey. You won't be alone. You might need them now. It will be good to come back. I won't be far away.* Usually I'd have dismissed them, but with end-less thoughts of Willow hurt going round and round in my head and my heart throbbing so hard I was fairly sure a heart attack was coming at any moment, they started to sound pretty compelling.

I was still worried about missing Willow if she came back to the flat, but in the end Naomi came to my rescue, volunteering to stay there and let me know straight away if there was any sign of Willow.

And now I'm on a train to New Haw. I'm not nervous, I don't have the brain space to be nervous. I perch Zara on the table in front of me, and she gurgles contentedly. I nabbed an empty table seat on the train and luckily no one has joined us. Maybe it's because they worry about sitting next to a baby who could start bawling at any moment – and by that I don't know if I mean me or Zara. I watch my daughter, her wide eyes looking up at me, then kiss her softly on the forehead.

Last night I lay in bed with Zara next to me, a cushion fort around her, and tried to sleep. I couldn't remember when I'd last slept without Willow. I don't know how long it took me to get to sleep, and then, almost immediately after I had just dozed, Zara started wailing and kept it up most of the night. It was already light when I fell asleep properly, and when I awoke it was to feelings of overwhelming guilt. How could I just sleep like that without knowing if my girlfriend was safe? Where she was sleeping and why wasn't it our bed?

After I read Mum's message, I tried my best with Zara: got her changed, fed her, packed a bag with nappies and wipes and clothes and her toys. I barely knew what to pack for myself, so flung some jeans and a few jumpers into a bag at random, then left with the pushchair. To the outside world I must have looked like a normal dad, taking his daughter for a walk.

I suppose I never was the most hands-on dad with Zara, because I worked, didn't I? Don't get me wrong, on weekends and evenings we'd do stuff as a three; we would have a lovely time – we would go to parks, playgroups, and I'd help out with baths and bed times. But thinking about it now, I never really knew her daily schedule – how often she needed changing, feeding, what she ate and when, and how much food was exactly the right amount. It's all a bit overwhelming, to say the least.

I trace Zara's face, running my finger softly over her soft wisps of thick curly hair, her nose, her lips. She has Willow's face. Her round brown eyes, her button nose, her rosebud lips – she's the spitting image. I just know she's going to have hair like her mother too. Lots and lots of beautiful, thick golden hair.

21

Zara's bottom lip is trembling now. 'Blankie,' she says quietly, but firmly. Shit. I hastily pull her into my lap, cradling her close to my chest like Willow always used to. I look around anxiously at the other passengers. They're all looking at me, waiting for the screaming to start. To our right there's an elderly lady, so frail she looks like she might break, with white hair. She looks sweet, kind-eyed, but she's probably also the type who would judge a young single father. Just behind her is a tall, heavily built guy, with olive skin and a thick beard whose eyes, only just visible through his salt and pepper mane, are fixed intently on me. He looks like he could be quite intimidating if he tried. Then opposite him there's a guy reading a newspaper, thick-framed glasses and freshly pressed suit. His eyes flicker nervously to Zara now and then.

'Blankie,' she says again. And then she screams. Her whimpers have become full tears. I pull her in closer to my chest and stand up.

'Sssh,' I soothe, 'let's find your blankie, shall we? That always helps, doesn't it?'

Shit. Shit. Where is it? Where's her blanket?

I am rummaging through the bag I brought for her, emptying everything onto the seat of the train, but I can't find it. I can't find Zara's blanket. I am filled with dread as the reality sinks in. I've left it at home. The home I can't bring myself to go back to without Willow there.

'I know, Zara,' I whisper, sighing as I stroke her hair. 'I miss her too, I really miss her too.'

And then I can't keep it in any more. I'm sat there on the train, tears streaming down my face, crying together with my one-year-old daughter.

All she wants is her mummy. All I want is Willow.

But where did she go?

# Chapter 5

## Willow

Then – July 2017

I can't believe I stormed out like that, and I can't believe I'm now wandering around at dusk, swigging wine straight from the bottle. It's reckless and it's dangerous. I barely even drink. In fact none of this feels like me at all. But then I've barely felt myself for five minutes since Gran announced we were leaving.

The wine is starting to go to my head and suddenly I'm cold and it's getting dark. Maybe I should just go home, make it up properly with Gran. But the thought of that makes me feel even worse. Then I spot a pub ahead of me and the headiness I felt a moment before morphs into a warm fuzzy layer of confidence. Maybe one more drink will be enough to put Gran and Brighton firmly out of my mind.

'Can I see some ID please?' the girl behind the bar says in response to my order of a vodka and Coke. I'm being refused alcohol because I don't look eighteen. Which makes sense, because I'm not eighteen. But, still, if the girl behind the bar knew how I felt right now, I'm sure she'd give me a drink.

'Do you think I'd be here if I wasn't eighteen?' I say. God, are my words slurring?

The girl stares at me, eyebrows raised. She looks about my age, but I don't see her flashing her ID about. 'You may well be eighteen, but I need proof of that,' she says, crossing her arms.

I fold my arms too, mimicking her. 'My name is Willow Allen. And I was born in 1987.'

The girl cocks her head slightly. 'So you're thirty?'

Damn. It's a lot older than I'd meant to say I was, but I can't exactly take it back now so I nod my head confidently. This is so unlike me. Usually just the thought of asking for a drink at a bar would be enough to make me hyperventilate. 'And if you refuse to serve me, I'll sue.'

'You'll sue?' I can't tell if the bartender is enjoying this or getting annoyed. Either way, she hasn't asked me to leave yet.

'Hell yeah, I'll sue, my family is full of lawyers.'

'Willow!' I hear someone shout a second before a pair of arms envelops me. I stiffen and I feel the person pull away. I turn around. The boy is tall, so tall he towers over me. It's hard to focus on him, because I'm still a little dizzy from the alcohol and the left-field embrace, but I can't help but notice his eyes: they're a deep hazel, almost hidden beneath a mass of heavy black curls. I don't know this boy. I don't know anyone here. But he's looking at me like we've known each other all our lives. How drunk am I?

'All right, you did the dare, good one! A tenner for you.' His voice is full of warmth as he winks furtively at me, before turning back to the girl at the bar, grinning. 'Sorry for annoying you, Hols, this is my friend Willow. She'll do anything for a dare.'

'Hols' looks unimpressed. 'She still doesn't get a drink without ID.'

'I know, it was a mere joke.' The girl rolls her eyes and stalks to the other end of the gleaming white bar. It sticks out like a sore thumb against the rustic brick walls lined with homely picture frames. Is this what the pubs are like in New Haw? All mismatched? Bit ugly? No theme?

I turn my head back to the boy, frowning at him. I am utterly confused. I don't recognise him at all – or am I deliriously drunk? I stare at him in silent confusion, waiting for him to explain, but he just returns my gaze, saying nothing, a smug smile on his lips.

I feel the corners of my mouth twitch, curling up into an involuntary smile. 'What the hell?' I begin. And then I'm laughing. And I can't stop. And he's laughing too.

Oh, wine, oh, lovely, lovely, wine.

We're outside in the lamplit garden, sitting on a cushioned leather sofa – I told you this pub is weird – sheltered from the rain by a wooden structure. We are sipping straight vodka from a flask he produced from his trouser pocket. His name is Dustin. I don't know him, and he doesn't know me. He just overheard my conversation with the bartender and knew I was going to get kicked out, so decided to save me from utter mortification and potential arrest, and come to my rescue. And I'm glad, because he is very nice, and we're talking a lot, and he is sharing his secret flask of alcohol with me, which is very kind. He's almost exactly a year older than me, as it turns out. He turned eighteen last week, and I've been seventeen for a couple of months now. He is wearing an oversized chequered jumper, with stripy trousers, and big leather Doc Martens. He stands out in a way I'd never dare to.

And he's on his own at the pub, just like me – though

everyone here seems to know him, so I suppose he's not really alone. Apparently, he's a regular here, he comes for the karaoke. They hold it twice a week, and tonight is one of the nights.

'So, I take it your family aren't all lawyers?' Dustin smirks, handing the flask back to me.

'Um, no, not exactly,' I say sheepishly. 'That was a bit of an embellishment.'

'So what do they do?'

I freeze. I can feel the familiar nerves and stomach-dropping dread. Are we going to talk about families now? Am I going to have to awkwardly dodge all the usual generic questions? Or worse, what if I end up giving too much away? I feel like the combination of the vodka and his hazel eyes could make me spill everything if I'm not careful. I give what I hope is an off-hand laugh and self-consciously brush the hair from my face. 'Um, well . . . '

'You OK?'

I look up at Dustin; he's watching me with a concerned expression.

'Look, I didn't mean to intrude or anything. You don't have to tell me about your family if you don't want to.'

'No, no, it's fine,' I say hurriedly. 'Sorry, I think I'm a bit drunk. I had the good part of a bottle on the way here.' I laugh awkwardly.

He arches an eyebrow. 'On a Wednesday? Now you're making me feel boring.' He's smiling again. I like his smile.

I grin back at him.

'Obviously, you have to have a bottle of wine on a Wednesday, catch up! That's what all the cool kids do now.'

'Oh, that's what they do? I'm always late with the trends,' he says, his eyes still not leaving my face. He's a funny-looking guy, really proudly wearing his mismatched clothes like they're all the rage. Is this his everyday attire? Or is this for the karaoke? He has a tiny hoop dangling from his ear, so tiny you wouldn't notice unless you really stare at it. And suddenly I realise I am staring. Shit. But then again, so is he. We've been staring for a little bit too long, so there's that pause. He realises and clears his throat awkwardly. 'Wait, this is so unfair.'

'What is?' I say. What does he mean?

'You already know my embarrassing hobby – karaoke. So what's yours?'

I'm so relieved that I don't even think before I answer. 'I like to knit!'

Did I really tell just him about my knitting? Wow. So cool, Willow.

Dustin eyes widen. 'Sorry, what? Are you secretly ninety?'

I bite my lip, trying to hold in my embarrassed laughter. 'It's actually fun. I'll teach you someday.'

'Is that a promise?'

I nod my head and wink at him. 'I always keep my promises.'

'And what brings you here tonight, when you could be having a wild night of knitting?'

I take another swig from the flask. 'Feeling pissed off at the world. Pissed off at people,' I say, thinking it'll come off cool and edgy. Instead it sounds whiny and I realise I've opened myself up to more questions. But Dustin just gets to his feet and offers me his hand. 'Sounds to me like you need to let off some steam. How's your karaoke?'

I take his outstretched hand. 'I've never even tried it. Like ever.'

Dustin feigns outrage.

'Must be a sign. Maybe you were meant to walk into this place.'

I bite my lip, feeling excitement flush my face. 'Obviously

a sign. You'd better do a duet with me though, I'll be super offended if you say no.'

He grins at me. 'One condition: it has to be an ABBA song.'

'I thought you'd never ask,' I say, before grabbing his hand and dragging him inside.

I can be anyone with him, absolutely anyone, cos he doesn't know me. He doesn't know the real me.

# Chapter 6

# Dustin

Mum stares at me from the doorway. She looks the same. Her cropped blonde hair might be shorter than it used to be, but it still has that slight off-centre parting that she'd always complain about. Only when I look closer do I notice the small signs of the two years that have passed. The extra creases around her brown eyes, shiny now with tears, and the slightly less pronounced cheekbones. For a moment she doesn't say anything, then I feel her arms around me, pulling me towards her, Zara still cradled in my arms. She smells exactly as I remember her: of lavender and fluffy towels.

'I've missed you, Dustin,' she whispers, her voice choked with emotion.

I'm thrown, I don't know how to reply. After this amount of time, I had expected a much frostier reception. More dramatic. More ... anything. Less ... this.

'I ... missed you too, Mum,' I mumble.

Two years without trying to contact me and she's acting like I've been gone a week. Thirty minutes I stood outside the house, pacing back and forth with Zara in her buggy, my stomach writhing like I was being eaten alive from the inside. And now this. Has she just decided to move on, forget any of it ever happened? I have so many questions, but I'm also so tired. So I just lean my head against her shoulder instead.

After what feels like hours, Mum shuffles us both into the living room, telling me to take my shoes and coat off and asking about tea and would I like some and did I manage to grab something to eat on the train. Before I even have a chance to answer, she calls Alicia from upstairs, and my anxiety comes flooding back. The living room has only changed a little in the years I've been away. I think the walls have been painted a brighter white, but there's still our cheesy family portrait on the wall. The wooden plaques engraved with *This is a home not a house* propped on the surfaces. The same diddy TV, that was always too loud or too quiet, impossible to get the volume just right. I am back.

My not-so-little sister – she's nineteen now – eventually comes downstairs, followed by a tall, dark-haired guy, who towers behind her. It is evident from the expression on her face that, unlike Mum, Alicia isn't about to sweep the last two years under the carpet. I walk towards her, not sure what I'm going to do. Hug her? Shake her hand? It doesn't matter anyway, because as soon as I approach her she backs away and, without saying a word, slides past me and sits on the sofa. Her boyfriend sits down next to her but not before he holds his hand up awkwardly and says 'All right, mate? I'm Elliot, Alicia's boyfriend,' as if I couldn't have worked that out for myself. I already know from her Facebook updates that he's called Elliot, but for the last year or so he's been Action Man in my head. Because he looks like an Action Man. Sharp jawline, electric blue eyes, messy hair that somehow looks carefully styled. It's like someone has put him together from plastic parts. I already don't like him. He just sits there, arm around Alicia, pulling her closer towards him protectively. He looks too perfect. At least he's introduced himself to me, I guess. My sister, on the other hand, is silent as the grave.

I was aware from Facebook that Alicia wasn't going to look like the round-faced seventeen-year-old I remember. But even so, seeing her in person takes me by surprise. Her once long, auburn hair has been dyed black and cut into a short blunt bob, revealing the monkey-like ears that stick out from the sides of her small head. She has decorated them with loads of tiny glints of metal, and the side of her nose and her septum follow this theme as well. Her rosy cheeks, the spray of freckles across her nose that have always meant she looks a few years younger than she is, are still very much present, but she has none of the charming innocence that used to characterise her, none of the wide-eyed curiosity. She folds her arms and glowers at me.

Mum sets cups of tea down on the coffee table, before flopping into an armchair with a loud exhale and a smile on her face, wiping another tear from her cheek. She's acting as if everything in her life has just come together, like everything is great and we are a happy family – long have been, and always will be. Then she sees Alicia's expression. Her smile fades away.

I look back at Elliot. The more I stare at him, the more I notice the wrinkles by the sides of his eyes. He looks a lot older in person.

'How old are you, Elliot?' I say to him.

Alicia's eyes widen. 'Seriously? That's the first thing you're going to say to us?'

I shrug. 'I'm just making conversation.'

'Oooh – biscuits!' Mum mutters, quickly exiting the room, because, of course, the absence of biscuits is what's making this otherwise normal situation so awkward.

31

I feel like Alicia's eyes are drilling into me. 'Why does it matter, Dustin?' she says coldly.

'I'm twenty-eight,' Elliot says quickly, obviously keen to defuse the tension.

I do the maths. Alicia quickly chimes in. 'It's really not that big of a deal.'

I shrug my shoulders. 'I didn't say anything.'

I wanted to, but I didn't.

'Well, even if you did, it's not like you were here to give your opinion so ...'

Something tells me that's going to be a familiar quip before long. I want to see Elliot's reaction, but he's just looking calmly at Alicia. Playing it very safe.

'So this is Alicia's niece?' he asks, though he's still looking at my sister, tapping her knee rhythmically with his finger.

I pull Zara closer to me, so she's leaning on my tummy rather than sitting on my knee. Alicia doesn't say anything, though she's now staring intently at Zara.

'Yep,' I respond. I feel almost self-conscious on Zara's behalf.

'I can't believe you have a baby, Dustin,' Alicia says slowly.

You're not the only one, I think. With everything that's happened these past twenty-four hours, I feel like I'm struggling to process it all over again.

Alicia grips Elliot's hand, leaning forward to get a proper look at Zara, and shakes her head slowly in disbelief – or maybe it's disgust. You know, I don't even recognise this girl. 'How are *you* a dad?'

'Little Zara is gorgeous,' Mum says, shuffling back in the room before I can answer, placing a plate of biscuits on the table.

I wonder how Mum already knew Zara's name, but I suppose Alicia has been keeping her posted on my social media.

I look down at Zara and her eyes look up at mine, her small

hand reaching out to grab my face. She is gorgeous, I don't need to be told that. My heart drops, like an elevator crashing through the floor of my ribs, coming to a stop somewhere in my stomach.

'Zara is *so* beautiful,' Mum says, as if she thinks I didn't hear her the first time.

'Just like her mum,' I whisper.

All three look at me sharply. I know I've given them an opening to ask about Willow. But I've already decided I'm not going to tell them about her disappearing, or the visit from the police or any of that. I know what they'd say. Well, what Mum would say at least. And besides, how can I tell them anything, when all I have is questions?

# Chapter 7

# Willow

Then – July 2017

I'm snuggled up on the sofa, hot water bottle on my belly, knitting another one of my blankets. Gran is sitting on the other sofa, a cup of her redbush tea steaming on the table, book still in her hands though she's not reading it because *Corrie* is on the TV. This is what most of our nights were like back in Brighton.

Gran and I are fine now. She was already in bed when I got in from the pub the other day but almost as soon as I shut my bedroom door I heard her pad into the kitchen for a glass of water and I felt a pang of remorse. She'd been waiting up for me. I started to apologise the next morning but she held her hand up and said we should focus on settling in and forget all about it. Which I have. For the most part ...

The settling-in part is proving more difficult. Brighton with its hustle and bustle feels very far away. Usually in the summer holidays I'd be walking along the pier, skimming pebbles on the beach and eating ice cream. Instead I'm inside doing nothing but knitting and drawing and watching daytime TV, counting the minutes going by and wishing for a way to speed up time. My room doesn't feel like my room. The fairy lights don't help, the posters on my wall don't help, the candles don't help. Even knitting obsessively doesn't help. I hug the hot water bottle closer to my tummy, and lean back into the cushions, pretending I'm actually paying attention to the TV.

I don't like how you have to drive to get anywhere here. In Brighton I could walk everywhere: to school, to the shops, to the beach, to the bowling alley. Here, I have to rely on lifts from Gee if I want to go anywhere. The flat Gran and I live in now is a bit bigger than the one we had at home. We have our own garden, a living room, and a dining room too. It feels more like a house. But still, it's got nothing on the period flat we had at home. It was small, but it was perfect for us. I miss the big sash window in our old living room, that I would push up and open, then crawl through to sit cross-legged on the balcony at night, watching the stars nestle perfectly in the sky, listening to the rush of the waves. Now I look out of the small square window of my bedroom and see street lamps, and houses, and there's no rush of waves, and no smell of salt. I miss my home. I miss Brighton. It was where I belonged.

I move to the fireplace, pick up another set of knitting needles and drop back on the sofa, sighing.

'Your tummy playing up, love? Shall I make a peppermint tea?' Gran's red-framed glasses are perched on the end of her nose.

'A little. But I'm fine, Gran, thanks.'

'You sure, sweetheart?'

I nod and look pointedly back at the TV. But I can still feel Gran's eyes on me.

'You're fitting in well here, right?'

'There's nothing to fit into, Gran,' I mumble. Gran has more of a social life than me; she's met people at bingo, at book club, at the country market where she helps out.

It's been a week since we moved and every single day I've had a text from Georgia asking if I want to go out with her and some friends. But I can never bring myself to go. It would be so awkward, everyone knowing each other and all the focus being on me as the new girl. All I ever wanted in Brighton was for people to include me, but now that Georgia is I realise I don't want that either. What do I want?

I hear Gran sigh. 'You're going to have to get used to it at some point, Willow.'

'Well it's not going to be for ever, is it?'

Gran doesn't reply and for a moment I think she's going to ignore me and go back to watching *Coronation Street*. Then she says, 'Sometimes a fresh start can be a really good thing. It was time for a change. And you know I wanted to be near Auntie Jayne and Georgia.'

I don't look up. What's the point? We both know the real reason we left Brighton.

I start stroking my necklace, fingers tracing the shape of the pendant.

'Is that a new necklace? I meant to say I noticed you'd started wearing it since we've left Brighton.'

Shit. I quickly drop my hand. 'Georgia got it for me. As a kind of welcome present.'

Gran smiles. 'It's nice you girls have the chance to spend so much time together now.'

'Yeah.'

Just then my phone pings. Text from Gee, the usual.

Hey, we are all going to Joe's house, do you want to come?

Soon she's going to get annoyed if I keep saying no to things. But this basically sounds like a house party full of strangers and I can't think of anything worse. Would everyone be drinking? Would they force me to drink lots too or question me if I said I didn't want to? Would they be doing drugs in the bathroom? What would I wear? How would I get home? What time would I get home? What if someone suggests me staying over? What if they don't have soap in their toilets? I've been to houses before that have no soap in their toilets.

But if I ask Gee even one of those questions I know she's going to roll her eyes through her phone and tell me to lighten up. But I can't. I can't lighten up. It's just not that easy sometimes.

# Chapter 8

# Willow

Then – July 2017

Georgia tricked me.

She texted me earlier asking if I fancied a film night at hers, something quiet and chill. I was surprised because quiet and chill is hardly Georgia's vibe at the best of times, let alone on a Friday night. She has so many friends, it makes me feel dizzy just thinking about how she keeps track of them all.

I haven't told Georgia about the boy from the pub – Dustin. She'd make such a big deal of it and it's not like I've spoken to him since that one night last week anyway. He liked the Willow of that night – drunk Willow, confident Willow. I don't know what he'd think if he saw the real me.

Georgia is grinning at me now, pleased with her deception. It is very clear we are not heading to hers for a movie night. She has pulled up in front of a field.

'What the hell, Gee?' I say. 'I thought we were just stopping by the shops to get popcorn?'

She rolls her eyes. 'This was the only way I could get you out. You're going to expire if you stay in that flat any longer. Besides, a couple of them will be in college with you in September so you should get to know them now.'

It's July. I don't even want to think about September yet.

Georgia gives me a shove. 'Come on. Out you get.'

The very last thing I want to do is step out of the car. But I can't just sit here like a sulky child. I get out, slam the door, and follow Georgia through the field. I honestly feel like I could kill her. What sort of people hang out in a field?

The grass is long and damp with dew in the twilight and my trainers are already soggy. I hate getting wet feet and now I'm worrying about ruining my trainers, and it's only adding to the butterflies in my stomach. I shove my shaking palms into my pockets and try to talk myself down – 'challenge negative thoughts' as Gran is always saying. What's the worst thing that could happen, Willow? You might say something stupid or be a bit awkward. They might not like you. Is that really the end of the world?

I hate Georgia.

Eventually we emerge onto a well-trodden path and ahead I see a group of people sprawled on various blankets and coats. There are cigarettes – cigarettes that don't smell of cigarettes – bottles of wine, plastic cups, and music blaring from a speaker. It's a proper little get-together; there must be fifteen people here, and because everyone is so loud and engrossed in various conversations, we manage to sneak up unnoticed. Thank God, is there anything worse than joining a party and have everyone turn to stare at you? I'm saying that like I know … I can imagine there's nothing worse.

Georgia parks me on the very edge of one blanket and pours me a glass of wine from a stray bottle. After last week's hangover, even looking at the wine makes me feel sick.

'Stay here, I'll be a few minutes,' she whispers in my ear and weaves herself through the people and patches of grass towards the guys at the end of the uneven circle we've formed. I sit quietly in my corner, staying very still and praying that nobody will notice me. So far so good. I take an inconspicuous look round the circle, trying to suss out Georgia's friends. It doesn't take me too long to get a sense of them. Basically they are all very loud, and they're all boys.

The two next to me – one guy with curly hair who has his back to me, another wearing a bucket hat – are half singing along (badly) to the Dido song blaring from one of their phones, half discussing some date one of them had the night before. I can't catch much of what the curly-haired guy is saying but bucket-hat guy has a deep voice and I can hear every word.

'Nah, it was a casual thing,' he says, taking a toke of a cigarette. 'I've got another date tomorrow so I'm not looking for anything too serious with Theo. It's all fun and games.' He leans back into the nest of coats and blankets and I shuffle backwards slightly, worried he'll catch sight of me.

I needn't have bothered, because the next moment Georgia is suddenly right beside me. And everyone's eyes are on her. 'Guys, I've got a friend with me, so be nice, OK?'

Oh God, now all eyes are on me. Why, Georgia? We had just made the perfect entrance. Snuck up nice and unnoticed.

'Wait, Georgia, you have a friend who's a girl?' bucket-hat guy replies incredulously.

Georgia rolls her eyes, before catching mine and smiling encouragingly. 'This is Willow, she's my cousin, just moved from Brighton with her gran. She's going to Norwood in September.'

Yay, don't remind me. Georgia turns to me. 'Most of these

guys were in my year so have just finished, but Liam ... ' she points to a boy with a mass of gelled spikes for hair, 'and Joe ...' this is the name of bucket-hat guy, it transpires, 'they'll both be there in September.'

I wave pathetically, feeling the blood rush to my face. Come on, Willow, just make eye contact and say hi like a normal person. Is it so bloody hard, just ...

'Oh my God – fucking hell, Willow, hi!'

Looking up, I see the curly-haired guy has now turned around and is grinning at me expectantly. My stomach flips.

It's the boy from the pub.

Dustin. I'm not sure how I could have missed it, with his curly hair – it's a little bit shorter than it was last week and pushed out of his eyes, but otherwise he's exactly the same. As I examine him more closely I can see he's wearing an almost identical outfit: the same chequered trousers, a dark blue jumper this time but still oversized and bobbly from too many washes.

If I wanted to disappear before, now I really want to. He leans in to give me a sitting-down hug, but I stiffen, pulling back. He also pulls away, confusion in his eyes. 'It's me, Dustin – from the pub last week. Remember?'

'Yeah, yeah I do,' I say a little too bluntly. I'm conscious of everyone's eyes on us, listening intently to this awkward exchange. I try to think of something else to say – anything at all – but my mind is blank.

'Well ... er ... it's good to see you again,' he mumbles, slowly turning back to Joe. Georgia plonks herself down next to us and I feel her eyes on me, studying me. 'You guys know each other?' she asks.

I shrug. Dustin stays silent.

Maybe I should have told Georgia about my drunken outing – given that she knows just about everyone in New Haw it now seems idiotic to assume she wouldn't find out anyway – but she would have had too many questions. I also, equally stupidly I realise, honestly never thought I'd see Dustin again. Yes, we chatted until two a.m. Yes, he walked me home. Yes, he gave me his number. But he was drunk. I was drunk. It was so obviously a one-time thing. Under normal circumstances it would never have happened. Especially not with me. I can barely ask for a bag at the supermarket, let alone chat to an attractive stranger in a pub.

Georgia's eyes are darting between us both. I can feel his confusion burning into me before he suddenly stands up and shouts, 'Anyone need another drink?'

The sun has finally set and the field is in darkness, but we're still here. I've been sipping on warm wine which has helped me loosen up a bit. I have continued to avoid Dustin, chatting to everyone in the group but him. Every now and then I catch him looking at me, and occasionally he has turned round to find me staring at the back of his head. I feel self-conscious, I don't know how to sit, and keep shuffling about from position to position. I suddenly have no idea what to do with my hands. Should I rest them on the grass, keep them folded in my lap? Why am I so aware of every tiny movement, and why am I not listening to anything anyone is saying?

Later, when Liam gets up to pee, I finally find myself alone. In my own silence for the first time all night, I breathe a sigh of relief. Although I've now realised how cold I am and I shiver.

'Do you want my coat?'

I look up to see Dustin and quickly look away again. Will he leave me alone, please?

'I'm OK,' I reply. 'Thanks though.'

'But aren't you cold?'

'Only a little bit.'

He slips his coat off and drapes it over my shoulders anyway. I shoot him a small thankful smile, which he takes as an invitation to sit down next to me. Great.

'You do remember me, don't you?' he says quietly.

'Yeah, I do ...' I mumble, purposely avoiding his eyes.

'Did I upset you or offend you that night? I thought we had a nice time.'

'No, you didn't do anything, it was a lovely night.'

'Well, I'm a bit confused then, because you don't seem too happy to see me.' He gives a weak smile. 'Everyone is always happy to see me. I'm not used to this, you see.'

There's a pause. It seems he's expecting a reaction; his smile falls, and I immediately feel guilty. I'm not trying to make it hard for him on purpose, but how can I tell him he's wasting his time?

'I promise it's not you,' I try to explain, shuffling a little further away.

'Hey, that's what they always say,' he says, with a smirk.

I frown at him. 'No. You were nice. It's just ... I am nothing like the girl I was that night. I was quite drunk. Very drunk. And I don't really drink often.'

'Don't worry – you weren't the only one who had a bit too much that night.'

He's clearly not getting it. 'Yeah but, it's not just that. I'm just ... I don't know ... different, usually. Quieter,' I say. I can feel my heart pounding in my chest, the heat rising to my cheeks. Why is this so stressful? 'I'm not sure I'm as much fun normally.'

'Well, I find that hard to believe. But you know ... I don't

43

mind being challenged,' he says. He says this so seriously and looks so determined that I almost laugh.

'Would you like to see my tattoos?' he says, as if this is a perfectly normal change of conversation.

'OK,' I reply, grateful for the helpline before I've even really registered what he has said.

He raises one eyebrow. 'You're in for a treat. Let's start off with my Capturing Nessie tattoo.'

I try to hide the sceptical look on my face. 'Capturing Nessie?'

He smiles proudly. 'My karaoke stage name.'

Who is this guy? I've never met someone so self-confident. He's exactly the same as the other night. He didn't have liquid courage.

'You mean I actually saw Capturing Nessie live in the flesh?'

He nods solemnly. 'Yes. Even better, you actually performed with him – aren't you lucky?'

I can feel myself trying not to laugh. 'Yeah, he was brilliantly terrible from what I remember.'

'That's what's so great about him, you'll never get a karaoke singer as bad as him.'

He rolls up the leg of his jeans to reveal a huge animated drawing of Nessie the Loch Ness monster on his calf, with the word 'capturing' inked across it in spiralling letters. Nessie is surrounded by other random drawings. An 8-ball, some kind of aftershave bottle? A bucket. I gently trace the outline of Nessie with my finger. I always find myself fascinated by tattoos. 'It's ... different. And having grown up in Brighton, I've seen my fair share of odd tattoos.'

'I know,' he replies. 'My mother is very proud of her son. He's achieving some great things, with his shit tattoos.'

I can't help but laugh again. 'I'm sure she is. You're a funny one, Dustin.'

'So I'm told, mostly by myself.' He places his hand on the grass, near enough to be touching mine. I'm not sure why I do it, and I instantly regret it, but I pull my hand back quickly. It's a knee-jerk reaction. Feeling my cheeks flush with the awkwardness of the situation, my hand goes automatically to my necklace.

'Sorry,' I mumble, slowly stroking the silver chain. 'That made me jump a bit.'

'Oh, don't worry, I jump every time I look in the mirror,' he says, circling his face with his finger. 'This here isn't a happy picture to look at.'

And then I'm laughing again. Why do I always seem to be laughing when I'm with him?

# Chapter 9

# Dustin

My room is exactly the same. They haven't touched anything. From the posters on the walls, to the *Nuts* magazine under my bed. I really should have got rid of that when I started dating Willow. Even the thirty gram bag of Amber Leaf tobacco in my bedside table drawer is exactly as I left it. I feel a pang of regret as it dawns on me what this means. They thought I was coming back.

Well ... I guess I did come back, in the end.

Mum asked if I was staying and I said yes. I feel like she already knew what my answer would be, because she didn't say anything. She nodded, trying in vain to keep a smile off her face, and then immediately announced that she was leaving to buy some baby stuff for Zara. I thought I'd brought the essentials, but Mum didn't think so. I figured it was best to let her get on with it.

I spent the afternoon in my bedroom with Zara while she napped. Going baby shopping with Mum felt like way too much too soon, and I'd rather be anywhere than downstairs with Alicia and Elliot. I am trying to process what has actually happened in the last twenty-four hours – how I have ended up with my baby daughter in my teenage bedroom – but nothing makes sense in my head.

I go back into detective mode. I call Willow. I call again, and again. Her phone is still switched off and I get her voicemail straight away. Immediately all the terrifying possibilities of yesterday come screaming back to me. What if she's been kidnapped and they've taken her phone? What if she did mean to run away but she dropped her phone and it ran out of battery and now she can't get home? What if she was hit by a car? I bring up WhatsApp on my phone and search for our conversation, buried under the panicked exchanges with Georgia and numerous other mutual friends. Her last seen was yesterday morning. She hasn't even been online. Frantically I add to my messages of yesterday evening.

Willow, let me know you're ok.
Call me?
Willow even if you don't want to talk to me can you just let me know you're ok?
For fuck's sake Willow I'm going out of my mind.

One tick only. They're not delivering. Why is her phone switched off? It's so unlike her. Willow is a worrier, to put it mildly. Usually she's glued to her phone, terrified of missing some message of distress from me or from Georgia. She's been much worse since Gran as well.

I consider for a moment, then I retrieve the card the police officers left me yesterday. A receptionist answers.

'Hi, um, I was wondering if I could speak to ...' I realise they didn't give me their official titles yesterday. 'Um, Nancy, please?'

'DS Francis?' the receptionist replies curtly. 'One moment please.'

I shuffle about whilst some tinny hold-music plays. Then Nancy's voice cuts through.

'Hello, this is DS Francis.'

'Oh hi, um . . .' Suddenly I realise I don't know what to say. 'This is Dustin. I was just wondering if you have any update on my girlfriend? She went missing yesterday. Her name is Willow Allen?'

'Dustin, hello.' DS Francis's voice is kindly, warm. 'It's good to hear from you. Did you end up finding someone to stay with you last night?'

'I'm at my mum's now.' God, does she think I'm about sixteen? 'I just wanted to know if you've been able to trace her at all.'

'We have filed a report, and once that has been processed we can assess what steps would be appropriate. Someone will probably try to make contact with Willow . . .'

'OK, so you'll tell me if you get in touch with her?'

There's a pause. I can tell DS Francis is weighing her words carefully.

'Not necessarily, Dustin. That will depend on what Willow tells us, and whether she wants us to pass on her contact details. We will need her permission to do that.'

I feel rage burning inside me. What do they think, that I'm some kind of threat to Willow? That she's actually run away because she's *afraid* of me?

I thank her and hang up. I can feel I'm starting to panic again, and I know that's not going to help. OK, think, Dustin, think. The police don't understand the situation, I guess it must happen a lot that women run away and don't want to be found. But they don't know Willow.

So what could have happened to her? Let's go through the possibilities one at a time.

Worst-case scenario: she's been kidnapped. It seems unlikely but people do get taken sometimes, right? Willow is young and she's pretty. What if it's one of those trafficking things? I clench my teeth, the thought of it, the thought of what she could be going through right now, it makes me sick. Is she even alive? Is she . . . I can't think about it. I can't.

She could have fallen, and knocked her head. Maybe she's got amnesia and can't remember who she is or how to get home. What if she's in a hospital ward somewhere and they have no way of identifying her?

Or, the only other explanation and, though I hate to admit it, the most likely: she left of her own accord. Willow wrote that letter, left her baby, left her boyfriend, without so much as a hint of why she left or where she is . . .

FUCK.

I angrily throw the phone and the clatter of it against the wall wakes Zara up. She starts crying. 'Sorry, sorry,' I whisper guiltily, picking her up and then reaching awkwardly for my phone with Zara clutched in one arm. 'Mama,' she mumbles sleepily and makes a grab for my nose. I clench my teeth. She seems to think 'Mama' is interchangeable for either parent. Which when I think about it brings a lump to my throat. Because maybe she will only have one parent from now on. I look at my phone. I can see Georgia has messaged, so I open up WhatsApp to reply and freeze. My series of panicked messages to Willow is still open. And they have two ticks. The message has delivered. Her phone is on. Before I know it, I'm calling her again and this time it rings. My heart freezes, my breath stops. It rings again. Come on, Willow, come on. It rings again. Then it goes to voicemail.

Well, shit.

# Chapter 10

# Willow

Then – August 2017

I look at my computer, where the screen shows Gee's face enlarged on video chat. She has her hair wrapped in a towel, and is clearly using the camera as a mirror because she's peering at it weirdly, eyes very wide, a mascara wand in one hand.

As much as I still miss Brighton, I'm glad Gran chose Surrey of all places. It is pretty great being this close to Gee, my only real friend. And my only cousin – sort of. Both of my parents were only children, which is pretty lonely when you also have no siblings. However, Gran wasn't an only child; she had a sister, who had a daughter, who then had Gee. So yes, technically she isn't my first cousin, but she is as close as it gets. Gran and Gee's gran were very close. They lived next door to each other in Brighton. And since Gee spent every summer with her gran, we would spend two glorious sunny months together each year, riding the Ferris wheel, spending a fortune's worth of two pence pieces on the slot machines, and making it our mission to try every ice cream flavour Brighton had to offer over the years.

Then Gee's grandma died when she was twelve and we saw less of each other. Until I moved to Surrey, that is.

'Has the screen broken or are you just not moving?'

'Sorry,' I mumble, 'I was distracted.' Readjusting my trusty hot water bottle, I try to make more of an effort. 'So you're seeing the Tinder guy tonight?'

Gee nods happily. 'The one in the picture I sent you. He's cute, right?'

I smile and nod obligingly. Of course he is. All the guys that like Gee are cute. 'He is.'

I start to ask her more about her date but she interrupts me. 'Right, so you know how you didn't reply to Joe's party invite, and rudely ignored me ...' She pauses to allow me to shuffle awkwardly before continuing: 'Well I'm giving you another chance. Liam's having a party tomorrow. You've been in Surrey for three weeks now, and that's your time up for moping around.'

I sigh. 'Gee, I'm just—'

'Dustin is going to be there.'

I stare at her. 'What? Why would that make a difference?'

She smirks at me through the screen, and I feel heat rising to my cheeks. 'Um, let's think ...'

'Has he said anything?'

Georgia pouts as she applies lipgloss. 'Nope, he didn't need to,' she says, smacking her lips together, looking proudly at herself in the camera. 'We were at the pub, which you were invited to, and bailed as you like to do, and he was busy being unsociable on his phone. So I asked who he was talking to, and it was you.'

I brush a stray hair from my forehead. Why am I sweating this much? 'Well it's mainly him doing the talking.'

'You kept that quiet, though, didn't you? Didn't tell me you were texting. Why wouldn't you tell your cousin that, Willow?' She's doing her high-pitched, false questioning voice.

I roll my eyes. 'Because there is nothing to tell, Gee. He messages me mostly, and I reply, because I don't want to seem rude, you know?'

'And you love it, because as much as you like to pretend you are a social recluse, you're not, and it's OK and normal to talk to people, and normal to enjoy it too. And I won't be offended that you don't always reply to messages, even if it is downright rude.'

'Hey, it's different with you, Gee.'

'No, no, it's fine, I see how it is.'

She's right though, I do enjoy having someone to talk to, it makes you feel like you matter. But then that's pretty dangerous, isn't it? Because once you start mattering to someone, they start mattering to you, and that means they can hurt you.

Luckily I haven't really had that with friends. I mean, there were people at school that I'd hang out with, eat lunch with mainly. I just sat closer and closer to their group till one time they were used to me sitting with them. I'd message about home-work too. But we'd never really do anything together and I'd hardly ever get invited to things, apart from the odd party the whole school was invited to, and even then I wouldn't always go. I suppose I probably didn't help myself: I am painfully shy and maybe some people mistook that for standoffishness. Though it's not like there weren't other factors at play. People love to gossip. And Brighton can feel like a very small place when you have something to hide.

Gee sighs heavily, interrupting my train of thought. 'I still think it's weird you both met at the pub before you knew the group and didn't tell me.'

'There wasn't anything to tell! I didn't clock that he would

52

be *your friend* Dustin, and anyway, I didn't think I'd see ever him again.'

'Well I'm glad you did, it's good for you to have a friend,' she says. Then she pauses. It's never a good sign when Gee pauses, it means she's going to say something that she doesn't want to say. And Gee is happy to say all sorts of things usually, so you know you're in trouble if she's hesitating. 'I just want you to be cautious,' she says finally.

'What? Why?'

I'm the most cautious person you could ever meet. I need to be a lot of things, but more cautious is not one of them.

Georgia looks like she's choosing her words carefully. 'I don't know, Willow, just be careful of getting too invested. Dustin is such a lovely guy and, like I said, it's good for you to have a friend, but don't put all your eggs in one basket, you know? Try talking to Liam or Joe a bit more at the party. They are much more your type. Quiet and chill, which is good for you. They're nice guys.'

'Type? What? Georgia, you've got it totally wrong—'

'Dustin is like my brother, yeah? He's a good guy too. But he can be reckless, he's only interested in himself.' Weird she would say that, because I've never met anyone who has paid me so much attention before. 'He just dates, all the time. Dating. Dating. Having sex. More dating. Sex again. He's never been interested in a relationship at all.'

'Hey!' I shout a bit too loudly. 'I'm not ... no ... That's not where this is going, I don't even ... Gee, you've got this very wrong.'

'OK, stop being dramatic, I was just trying to warn you. Anyway, I have to go, I'll see you tomorrow and help you plan what you're wearing to the party, OK?'

'No.'

'OK, sweet, two p.m., sounds good, sweet, see you tomorrow.'

She hangs up.

I stare at the now blank computer screen, puzzled. She stresses me out. What has Dustin been saying? What has the group been saying? Why was she deliberately trying to steer me away from him? Is there some truth in what she was saying? Maybe he's like this with everyone, and I'm not special at all.

My phone pings.

It's Dustin.

So I hear you're coming to Liam's?

I roll my eyes. For all her protestations about being cautious, Gee talks fast, doesn't she?

# Chapter 11

# Dustin

I've been back in Surrey for approximately seven hours; however, Mum is acting like that's the amount of time I've been gone for. She called me down to dinner, like old times. Except it's not old times.

And now I'm sitting at the table with Alicia, Mum, Elliot and Zara, who is strapped into a new high chair that Mum brought back from her shopping trip. As I prod my shepherd's pie, feeling the cold wall of Alicia's silence, I try to recall my reasoning for coming here again. What did I think this would achieve? Why did the police think this would be good? Since when do I listen to Georgia? Spending time with my family is going to do anything but make this easier for me.

'So, what do you want from us then?' Alicia says, breaking the silence.

'Alicia,' Mum hisses, her eyes darting from me to Alicia and back again, as if she's afraid I'm going to disappear before her eyes.

'No, Mum,' Alicia says, her face serious. 'Unlike you, I'm not going to pretend things are normal. He can't just come here after two years with no contact and expect things from us.'

Mum's face tightens. I can almost hear the voice in her head, convincing herself that if she keeps thinking everything is perfect, maybe somehow it will be.

'I don't want anything from you,' I say calmly.

'Well then,' Alicia says with the same icy tone, 'why are you back?'

'Look.' I glance desperately around the table again, my eyes resting on Elliot. I still don't like him, though I can't find a proper reason why, which makes it even worse. 'Can't we wait till Elliot goes home? We don't need to talk about it now.'

Alicia gives a slight smile. 'Elliot's already home.'

'What?' I realise I've spoken too loudly, because Mum winces.

Alicia doesn't drop her gaze. She speaks slowly, enjoying the words; she's practically rolling them around on her tongue. 'Elliot moved in five months ago, it's closer for his work.' I turn to Mum, who has that compact smile glued to her face. Elliot lives here? I can barely get my head around it, Elliot lives *here*? What the hell has happened since I've been away? I think back to the last time I saw Mum before I left. The argument we were having. And now all of a sudden Elliot's living here and that's completely fine?

'Anyway, stop stalling, Dustin. What do you want from us? Because you'll soon learn that you're not going to get it, and then you can leave again.'

I take a spoonful of shepherd's pie and chew slowly. Is this really my sister?

As I watch her glare angrily at her plate, I am suddenly reminded of a different Alicia. Younger, mellower, happier. She's laughing – head thrown back, tears streaming down her face. Next to her Willow is laughing too. She's doubled over, arms clutching her stomach. I can't even remember what they found so funny. And then Willow was wiping her eyes and she looked at me and she smiled, and suddenly I realise how long it has been since I saw Willow smile like that.

'Dustin.'

Mum pops me out of my bubble, and I look at her, confused.

'I asked how old Zara is?' she says with a smile.

'Oh.' I still can't get Willow's face out of my head. 'She's fifteen months.'

'Oh, that old? I'm surprised, because she is a very quie—'

'Quiet baby, yes, I know. The doctor said it's fine,' I snap.

'Does she walk yet?'

I look at Zara consciously. 'No, not yet, but she can stand if she leans on things. She's a thinker. Likes to take her time and check she's doing it right.'

'Oh – well, she is definitely not taking after you; you were a very quick learner, walking and talking by one. A very smart baby.'

She probably means it well, don't rise to it, I think.

'Well, I was thinking, I could look after her for you, if you need to go back to Brighton? I'm assuming you have things you need to sort out there. Were you working?'

'Oh no, I've quit my job.'

That's *almost* true. When I called them up this morning to tell them I wouldn't be coming in and I didn't know when I would be, they were fine about it. Said to take all the time I need, and then they signed me off work for two weeks. So I won't need to be going back to Brighton anytime soon. I can't imagine waking up in our empty flat, dropping Zara at some sort of daycare, going to work.

'So, what are you doing for money?' Alicia asks.

Mum looks uncomfortable. 'Money is still a bit ...' She

pauses, reluctant to say more. I know she will be short on money, she always has been. But then she just spent a ridiculous amount on Zara at the shop, and that surprised me. Mum starts muttering again. 'You know, money and that ... For us things are still quite tight—'

'No, I have savings, enough to tide me over until I sort myself out.' I do have a nice amount of savings, even with the disappearance of our Disney fund box. I still haven't told Mum about Willow's disappearance and I don't plan on doing so. I don't want to give her any excuse to start criticising Willow. My life won't start again until I have her back.

'See, I know you hated it, but I did always tell you how good saving always was,' Mum says. 'When you were younger—'

'Where's Willow then?'

Alicia's question cuts the conversation dead. I flinch. I knew it would come – it was a miracle I'd avoided it for this long. And suddenly it dawns on me how many times I'll have to answer this question over the coming months. Everyone will notice the gap in my life, the hole in my heart, the missing person. I can see Mum giving her a warning look, that Alicia comfortably ignores. I take a deep breath. 'Willow ... Willow and I ... well, I broke up with her.'

'Well obviously, but what happened? I thought she was the love of your life and all that?'

I grit my teeth. She *is* the love of my life. I feel my nose start to burn, and quickly busy myself with feeding Zara another spoonful of dinner. 'I just need to work out my life a bit, and I can't be there in Brighton,' I say, ignoring Alicia's questions.

'So now you're not with her, you come back running to us ... your second best. I see how it is.'

'Alicia,' Mum hisses.

'No, Mum!' Alicia stands up, slamming her fist on the table.

58

Zara immediately starts crying, and I wish I could do the same. I lift her out of her high chair and onto my knee, jiggling her up and down, hoping it'll distract her and she won't just throw up all over me. Elliot puts his hand on Alicia's, trying to soothe her, but she jerks it away. 'No!' she shouts again. 'I'm not going to pretend this is normal and this is OK, because it's not normal and it's not OK. He can't just leave for two years, no contact, apart from accepting my Facebook friend request, that I sent just so I knew he was fucking alive.' She turns to me. 'You know, I would always be looking out for your friends, hoping I'd see them in town, so I could get information about you, ask how you were, ask if you were OK. But then I stopped. Because *you* were always OK, Dustin, *you* were just fine.' She steps away from the table and I notice with horror that there is a tear dripping down her cheek. Zara continues to wail, louder and louder, as if this situation weren't difficult enough already. I start cradling her, taking deep breaths. I don't need this.

Alicia takes a deep breath, and I can see the physical effort she makes to compose herself. She ignores Zara and turns to Mum. 'Mum, this is your house, and if you want him to stay here, you're a stronger person than me. But he is not my brother, and I don't think he is your son. He can't only want us when he's struggling. That's not how it works. That's not family. He's not our family.'

Then, wiping her eyes with the corner of her sleeves, she storms upstairs. Elliot clambers out from the table after her, awkwardly thanking Mum for dinner before leaving. Then it's just me, Zara and Mum. After sitting for a few minutes, trying to quieten Zara, I look at Mum. She stares at her food, her bottom lip starting to shake.

Fuck.

I get up, the chair squeaking on the wooden floor.

'Sorry, Mum. I shouldn't have come. I'm sorry.'

Mum looks up, her eyes wide. I walk quickly into the living room and gently place Zara down in her new carrycot. I can sense Mum behind me.

'Wait, Dustin,' I think I hear her say. I ignore her and go upstairs, where I grab my duffel bag and start shoving everything of Zara's into it. I go back downstairs, pick up a screaming Zara again and sling the duffel bag over my shoulder. Mum is still standing in the living room. 'No, Dustin,' she whispers.

'I really shouldn't have come here,' I say, as I go towards the door.

I have one hand on the door handle when she grabs it, forcing me round to face her. She looks up at me, her eyes wide, pleading. 'Please don't leave me again, Dustin. Please don't leave. I can't deal with you leaving again.'

And I pause. Because I know those are the exact words, with the exact same tone of desperation, I'm going to have to say to Willow when I see her again.

# Chapter 12

# Willow

Then – August 2017

I'm on my way to the party. Yep, I'm just as surprised as you are.

Gran could tell I was stressed before I left the house.

'Do you want a lift?' she asked, as I was rummaging through the alcohol cupboard in search of booze that seemed cool enough to take. Pimm's circa 1995 wouldn't do. How did that even make it through the house move?

I popped my head up to look at her. 'I'm OK, thanks, I'm walking there with Gee.'

'Well be careful, I don't like the idea of you girls walking alone in the dark. Stick with her.'

'I would never walk alone, don't worry,' I lie. I mean, if Gran can, I can, right?

She smiled at me. 'Have fun tonight. I'm so excited for you. The heart that loves is always young.'

I can't help but smile back. Gran is always repeating things she read in a book, or else picked up somewhere.

But now I'm here at the party, and the more I think about

the phrase the more I wonder what the hell it means. What's so great about being young? 'Young' just seems to be code for a whole lot of stress and worry. Gee is off with some boy, and I'm standing next to Joe, drinking an awful vodka and Coke concoction from a plastic cup. I have a horrible feeling Joe is bored of standing with me. Dustin is chatting to some girl across the room and I know I am staring at him. Everyone around me is having the time of their lives and I feel like I want to curl up into a ball and disappear. I had the usual butterflies walking up but now my stomach is churning so much I worry I might be sick. I'm going to cry in a minute, but if I walk away I'm worried people are going to look at me, and my breath is getting shorter and raspier. Count to ten, Willow, count to ten. But I can feel it brewing, a full-blown panic attack is going to come crashing down on me any moment now.

I want to go home. I want to go home. I want to go home.

'Why?' Joe is looking at me. I didn't know I said that out loud. He looks across the room at Dustin. 'What, because of that?'

'What? No!'

'Someone's jeeaa-lous,' Joe drawls in a teasing, drawn-out way. I could hit him.

'No!' I shake my head vigorously.

Dustin now has one arm round the girl, and she giggles, jokingly punching him on the other. She is pretty. Long auburn, wearing a sparkly blue jumpsuit. She looks like a modern-day Disney princess.

'It's his sister.'

I throw my head back to Joe. 'What?'

He laughs at my response. 'The girl he is with is Alicia, his younger sister. Don't worry.'

'I wasn't worrying.'

Joe takes another sip of his beer. 'Whatever you say, Wills.'

He barely knows me, and he calls me Wills. I've never had a nickname before.

Joe starts walking away, and I'm on my own, so I use the opportunity to go to the toilet and assess what I'm doing next. The panic is still there, lurking. I place my cup on the floor and start walking quickly. Weaving through people, eyes lowered, and it's going well until I bump into someone. I look up, embarrassed, and am beginning to apologise, when I see it's Dustin.

He smiles. 'Hey, you.'

I just gawk back.

'You never replied to my last message,' he says in mock accusation.

But I just stay silent, worried if I say a word, I'm going to break down. I'm not feeling good, I just want to go home. My heart is pounding and I am shaking all over.

Dustin frowns. 'You OK?'

'I just need ... I just, I just need some air.'

He nods his head, smiling again. 'Gotcha! Put your hand on my shoulders, I'll lead the way.' So I do, and he leads me out, and as soon as I step outside I instantly feel better.

He directs me to a bench and sits down next to me. He doesn't say anything, maybe sensing that I need silence right now. I close my eyes, stroking my necklace. I can feel the panic attack subsiding.

'I like that necklace.' I drop my hands and look back at him, startled. I need to stop bringing attention to this necklace.

'Thanks.'

'I notice you always wear it. What's on it?'

'It's an angel,' I say quickly. He doesn't say anything else, and I'd rather just say it all now than him asking questions later. 'It's for my parents.' I am almost rushing to get the words out.

'Oh,' Dustin says. It's rare for him to be so short of words.

'Georgia didn't tell me anything about your parents, she just said not to mention them. Sorry I didn't mean to—'

'They're not in my life any more, but I like to think of them as angels looking out for me.' He's unusually quiet, which makes me unusually talkative. 'I think that angels are always there in everyone's life. Maybe it's a person you lost, someone who is gone for ever physically, but who is always somewhere looking out for you. I think anyone can be an angel – everyone has a bit of good in them, despite the things they do, everyone is a little bit of an angel.' My words are garbled. Am I even making sense? What must Dustin think, with me babbling away like this? And now I can feel tears start to form in my eyes. Great, that'll definitely make this less weird.

'Yeah, totally,' Dustin mumbles. I don't think I've ever seen him so lost for words. Eventually he says, 'I'm sorry about your parents, Willow.'

'Thanks. These things happen.'

'I know, but still that's really sad. I'm so sorry.'

We are silent for a minute or two. It's so peaceful out here, the party just a distant hum through the closed door.

'My gran says, there's good times and hard times in life; when you are going through a hard time, that just means there's good times coming.'

Dustin seems to consider this for a moment.

'I know what you mean. Like my dad has never really been in mine or my sister's lives. He left, not long after my sister was born. He didn't like the fact his life totally changed, he didn't like responsibility, the financial struggle, any of it, I guess. And sometimes it would make me so mad, so annoyed – I'd think, why can't I have a dad like everyone else? But eventually I knew I couldn't dwell on it. This is my life. I should take what happens and live with it. And the good news is I know I'll never become my dad. I would never walk out on my family. I'd never hurt my mum and sister the way he hurt me . . .'

Oh wow. 'You get it,' I say.

He frowns. 'I used to feel so unlucky, then I hear you've lost both of your parents and I feel selfish. I am very lucky.'

'You can't compare, Dustin. Every life is different. I guess it's just about not letting what's happening in your life take over and completely weigh you down.' I smile. 'Besides, I think certain people bring good times with them.'

His mouth twitches. 'I think they do.'

I spend the rest of the evening with him. He's easy to talk to. He makes me calmer. He asks me questions about myself and seems genuinely interested in my answers. And suddenly I'm telling him all the things I've never told anyone else. About how nervous I am about college, and yet how education is really important for me. How I think the lack of qualifications didn't help my parents, and I don't want to be the same. I want to make my gran proud. How I want to go to uni, study graphic design. How there's something amazing about creating something, having control over the product you make. There's not a lot you can control in life, so having control over your job, and everything you do day-to-day would be pretty cool. Dustin says he's not as set on what he wants to do for a career, he's taking a gap year to figure it out. He knows all he wants is to be happy every day he goes into his job. He doesn't want to be stuck in a job forty hours a week if it makes him miserable, if it brings him down. He says his mum is worried about his lack of direction but he's not. He is confident he will find a job this year, but if he doesn't he will go into uni, or he will get an apprenticeship. He says positive thinking is the way to success. I say I could see him doing sales. Apparently a lot of people tell him that.

Late in the evening, when someone suggests karaoke, we grin at each other.

'Do you think Capturing Nessie might put in another guest appearance?' I ask.

'I think it's entirely possible,' he replies with mocking solemnity.

The cheers are deafening when he gets up to sing and he pretends to get shy which makes everyone laugh. I can't take my eyes off him. How does he do it? He seems so relaxed, so completely at ease with himself and with his audience. I linger at the back, watching him. He doesn't look at me, too caught up in the music, until the third song. Suddenly he meets my gaze, and he doesn't look away once during the whole song.

# Chapter 13

# Dustin

I wake at four a.m. to Zara screaming 'Blankie,' at the top her lungs. Unfortunately for Zara, I'm pretty crap, and I forgot blankie, so rocking her in my arms was my only hope. I try not to listen for sounds of Alicia and Elliott stirring in the next room as I gather her up into my arms and head downstairs. After an hour of walking up and down the kitchen with the door to the living room closed in an effort to muffle her wails, trying and failing to get her to take a bottle, I finally lose the will. I put a jacket over my pyjamas, bundle Zara into a coat, and carry her into the living room. I am just getting the pushchair ready when I hear footsteps on the stairs and there in the doorway is Mum. Bleary-eyed, hair scraped back, a dressing gown wrapped tightly around her silk pyjamas. She looks from me to Zara, half strapped into her pram, and I register the fear in her eyes.

'I'm just going for a walk,' I say quickly.

She blinks slowly, as if trying to decide whether she believes me or not before forcing her lips into a tired smile. 'Oh well, do you want—'

'I'm fine, Mum, honestly.' I try to look reassuring.

She nods. 'OK, well, have a nice time, breakfast will be ready for when you are back.'

It's a clear message: I'll be waiting for you, just in case you're thinking about leaving again.

It is barely light outside and my breath frosts in the crisp morning air. I pull Zara's hood closer around her little cheeks and head for the park. It's so quiet and peaceful – there's nobody about, and for the first time in two days, I feel something close to calm. I walk past the White Hart, the Co-op at the corner of the road; I turn right and there's the pizza shop, next to the bus stop. Nothing seems to have changed here, nothing at all. If I didn't have Zara with me I could almost believe the last three years hadn't happened.

She has finally quietened down as well and is gurgling away happily in her pram. I turn into the gates of the park and am immediately hit by a wave of memories. Sitting under the trees, smoking weed with Joe, Tony and Liam, talking excitedly about a string of meaningless dates, completely clueless that I would soon stumble into Willow at a pub and my life would change for ever.

I park the pram next to a bench, sit down and retrieve my phone from my coat pocket. I check Willow's social media for her 'last seen's. She hasn't been online since the morning she left. I call her for what is possibly the thousandth time in under forty-eight hours. It rings, it rings again, and then it goes to voicemail. It's not ringing long enough. I'm being cut off. Is it Willow? Or has someone else got her phone? If it is Willow why won't she speak to me? Let me know she's OK at the very least? I feel so helpless. Is she mad at me for something I've done? Or is it something she's done? Constant messages don't work. Nothing works. I drop my head to my hands, massaging my temples. I just don't understand.

I suddenly feel so angry that my hands clench automatically into fists, and I realise this isn't helping me. The more time on my own, the more time I have to think, and thinking is getting me nowhere fast. I get up and start walking, pushing the pram with so much force that Zara turns her head to me in surprise. I am suddenly tired and hungry and can't think of anything better to do than head home. I am walking so fast I'm practically trotting. The faster I move my feet, the better. The more I focus on counting my steps, the more the questions in my head seem to recede. 1. 2. 3. 4. 5. 6. 7. 8. 9—

What the . . .

I'm momentarily winded as Zara's pram collides with something solid, and the handles ram into my stomach. I'm at the corner of Mum's street, and I look up to see a bulky guy with a full salt and pepper beard. He's easily over six foot and wearing a heavy dark coat. For one split second I am sure I recognise him, but as his light blue eyes meet mine I realise I can't place him.

'So sorry,' I mumble, very aware of his size and the fact that I have just rammed a pram into him.

He doesn't say anything. He just stares at me and I can feel the back of my neck grow hot. For a moment we stay locked like that, then I awkwardly manoeuvre the pram around him and dash into the driveway of Mum's house.

Only once I've got the door open do I check Zara for signs of any injury in the collision. She seems fine. As I wheel the pram inside I look instinctively over my shoulder for the bearded man. But he's nowhere to be seen.

# Chapter 14

# Willow

**Then – September 2017**

After spending days when we first moved to New Haw worrying about how I would fill the remaining five weeks of the summer holidays, I am somehow starting college tomorrow and I'm stressed. I have two huge spots on my face, my stomach is playing up so badly that I haven't been able to touch anything since breakfast, and my hands are cracked and flaky because I've washed them so many times.

Dustin messaged me earlier:

Good luck tomorrow, it'll be fine.

It's not going to be fine, I don't know anyone.

You know Liam and Joe. And then you can make friends.

I can't make friends.

Oi, so what am I then?

I was too distracted to reply. I put a face mask on. Washed it off, washed my hair, plaited it, applied spot cream to my forehead. Made a cup of peppermint tea. Now I am wrapped up in a dressing gown, watching back-to-back episodes of *The Office* on my laptop. I know if I try and watch TV with Gran she'll end up interrogating me on how I'm feeling about tomorrow, or attempting a pep talk and I just can't face it. So I'm curled up on my bed instead, knitting and trying to relax. Just relax, Willow, and be normal for once in your life!

My phone pings.

It's Dustin.

Front door, two minutes.

I stare at the message, baffled. Did he mean to send that to me? Was it meant for someone else? I wait for the 'Sorry, wrong chat!!' message but it doesn't come. Curious, I go to my bedroom and pull back the curtains. There he is, strolling down the road, holding something in his hand. I can't see in the darkness. Oh my God. What? What is he doing there?

I rush to the living room, where Gran is snoozing on the sofa, and open the door before he manages to knock. He has the dorkiest grin on his face, and in his hands is a bunch of flowers. He offers them to me and I notice that the stems are uneven and he's wrapped them in newspaper. It looks like he has just picked a big hole in someone's garden.

'Why are you here?'

He gestures towards the flowers. 'I'm here to wish you good luck?'

I try to process his reasoning. Is this a joke? What is he

71

thinking of, showing up at my house with flowers like he's in a Ryan Gosling film? How does he even know where I live? Aware that Gran is still snoozing, I hastily step outside and pull the door shut behind me. 'I'd let you in, but we might wake up my gran, and then she will start asking a hundred questions and she also—'

'I wasn't expecting to come in, the weather's nice out here anyway,' Dustin says, smiling at me.

'OK, well ...' I walk towards the small green opposite our building and sit down, motioning him to follow. I don't know what else to do.

'Willow, I know I surprised you and all, but you don't have to come out armed,' he says with a chuckle.

I look down and realise I'm holding my knitting needles.

Oh shit.

'Sorry, I didn't even realise I brought them out with me ...'

'Oh wait, is this my first knitting class?'

'What?'

'You promised to teach me. Remember? The night we met?'

'Oh yeah. Maybe next time.'

Dustin grins, digs his hand into his rucksack and gets out a bottle of water. He swigs from it and offers it to me. I shake my head.

'How did you know I live here, anyway?'

He arches an eyebrow. 'How do you think?'

I roll my eyes. 'Georgia.'

I look down at my hands. The flowers he's brought are a real mishmash of colours and scents – they smell beautiful. I don't think I've ever been given flowers before.

'Thank you for these, it's super sweet.'

He shrugs. 'I know you get nervous about things, so I thought this might help.'

He says it like it's nothing, like this is the kind of anxiety everyone experiences now and then, but he must think I'm crazy really. 'I know, it's ridiculous how nervous I feel,' I say, forcing a laugh that sounds so fake I instantly cringe. 'Sometimes I think I just shouldn't bother. Like it's not worth the stress.'

'No!'

Dustin's response is so forceful that I start. I wait for him to apologise but he doesn't. Instead he says quietly: 'Don't ever say that, Willow. This is super important. This is your future. All that stuff you were saying at the party, about how design makes you feel in control when you don't have control over your life? But you do, Willow, *this* is control. You can't let irrational worries get in the way.' He hesitantly reaches for my hand and this time I let him take it. It feels good. 'I believe you can do this, you really just need to believe in yourself.'

I look at him.

'I think I'm starting to.'

There's silence, his eyes on mine, mine on his and I am suddenly overwhelmed by the desire to move closer to him. It's like an itch I'm burning to scratch. And suddenly, I realise, that desire is all I'm feeling. All of my nerves about college have evaporated. In the end it wasn't the peppermint tea, it wasn't the knitting, the spot cream, or the face mask that helped. It was— Oh. My. God. The spot cream. The spot cream is still on my face.

In horror I put a hand to my forehead but Dustin doesn't say anything. He very slowly moves my hands away and gradually our heads move closer together, until finally our lips meet.

# Chapter 15

# Dustin

I'm barely through the door before Mum is there, rushing to help me steer the pushchair around the staircase. 'How was the walk?'

'Umm ...' I'm still thinking about the salt and pepper guy. Did I know him? He was looking at me so strangely. 'Fine, yeah, it was fine.' I wrestle Zara out of her pushchair.

'I can hold her,' Mum says, extending her arms to take her from me. I shield Zara from her instinctively.

'It's OK.'

Mum doesn't let her smile fall. 'OK, well, you go into the warmth, I'll sort out the pushchair,' she says, shimmying past me. I go into the living room carrying Zara, and sit on the sofa. It's quiet. Alicia and Elliot must not be up yet. Then I notice it. On the coffee table, a brown parcel. My name is scrawled on the front in block capitals. DUSTIN.

No address.

No postage stamp.

Weird.

'Oh yeah, that arrived for you,' Mum says behind me, causing me to jump. I didn't realise she was already in.

74

'Sorry, what?'

'That came whilst you were out.'

'Came for me? What do you mean? Did someone deliver it?'

'Well I suppose they must have done, as it's way too early for post. I was just putting the rubbish out ...'

Looking out to see if I was on my way back, more like.

'And I just tripped over it on the doorstep.'

I look down at the parcel, focusing on the handwriting. It doesn't look like Willow's usual loopy hand, but then it's hard to tell with block capitals. Did she post this? But how does she know where I am? In fact, how does anyone know I'm here? My friends from work know I've come to Mum's, but they don't know where she lives. And anyway, there's no way they'd come all the way from Brighton and not stop by. Georgia and the gang? But again they'd just pop round. Or message me, even if, I think guiltily, I am avoiding their messages. I pop Zara down on the floor and sit next to her, carefully stroking the parcel.

'Come on, I'm excited, I want to know what it is,' Mum says.

I ignore her. Does she really not think there's anything weird about this?

I finally decide to open it, ripping it open with the same bated force with which you rip off a plaster, and stare in disbelief at what is exposed in my lap.

'Ooooh, that's nice,' Mum says, peering over my shoulder. 'Is it a baby blanket? It looks like nice quality.'

A lump is stuck in my throat. I pick up the blanket, trying to stop my hands shaking. 'Yeah, it is,' I say quietly. 'It's Zara's. She loves it, can hardly sleep without it.'

'Ah, how sweet,' Mum says. 'Well I'll go and see to breakfast, shall I?'

She pads into the kitchen and leaves me stroking the blanket.

The blanket I definitely left in the Brighton flat yesterday morning. How the hell is it here now?

Zara has clocked the blanket, and her wide eyes stare at me in excitement. 'Blankie!' she says.

'Did Mummy send this for you?' I whisper. She reaches out for it and I give it to her. Her little fingers close around the wool happily. I watch her in a sort of daze. Maybe Willow went back to the flat? Maybe she guessed where I'd be and this is her way of telling me she wants me to come home? Cryptic, admittedly. But then Willow's behaviour has hardly been straightforward these last couple of days.

I ask Mum if she could watch Zara and she's thrilled. I go to the bathroom upstairs and splash cold water over my face. OK, think, Dustin, think. If Willow delivered this by hand maybe she's still in New Haw?

I check my phone. No messages but perhaps she's waiting for me to make the next move now. I call her.

No answer.

Then I call Naomi.

'Hey, Dustin, you OK? Any news?'

Not the response I was hoping for.

'Um, no, not yet. Listen, Naomi, are you still at the flat?'

'Yes, they let me work from home today. I said I was keeping an eye on things for you.'

'Has Willow been back?'

There's a pause before she answers.

'No, Dustin,' she says quietly. 'No one has been back.'

I can feel my breath getting caught in my throat. Stay in control. 'When did you get there again?'

'After work yesterday.'

I left the flat in the morning, about eight a.m. I had walked around town with the pushchair for a good hour and a half trying to psych myself into getting on that train. If Naomi didn't get there until the evening that means there was a good window of over ten hours when no one was in the flat. Which means ...

'Oh my God. I think Willow has been back, I think she came back to the flat. OK, Naomi, I need to get back to Brighton. I'm leaving now, so I'll—'

'Woah.' Naomi has to raise her voice to cut through my babbling. 'Dustin, calm down, I don't understand what you're talking about.'

'Naomi, she has been there. Maybe when you were at work yesterday. Zara has this baby blanket – Willow actually knitted it for me years ago, but Zara adores it. Well, I accidentally left it at the flat ...'

'Yeah ...'

'And I just found it on the doorstep here. And Willow must have brought it – who else knows where to come? Honestly, Naomi, I'm telling you ...'

'Dustin, I—'

'Because I left the blanket at the flat yesterday morning.' I am aware that I'm shouting like a madman but am powerless to stop myself. 'So Willow must have come back to the flat, realised where I was and—'

'Hey, Dust—'

'And known how much Zara would miss the blanket. I mean she's not answering my calls, but maybe if I came back—'

'Dustin!' she shouts, shutting me up. When she speaks next her voice is calm and controlled. 'It's OK. Look, if she went and posted it, that might mean she's in the area. OK?' I nod my head, forgetting she can't see me. 'I mean it's a bit weird, I don't see why she wouldn't just talk to you. But honestly, I don't know if coming back here and waiting around for her is the best thing for you. I honestly think you'll drive yourself crazy here, and at least where you are you have your mum to help with Zara. Look, you stay there, stay with your family. I'll stay here, and I'll let you know. I'll stay here for the rest of the week while you try to work out what to do. Stay calm, OK? If you need me to come see you let me know. OK?'

I swallow heavily. 'OK.' Now that she says it, the thought of pacing up and down the Brighton flat on my own for who knows how long till Willow comes back isn't that appealing.

'Work is fine with me working remotely for a bit; they've also said you can do whatever works best for you. Like, if in a couple of days you want to work from New Haw or something.'

'I can't even think about work.'

'OK, but—'

'I can't.'

I hang up. I know I've just been a dick to Naomi. And she's doing me a massive favour at the end of the day. Guilty, I tap out a text to her:

Sorry, still feeling kind of overwhelmed with everything.
Hugely appreciate you being there.

Her reply comes back instantly.

Don't worry at all. I'll let you know if I hear anything
from Willow x

'I don't care. I don't want him living here.' My sister's voice booming from her bedroom greets me as soon as I open the bathroom door.

'Alicia—'

'No, I don't want him here. Two years, Elliot. Two years!'

'I know, but, like, you've got to think about your mum.'

'Oh, don't bring Mum into this, it's obvious why Mum is pretending things are OK.'

'I know, I'm just saying, I mean he is still your brother.'

'Yeah, that doesn't change the fact that he's a selfish arsehole. I don't care if he broke up with Willow. I just accepted that I wasn't going to see him ever again and then he decides to pop back into our lives as soon as it suits him. It's not OK.'

I wonder if that's what will happen with me and Willow. Just when I accept she's gone, she will come back. I don't think so. I won't ever be able to accept she's gone.

'It's not fair, Elliot, I didn't do anything. I didn't deserve for him to cut me out too.'

Elliot doesn't reply and I'm fairly sure I can hear Alicia crying.

I go to my room and close the door. For the first time I understand how Willow might have felt. I want a magician to do a vanishing act on me. That would be nice right now.

# Chapter 16

# Willow

Then – September 2017

The college is so much bigger than it appears from the outside. It's a labyrinth of corridors shooting off from corridors, and they all look the same. I bring up the email on my phone again, the one from my new head of year stating the room number of her office, where I am supposed to go.

Dear Willow,

We're very much looking forward to welcoming you to Norwood next week. I hope you've had a chance to feel settled in New Haw.

Given that you're joining us halfway through your A-level course I think it might be helpful if you arranged a quick catch-up session with each of your tutors in your first week, just so you can talk through the modules you took in your old college and how you're feeling about each subject. I can see your AS results were very strong, congratulations, and I hope you will find Norwood a place to build upon your already excellent achievements. Your Design teacher from your last school spoke of you in particularly glowing terms and I'm excited to see what you do with that subject this year.

On your first day, I wonder if you might pop by my office first thing so that we can meet each other and I can talk you through your timetable. My office is Room 3:05 on the third floor.

I also wanted to say that we are aware that circumstances haven't been easy for you over the last years, but I hope you know you can always talk to me or to your tutors if you need extra support.

With best wishes,

Miss Ingram

It was a nice email – raised a lot of questions in my mind as to exactly what Gran had said to them, but kind. The thing is, I'd much rather have slipped into the back of the classroom, as inconspicuous as possible. But I want to start things off well, and failing to show up to the first appointment with my head of year is not going to be the best start. And I need to ace this year.

Which room is this? 3:08. But I've just passed 3:03 and 3:04 and there was no sign of a 3:05. Where the hell is it? I can feel the panic rising again. God, if only Gee or Dustin were here. Breathe, Willow, just . . .

Two hands grab my shoulder and I jolt and turn round.

It's Liam. He smiles at me goofily. 'Hey, Wills. How you finding the college so far?'

'Scary.' I exhale. 'I'm the new girl.'

He shrugs. 'At least you're not the one who couldn't pass last year.'

I nod my head, trying to count the doors down the corridor: 3:07, 3:09 ...

'Do you need help?'

'I'm looking for the head of year, Miss In—'

'Miss Ingram? Yeah, I gotcha, literally just round that corner, turn right and follow the corridor right to the end. The room numbers here are so stupid.'

I look up to him gratefully. 'Thanks, Liam.'

'No problem. Now I would stay and take you, but I try to avoid Miss Ingram at all costs.'

'Oh no, it's fine, I got it.'

I say goodbye, Liam dashes off, and I head in the direction he pointed. I'm definitely going to be a few minutes late, and I'm also trying to ignore the stupid questions and worries in my head.

Dustin and I kissed. The warmth bubbles in my belly as I think of it again. We kissed. Try to ignore it, Willow. But we kissed, doesn't that mean something? But then I remember what Gee said Dustin is like. He's a dater, he's a flirter, what would he see in me? He probably kisses loads of people.

Now, Willow, what you need to understand is, kisses aren't a big deal for a lot of people. They don't mean anything. Don't overthink it. Stop focusing on the way his lips felt on yours, his hand stroking your hair, your ear, the back of your neck. The tiny goosebumps all over your body. Stop obsessing over it.

I thought he might text after we parted ways last night – he usually does – but no message came. Now I'm worried it's going to be weird. I don't want it to be weird, I care about Dustin a lot. He makes me feel like I matter. What if all that is ruined now?

I reach the door with a sign that says 'Miss Ingram'.

Deep breaths, Willow, deep breaths.
My phone pings.

Good luck today! You'll be fine! You got this!

It's Dustin.
I bite my smile away, and knock on the door.

# Chapter 17

# Dustin

Alicia and Elliott are still arguing and, fed up of hearing myself described as a selfish arsehole over and over again, I eventually go downstairs. Mum is fussing over the hob, Zara's gurgling happily in her high chair, a bowl of porridge in front of her, and there's a big spread of breakfast on the table – juice, sausages, bacon, croissants, fruit. Guilt gnaws at my stomach. As much as it pains me to admit, this is just as much the mum I remember as the controlling mum I've seethed at over the last few years. Always generous, always going the extra mile. It doesn't mean she was perfect – far from it – but the way she's acting now, it makes it harder to remember how we got to me leaving and not coming back for two years. Mum forced me out – that's the way I saw it at the time. I felt like I had no other option.

A thought hits me. Is that how Willow felt? Like I'd left her no other option? But that can't be right – when I left Mum behind I wasn't happy. Willow and I were happy. Weren't we?

'Mum, you didn't need to,' I say, motioning to the food, sitting down in the seat next to Zara's high chair and stroking her cheek absent-mindedly. We used to have breakfast together, if I had time before work. The three of us, Zara usually on Willow's lap after refusing to settle in her high chair and pushing her porridge onto the floor. I would cook eggs, make us both a coffee. Little normal things you take for granted. My heart hurts. Stop thinking about it, it does no good.

'It was no effort,' Mum lies, popping the kettle on. 'Coffee?'

'I'm all right, thanks, Mum.

'Oh, don't act like you can begin to understand, Elliott!' Alicia is shouting so loud now that even from the kitchen we can hear every word, crystal clear. 'You have no idea what it's like to have a brother just abandon you for years.'

'Tea?'

'No, thanks.'

Mum pauses, as if my answers have ruined her plan, before she awkwardly sits down opposite me.

'I should probably see what Alicia and ...' Mum begins but with almost impeccable timing, Alicia stomps into the kitchen. She's dressed in black jeans, red boots and an oversized jumper. I follow her eyes to the spread on the table, to Mum, to Zara, while she studiously avoids looking in my direction. 'Staying for breakfast, Lis?' Mum says, as if we hadn't both heard her screaming the house down just moments before.

Alicia glances at me. 'No, I'm late for college,' she mumbles, before walking out the room and shouting up the stairs for Elliot.

I turn to Mum, confused. 'Alicia's still at college?'

Mum nods, clutching a cup of tea between her hands. 'She's retaking her A-levels.'

Oh. Alicia was always so good at school. A straight-A student. What happened there? And how does someone who still goes to college meet a twenty-eight-year-old like Elliot?

'And Elliot is a personal trainer, they met at the gym.'

Did Mum read my mind?

Mum stares at her untouched breakfast. I have zero appetite, so I decide to help by trying to spoon Zara some porridge, but she turns her face away.

'Mum ... I'm sorry me coming back has made things difficult.'

Mum tuts. 'Don't be silly. I'm so happy to see you both.' She wants to say something else but is holding back. Now that really isn't like the Mum I know.

'Is something wrong?' I ask her.

Mum stutters slightly, clearly nervous about what she has to say. 'I just ... I just wanted to check that Willow is OK? That she isn't missing her little girl.'

I look down awkwardly. Mum is trying to be subtle. She wants to know more, but she's failing at not making it obvious. I can't tell Mum the truth, but I need to give her something so that she doesn't pester me with questions. 'We thought it'd be best for me to look after Zara for now, because I quit my job, so I have the time. And she's away for a couple of weeks. She just wanted to clear her head.'

That sounds plausible. I'm hoping this will buy me a little bit of time.

Mum nods her head like she totally understands, and is OK with that lack of information. 'So quitting your job was unrelated to breaking up with Willow?'

'Yeah, bad timing.' Another lie. 'My head's just a bit of a mess, and I really need to work some things out.' Not so much of a lie. 'So I came home to do that. I'm sorry it seems like you're my second option, or if it seems like I'm using you guys ...'

Mum reaches across the table and places her hand on my shoulder. 'We're family, family comes first, we will always be here,' she says firmly. 'You can stay as long as you like. I'm just glad you thought of us.'

She smiles appreciatively and I nod, pretending it had all been my idea, that I had every intention of turning to them before the police, people at work, and Georgia practically forced me to go see my family.

'Family is for ever, Dustin.'

She takes my plate and sets about filling it, whilst I feel a little sick thinking about the last time I heard her say that.

# Chapter 18

# Willow

Then – November 2017

I'm doing very well at Graphics, I'm doing well in English Lit, not doing so well in Sociology. But it's OK. I've been at Norwood for almost three months, and I'm surviving it. I wouldn't say I've made friends as such. There are people I talk to, and mostly I sit with Liam and his friends at lunch. But outside of college I see Georgia and the rest of the group quite a bit. I see Dustin a lot. I talk to Dustin a lot. All the time, actually.

It's mid-November, and I'm just coming out of the college gates all bundled up in a coat, and he's there. Dustin. Leaning against the lamp-post, wearing his coffee shop apron over a thick jumper, grinning at me. I find myself running up and hugging him. This is our routine. Dustin now works in the coffee shop round the corner. Not his forever job, he claims, but apparently it keeps his mum off his back. So he tries to do the shifts that end in time for him to meet me by the gate at four p.m. He looks almost dashing in his stupid coffee shop uniform. He can pull anything off. And then we might see the group, or we might do something just us two, or he'll walk me home. Dustin is a laid-back guy. Not much of a one for rigid plans.

I don't know how this happened, but we are here now. I think we're dating though neither of us has rushed to put a label on it. We just couldn't stop talking to each other. At first I would go out to the pub with the group, just so I could see him. And then we started doing stuff just us two. And now we see each other nearly every day. I don't want to think about the situation too much, because it's a good thing right now, and I know good things don't last for ever. Which scares me, so I just try to put it in the back of my mind and enjoy it. It's like Gran is always saying – when you're walking you can't look too far behind or too far ahead, otherwise you'll stumble. I'm not usually very good at following that advice, but there's something about Dustin that makes me feel different. Stronger. Not fearless, exactly (I don't think I'll ever be that), but less fearful certainly. I am a different person when I'm with him.

'How was your day?' he asks, taking my hand in his.

'Good,' I reply. What I want to say is 'It was good, but infinitely better now you are here and I wish you were with me every second of the day.' But even I know that's too much.

'I found out when the Reading University open day is,' I say.

I never thought I'd go to university away from home. When we were in Brighton I always hoped I might go to the university there one day, but when we came to New Haw I faltered. Moving away from Gran into halls full of strangers. I couldn't imagine anything worse. But my Graphic Design teacher, Mrs Layton, took me aside two weeks into term and told me that I should be seriously thinking about taking design further. Had I thought about further study? So I started thinking about it again. I've looked at Winchester, Southampton and Reading.

Reading is my favourite. I'm not sure why, the website just connected with me. I could see myself going there.

For the first time ever, it feels as if things are starting to come together in my life. Fragments slotting together to form a whole. And sometimes I feel overwhelmed with excitement and relief at the idea that the future could actually be bright and interesting. But then the guilt sets in. Doesn't moving on mean moving away? From Brighton, from everything there? I think about my parents. How would they feel at their little girl going to university? Would they be proud?

'Aw, that's great!' Dustin's eyes are bright with excitement. 'Can I come with?'

I'm taken aback, but flattered. 'Of course, I'd love that. Gran's coming too.'

Dustin stops walking, raising an eyebrow. 'So when do I get to meet this gran of yours? We can't all go to Reading together if she's never even met me.'

Dustin has never been to our flat, or at least not inside it. I've never been to his house either. I'm not sure why. I can't imagine introducing Gran to anyone, having someone else cross the threshold of our private sphere. For years it has been just the two of us. And what if Gran doesn't like him? I couldn't bear it if she doesn't. I'd rather the unknown than her disapproval. Though as I look at Dustin now, his easy smile, his wide-eyed earnestness – it seems impossible that anyone could ever dislike him.

'When I get to meet your mum,' I retort.

Dustin's reaction confuses me, however. He doesn't smirk back. For a split second a frown creases his forehead and it's obvious there's something he can't bring himself to say. Shit, have I misread this completely? But then that grin is back, and he's the same old confident Dustin again.

'OK, deal,' he says. 'But I want to go to your gran's first. I want her to approve of her granddaughter's boyfriend.'

'Sorry, her what?'

Suddenly he blushes so hard I think his whole face is about to turn crimson. 'I just thought ... aren't we ... I mean, if that's OK, of course?'

I kiss him.

# Chapter 19

## Dustin

After breakfast I mope for a bit but I can't settle to anything. There's nothing on TV and without many of her toys here Zara soon gets cranky and restless so I decide to take her into town.

The town centre is in the opposite direction from the park, which is unfortunate because it means encountering a new lot of familiar yet foreign spots. The Sports Direct where I whiled away insane amounts of time as a teenager. The Wetherspoon's where I'd go with the lads on weeknights, winding up in McDonald's in the early hours and creeping home just before sunrise and Mum's alarm. Weeknights when Willow couldn't come out because of college the next day. Most of my experience of this town was a life pre-Willow, so why does everything seem to be tainted by her? The Pizza Hut where I had my seventh birthday party is also the Pizza Hut where Willow and I occasionally went for Saturday lunch after a Friday night at the pub. We'd order ham and pineapple. Her favourite, and after a while it became mine.

When I get to the high street I survey the line of shops.

'Where shall we go, Zara?' I mutter. Then I spot an

Entertainer I don't remember being there before. Perfect. I spend maybe twenty minutes steering Zara through the aisles. I glance down at her every so often to see her expression, but nothing seems to be grabbing her attention. I guess she's a bit young for everything in here. Eventually I give up and push the pram into a coffee shop, sit down dejectedly. How am I going to do this for the rest of my life? Life is short so you have to make the most of it has always been my mantra. Now, for the first time, life seems to stretch ahead of me endlessly. OK, one step at a time, Dustin. I just need to get through the next hour, then I'll focus on the next, and eventually this day will be done and that'll be one less day to endure. I look at the time on my phone. Thinking about it, maybe an hour is a bit long. Maybe I'll just focus on getting through the next twenty minutes instead. I feel like someone told me that once; I can do twenty minutes.

They have a high chair in the corner so I grab and it and wrestle Zara into it. I'm still manoeuvring her right leg through one hole when the woman behind the counter – a kindly lady in her late fifties – asks what she can get me.

'Erm,' my mind has gone blank, 'can I have an almond milk caramel latte, please?'

Willow's drink. Why the hell did I order Willow's drink?

'Coming right up, dear.'

'Um, actually ... ' I say but she's already bustling away.

I sit down miserably. When she brings it I stare at the mug for a while before taking a sip. Ergh, it's gross. It's so sweet, how the hell did she drink these things? I swill the sickly milky liquid around and then push it away. At least Zara is sitting quite happily in her high chair.

I don't know how long I stare absent-mindedly out of the window before I see it. A flash of golden hair, long, but not too long, naturally wavy. Oh my God. I jump up and race outside.

And there, I see her. A girl dressed in an oversized sweatshirt, leggings, socks with sliders, walking away from me. She's already halfway down the pavement on the other side of the street. Is that ... is that Willow? I am running now, weaving through the people, my eyes never leaving her, my heart thumping in my ribcage. I am forced to stop for a cyclist. She's getting further and further away, I'm going to lose her. 'Willow!' I hear myself shout.

But she doesn't turn, she is still walking. Did she hear me? Is she deliberately ignoring me? 'WILLOW!' my voice booms through the street. Multiple people stop, turning around to stare at me, including Willow. She stops, turning around to look at me, and my heart sinks. I grind to a halt. I've reached the other side of the street and now I'm closer I see it's not her. It's someone totally different. She frowns at me.

'Sorry,' I gasp. 'I thought ...' *I thought you were my girlfriend, the mother of my child, the love of my life.* 'I thought you were someone else.'

And then I'm turning around and walking away. People are still staring but I can't bring myself to feel embarrassed. There's no room for shame in the swell of misery and helplessness inside me. As I'm walking home I pass a couple, arms linked, pushing a baby in a stroller. Then another couple swinging a toddler between them just a bit further down. Christ, I swear it's like the universe is trying to rub it in my face – how many happy, normal families there are out there. How I'm not one of them. How Zara won't grow up feeling safe and loved between two parents.

Zara.

My stomach lurches.

*Shit.*

I forgot her.

I run back to the coffee shop, practically elbowing people out of the way on the pavement, burst through the door and find a lady holding a screaming Zara in her arms. She's locked in discussion with the woman behind the counter and they're both frowning anxiously. I rush up to them, dazed with panic.

'That's my daughter,' I shout and try to grab Zara, but the lady holding her pulls back protectively.

'It's my daughter, I swear,' I say, pushing the words out though I can barely breathe. With trembling hands I retrieve my wallet from my back pocket and take out the photograph tucked inside it. The photo of me, Willow and Zara. 'Please.'

The woman's eyes soften and she hands Zara over to me, who instantly stops screaming. I squeeze her so tight I feel I must be hurting her, but she snuggles into me. 'Don't worry, I am a mum of three kids, it happens,' the woman says, giving me a reassuring smile and leading me over to a table. The woman behind the counter follows.

The lady who had been holding Zara explains they were just about to call the police, and as soon as I hear that I break down. I'm crying so hard I can barely get the words out, but I tell her about Willow leaving, about how the police aren't helping, about moving in with my family and my sister hating me, how I feel paralysed. It's all so scrambled and muffled by my tears that I'm fairly sure they can't understand a word. But they listen and nod and one of them puts an arm around my shoulder, patting my hand sympathetically. Then I have nothing more to say and the woman behind the counter goes back to her station. The other waits quietly with me till I've calmed down. Zara is looking up at me with anxious eyes and I stroke her beautiful face. I can't believe I forgot my daughter. I could have lost her. Then I would have lost both of them.

'You probably think I'm an awful dad.'

She shakes her head. 'Not at all! You were barely out of the door before you came back. Don't be so hard on yourself.'

She ruffles Zara's hair and orders me a cup of hot, sweet tea.

Later, when I have finally stopped crying, I thank them both and try to pay, but the woman behind the counter shakes her head and says to forget about it.

I walk back home, pushing the empty stroller with one hand, the other clutching Zara to my hip. I don't want to let go of her quite yet.

When I get home, Mum is instantly there at the door, smiling like she hasn't seen us for days.

'How was town?' she says.

I look at her, still feeling panicked, sick, and out of breath. My heart hasn't stopped thumping in my chest. But I force my mouth into a smile. 'It was lovely. Good to be home.'

# Chapter 20

# Willow

Then – November 2017

There's a knock at the door, and I rush to the living room, leaving Gran to set the table. I open the door, hoping my nerves aren't written all over my face. Dustin stands there, bottle of wine in one hand, a bunch of flowers in the other.

'Hello, you,' he says, planting a kiss on my cheek, before confidently stepping past me.

Gran was thrilled when I asked if Dustin could come for dinner. 'Oh, I get to meet this mysterious Dustin,' she said and two seconds later had whipped out her diary to check when she was free in between her bingo, book club, knitting group and the country market. We decided on a Tuesday evening, and when I asked Dustin if he was free, he told me it was a stupid question.

I introduce him to Gran, who beams excitedly as he shakes her hand – very formal. But before too much conversation is exchanged, I drag him to my room. He flops back onto my bed, arms folded behind his head. 'Exactly how I imagined.' He smiles.

I frown at him. 'Is that a bad thing or a good thing?'

He shrugs. 'It's just a thing,' he says, propping himself up on one elbow, his eyes scanning every inch of my room. Then he notices my knitting basket at the foot of my bed and grins. He leans forward, picking it up. 'This is the famous knitting basket?'

He picks out a yellow half-knitted blanket, staring at it. 'This your next project?'

I snatch it from him, glaring. 'Well it was going to be for you, but now you've ruined it.'

'Noo,' he whines. 'I'm sorry. I'll forget I ever saw it. It'll be a perfect surprise.'

'Shut up,' I say, rolling my eyes, but I know I'm smiling.

Thirty minutes later we are sat around the small fold-out table Gran got out from the garage just for the occasion. She made salmon fillets, new potatoes and broccoli. Dustin inhales it like he hasn't eaten in about three months and Gran, delighted, piles more potatoes and veg onto his plate. Dustin and I did most of the talking – about college, the Reading open day in a couple of weeks, Dustin's job at the coffee shop and his plans for the future. Gran mostly sat and listened but I could tell she was so happy. Happier than I've seen her in years.

'That was amazing, Mary, thank you so much,' Dustin says, and gets up to start clearing the table.

'Oh, you sit down and leave that to me.' Gran smiles, taking the plates from him. 'It was my pleasure. You're welcome anytime, Dustin, you're such a gentleman.'

She turns away and Dustin beams at me, so obviously pleased with himself I have to suppress the urge to laugh.

Dustin stays over in my room (Gran, to my amazement, doesn't even offer to make him up a bed on the sofa) and as we lie tucked up under the duvet it strikes me that he is the first person to ever share a bed with me. Even when I stayed at Gee's, or she stayed with me, one of us would be on the blow-up bed. I've always liked my own space. But now as my head rests on his chest and he runs his fingers delicately through my hair, I couldn't feel better.

'Thank you for coming tonight,' I say.

He kisses me. 'Thank you for having me.'

'So your house next, right?'

Dustin pauses. I can feel his body tense.

'Yeah,' he says, and he slackens. 'Yeah, of course. We'll have to sort that soon.'

# Chapter 21

# Dustin

It's Monday evening now. It's been one week since she went missing and I still haven't heard anything from Willow. In the past week I have called Zara's daycare, the dentist Willow went to, and her GP. I even called her hairdresser she went to once. They couldn't tell me anything. Georgia still hasn't heard anything either. I know she and her mum must be worried sick, they're Willow's family, after all, but Georgia is only ever calm when she speaks to me.

'There's nothing more we can do now,' she says.

And she's right, I guess. She and I designed a missing poster and sent it to Naomi, who, with the help of my work friends, plastered them all over Brighton – pieces of paper with Willow's picture taped to lamp-posts, shop windows, wherever we can think of.

'We should put them up here,' Georgia said. 'Especially if you think she might have come here with the blanket.'

But I refused.

'If she's deliberately avoiding us, missing posters will just put her off coming here,' I said firmly, knowing that what I was saying only half made sense. The real reason, of course, was that I didn't want Mum, Alicia or Elliott seeing them.

Though it is more painful than I ever imagined anything could be, I am starting to accept what the police and Georgia seem to think. Willow wasn't abducted, she left me.

Mostly I think this because she has blocked me from everything on social media. I was checking her socials about ten times a day and one day I just couldn't see her any more. She has blocked Georgia too. She has even blocked me from Twitter, though she's only ever tweeted once or twice. Or maybe she's deleted herself from all of these platforms. Either way, when you search her name there's nothing there, like she never existed.

But she does exist. She will always exist to me.

Zara is grizzly. She's been grizzly all morning.

'Please stop crying,' I beg. I can feel anger bubbling and feel instantly guilty. Willow probably never got angry with her, and she was on her own with her a lot. Why did Willow ever think I'd be a better parent?

Zara doesn't stop crying.

This has been the longest week of my life, like an ongoing nightmare. The life I used to have doesn't exist any more. I don't work. I don't see or talk to my friends. I'm back living with my family. My sister hates me. She has barely spoken to me since she and Elliott argued.

I'm not even sure how my mum feels about me being back. Most of the time she acts like she couldn't be happier and everything's just perfect, but on a couple of occasions I've come into a room to see her hastily stuffing a tissue into her pocket, red-eyed and sniffly. I sleep in an empty bed, cuddling a pillow next to my body. I'm looking after my baby all on my own. I have no clue what I'm doing.

I'm sitting on the kitchen floor, Zara in the high chair. She wails, her puffy red face scrunched up, tears streaming down her cheeks. I stand and try again to pop a spoonful of food into her mouth. She spits it back out again.

I grit my teeth. It's not fair. I want to cry all the time too, but I can't. I have to be a dad, I have to have my shit together. Doesn't Zara realise that?

She stops crying. I look at her, her big brown eyes watching me, her lip trembling.

'You OK now?' I ask, wiping my tired eyes. Zara starts shaking her head. Her bottom lip juts out. No, no, no. Don't cry, don't cry again. I'm not sure I can take it any more.

I can feel sweat trickling down my forehead. 'Come on, Zara, how about something to eat, eh?' I spoon some of the pureed mush onto the stupid plastic spoon, pushing it up to her mouth, but she clamps her mouth shut and turns her head away. 'No!' That's another one from her limited repertoire of words. Possibly her first actually.

'Just eat the bloody food!' I slam the spoon on the table.

Damn it.

That was loud. And aggressive.

Too loud and aggressive. Zara looks up at me, eyes wide, blinking, and then the screaming starts. She lifts her arms up this time, screaming loudly, throwing herself against the sides of her high chair. I go to pick her up but she just screams harder, scowling at me with accusing eyes.

'You all right, hon?'

I turn to see Mum standing in the doorway. Her hair is tied back into the smallest bun, neatly ironed sheets folded over one arm. As I see her staring at me, I realise how thankful I am to see her. I realise why I'm here. My heart sinks as I swallow the bile in my throat. I need my mum.

I shake my head. 'I don't know what to do,' I whisper, pulling on the neck of my T-shirt. 'I don't know how to make her stop crying.'

Mum smiles gently. 'It's OK, hon, babies cry.' She moves forward, places the sheets over the back of the chair and stretches out her arms towards Zara. But then she pauses. I know Mum wants to hold Zara, but instead she calmly instructs me. 'Pick her up and hold her close to your chest.'

The last thing I want to do is bring the crying closer to me.

'It's all right, it'll calm her down.'

'No, it won't. She wants her mum.'

'Pick her up, Dustin.'

I bite my tongue, and slowly lean down and lift Zara up out of her chair, holding her thrashing body away from me.

'Now bring her closer to you, that's it.'

I carefully pull her onto my chest, hand under her bum, the other around her body.

'Great, now gently rock her.'

I start swaying, and I feel Zara start to relax and her moans grow quieter. I look up at Mum. 'Thank you.'

'Woah, you look like shit.'

We both turn to the door, where Georgia is standing dressed in leather knee-high boots, leather jacket and shorts, though I'm not sure it's strictly the right weather for that.

'What are you doing here?' Georgia lives in Surbiton now. She didn't tell me she was coming back to New Haw. She didn't tell me she was popping round. I would have made sure I was out.

'Your delightful sister let me in. She's changed a bit,' Georgia says, never one to mince her words. She waves at Mum. 'Hey, Carol.'

'Hello, Georgia,' Mum says with a thin smile. She's not Georgia's biggest fan. 'Would you like a cup of tea?'

'Aw, that'd be lovely,' Gee says brightly. 'My mum passed you at the supermarket car park the other day, she sends her love.'

'Oh how lovely,' Mum says, imitating Georgia's chirpy tone. 'I'll pop the kettle on.'

Once Mum's back is turned and she's busy rummaging with cups, Georgia's fake smile drops. She rolls her eyes and turns back to me.

'You really do look like shit. Have you been eating?'

I glare at her. I've always had a weird relationship with Georgia. She's one of my closest friends and yet every time we see each other we somehow manage to piss each other off. Like brother and sister annoying the hell out of each other, but with plenty of mutual affection deep down. I had worried my dating Willow would put a strain on my friendship with Georgia, but it didn't. If anything it made it better. We became the three musketeers.

'What's up, Georgia?'

She rolls her eyes again. 'Why are you calling me Georgia?'

'I don't know, it just reminds me that she—'

'That Willow called me Gee?' She tuts. 'Oh, Dustin, stop being so mopey.' I look hastily back at Mum, who stiffens but doesn't interrupt. I shoot Georgia a warning look and she cocks her head to the door, motioning for me to follow her.

I don't know why I do, but I let Georgia lead me through my own house to the hallway. She stops at the stairs and sits down, indicating for me to do the same. 'Dustin,' she says calmly, 'this can't go on.'

'What?'

'You can't keep ignoring everyone's texts and phone calls. It's all on your terms at the moment. You ask about Willow, we reply, then you ignore us again. You ignore us trying to help, trying to talk, trying to be there for you. We want to see you.'

When she means everyone, she means the group. I don't talk to the group that much. We kind of drifted when I moved away. Don't get me wrong, I love them to bits, but my life in Brighton was a bubble. Mine and Willow's perfect, satisfying bubble. So I did neglect the group, I would rarely chat to them, I would rarely see them, unless they came down and visited us in Brighton, and that happened less and less frequently over time. Georgia was the exception, though. I would see Georgia about once a month, Willow stayed in touch with her more regularly than that, and Georgia would come to stay.

'OK, well, congratulations, you have seen me. What now?' I say, shuffling Zara onto my hip.

She looks at me for a second. 'I'm going to take you on day release.'

I don't know if Georgia is playing a game with me, but she's taken us back to our regular pub. The White Hart. I haven't been here in two years, and the last time I was here was with Willow. It's the pub where she and I met. Bringing Zara here without Willow is horrible. We always talked about coming back here with her one day, maybe on her eighteenth birthday for her first drink. Giving her the whole 'This is where we met' story. I always thought it was unlikely to ever actually happen. Then again, there are a lot of things I never thought would happen and I turned out to be pretty wrong about some of those.

'You bringing your baby in this pub is strange, right?' Georgia says, slurping on her rum and Coke.

I frown, taking a sip of my pint. Mum tried to convince me to leave Zara at home, she'd happily have looked after her. But nope. Mum always offers to take her on walks, but I can't bear to be away from her. And what if Mum loses her like I almost did? At least I don't have to worry when she's with me.

'Are you going to have cuddles with Auntie Geebean?' Georgia says in an annoying high-pitched voice, lifting Zara off my lap and onto hers.

She looks at me, proudly. 'I love her. I always love seeing her.'

I nod my head, taking another sip.

'How is it being back home?'

I shrug my shoulders. 'Well, it's not the best of circumstances. And Alicia hates me. She doesn't talk to me.'

'No kidding. You guys used to be pretty tight before you cut her out,' she says.

'I didn't cut her out!' I say angrily. 'You know what happened.'

Georgia arches an eyebrow in an infuriating way.

'What are you saying, Georgia? You think it was all my fault?'

'I didn't say that.' She says it with an air of finality and turns her attention back to Zara, making it clear she's not going to let me drag her into an argument. She starts bobbing Zara up and down and I think about warning her that Mum fed her just before we came out.

But I stay silent. If Zara throws up, Georgia's cleaning it up.

There's a pause. 'How's your mum?' she asks.

'OK, actually. It's weird. She's being really nice.'

Georgia smiles, a fake smile. 'Well, that's good,' she says. She's never liked my mum much either. They're just both strong personalities, I guess. Whereas Willow was the total opposite – mellow and eager to please – so it should have worked.

I don't like the silence, and every question Georgia asks

106

scares me, so I decide to take control of the conversation. 'How's your job going? How's living in Surbiton?'

Georgia sighs. 'I'm already bored of commuting into London, and I've only been doing it for a month. But it's nice to not live at home, though I'm staying there tonight.' Her face softens slightly. 'And I can stay at home longer, if you need me to, you know that, right?'

I nod. I do know that. 'Thanks, Gee.'

Georgia smiles, then she pulls a face and holds Zara up in front of her. 'I think she's done a poo.'

'Great.' I reach for the pram to pull out the changing bag.

'You should come see the others; they miss you. It'd be a nice change, actually seeing everyone in Surrey for once.'

I roll my eyes. 'Yep, rather than everyone going to Brighton, paying for a hotel or getting the last train home. I know. You always say this, but it doesn't look like I'll be going back to Brighton at the moment so you don't need to worry about that.'

Georgia ignores my gripe. 'We've dispersed a bit but most of us still make it back here every few weeks or so. It'd be nice to be back together again.' She grins at me. 'Obviously it's not nice circumstances. Obvs.'

I have to say this. It's starting to piss me off.

'How are you so calm about all of this, Georgia? Do you not care about Willow? Aren't you frantic?'

She narrows her eyes at me.

'Of course I'm worried. She's my cousin and my best friend. What she's done is really fucked up, and I have no clue why she's done it. Or where she is. It's not like her and I'm really worried.'

Though we've had this conversation, the certainty with which she talks about this being Willow's decision still stings. Even if I think she's probably right.

'But right now we've done all we can. And honestly, Dustin, I think she'll come back when she's ready.'

'Yeah?'

'Definitely,' Georgia says and smiles down at Zara. 'She needs to come back for this little stinker.'

What about me? She needs to come back for me.

# Chapter 22

# Willow

**Then – February 2018**

We've been going out officially for a good few months now. He still hasn't invited me round to his house and he comes over here all the time. He talks about how much he loves Gran and how at home he feels here, which is a good thing, of course, but I don't understand why he hasn't returned the invitation yet. What is he afraid of?

Music is playing through my room, as I stare at myself in the mirror. My outfit has a 'flung-together appearance' as Gran would say. Velvet shorts, an oversized shirt, and my DMs. All from the charity shop. This looks OK, doesn't it? Yeah. It looks OK. I look OK.

'The door,' Gran shouts.

I turn the music down, running to the door to let Dustin in. His eyes trace every inch of me before he says, 'I like your outfit.'

'Thanks,' I say, trying to hide my smile.

Dustin walks in, seeing Gran on the sofa, knitting away. 'Oh wow, Mary, you're looking as stylish as ever. I'm going to have to get some style tips from you.'

Gran chuckles. 'How are you, Dustin?'

'I'm better now I'm here.'

Gran shakes her head, smiling. 'Make sure you two stay safe – you have to be careful walking around at this time of night.'

'I will always protect her,' Dustin says, flinging his arm around me.

I roll my eyes, and drag him towards the door. 'OK, that's very sweet, but can we go please?'

Dustin drops my hand dramatically, and stares at me. 'What's this, Willow? Keen to go to a party and socialise? Never thought I'd see the day.'

I sigh, and Gran decides to chime in on the joke. 'I know, Dustin, tell me your secret. I've obviously been doing the wrong thing for all these years.'

'Well, Mary, the secret is, I'm such bad company that she is now desperate to spend time with ANYONE but me. So now she likes going to parties.'

'Ah. I see, I never had that issue. Willow likes my company.'

I roll my eyes again. 'All right, all right, very funny, guys, can we go now ... please?'

'Liam, where is the craziest place you've ever had sex?'

Liam stares at the group. He's blushing and his eyes are flicking towards the rest of the room. 'Um, I ... er ... Dare, I change my mind – I want a dare.'

We are at Liam's house, and even though we got here relatively early it's already pretty crowded. I realise with a warm jolt that I know or at least recognise most of the people here now. A few of them I know from college, such as the girl Liam has been trying to flirt with all evening. Charlotte's pretty and seems sweet from the few times I've spoken to her, but we don't talk much. Then there is her twin brother Luke, and her friend Sandy. Harrison comes back from Birmingham University for occasional weekends, and then of course Gee is still here. She opted for the University of Surrey, so she didn't have to move out 'and live with gross strangers' as she puts it. There's Joe, who is taking a gap year like Dustin. He's been on a lot of road trip adventures recently and is telling Tony, also home from Exeter for the weekend, all about it. I guess you could say we're kind of a loose gang. It's the first time in my life I've ever had anything that could even vaguely be called a gang.

Since we're here all the time, Dustin and I are by default the core of it and this has been the first time in a while that everyone has been around. We are celebrating with a game of Truth or Dare, a great favourite of theirs and one I had never played before I became friends with them.

Liam is currently giving Tony a blindfolded lap dance, which is very entertaining. I almost choke on my drink as I watch. Dustin places his hand on mine, I lace my fingers through his. We try not to be too couply with the group. At the beginning we didn't even tell anyone we were dating. My fear was that I would just become Dustin's girlfriend that way, rather than part of the group in my own right. But then we got drunk one night at the pub, and ended up kissing in front of everyone, which put paid to that little secret. Everyone was super nice about it though. They still feel more like Dustin and Gee's friends than mine, if I'm honest, but I don't really mind. It's much better than anything I've had before.

I see Gee watching us silently. For someone who loves talking,

111

she doesn't say much about our relationship. I have a few theories about this, though none that I'm ever planning on running past her. It could be that she's trying to respect our privacy, and worries that making a big deal out of it will make us uncomfortable. That doesn't feel much like Gee though. Perhaps she doesn't like that I'm dating her friend. She feels left out now. Or maybe she is already worrying about being caught in the middle if we break up. Perhaps she's convinced it's only a matter of time before we do.

I'm so afraid it's the last one.

'Aw, look at you guys,' Joe says, his attention drawn from Tony and Liam to Dustin and me. 'You're like a proper little couple.'

Dustin says nothing, but he squeezes my hand tighter. I feel the blood rush to my cheeks.

'You guys are pretty serious, right?' Harrison chimes in.

I glance at Dustin. 'Yeah, of course,' he says confidently.

'Dustin in a proper relationship,' Joe says. 'Never thought I'd see the day.'

I notice Georgia turn to look at Joe, who sits next to her, but she doesn't say anything.

'So have you brought her home yet, Dustin?' Harrison smirks. 'What did your mum say?' He and Joe burst out laughing and in my confusion I turn to Dustin. He is shaking his head and smiling, but it's a smile that doesn't reach his eyes.

What's the joke here?

# Chapter 23

# Dustin

'Can you remember all our games of Truth or Dare?' I say to Georgia. We've lapsed into silence since she mentioned Willow coming back. 'Here, every time someone had a free house. How did we not get bored of it?'

'I know!' Georgia says, covering her eyes. 'We were so young and easily amused. Now look at us. We're old, Dustin.'

'Yep,' I say, quietly.

'We are all adults now. You are an estate agent and a *dad*, Joe's doing a masters, Liam's an accountant. Even Tony got that design job he applied for recently. Harrison is training to be a teacher. It's all changed.'

'Yeah, and you have a fancy job in London.'

Georgia smiles. 'Yeah, we're all grown up now. We all had to follow suit once you had a baby.' She grins, but as she scans my face, her smile drops. 'I hate what she's done to you.'

I'm now holding a sleeping Zara in my arms. Georgia's a few drinks down, and I think she's drunk. So this is why she wanted to walk to the pub and not drive. 'What do you mean?'

Georgia moves her hand forward and touches mine. 'You're so sad, Dustin.'

I exhale heavily. 'What do you expect? I can't pretend everything is fine like you.'

I feel the tips of her fingers on my chin, lifting my face to look back at hers. 'Everything is not fine, I'm really not OK. I'm just pretending I am. Fake it till you make it, and all that. Sometimes it's the best way.'

'I wish I could fake being a good dad. But I can't even do that.'

'You *are* a good dad,' Georgia replies firmly.

'Honestly, Georgia, I realise it now – I've never spent much time with Zara. Yes, I was working a lot but also I went out too much. It's just a fact: I'm not a good dad, I don't know what I'm doing. And it's like half the time I can barely even think of Willow because I'm so busy with Zara. Then the other half I don't even want to do anything for Zara because I'm so caught up with everything with Willow, and I just feel like I'm walking—'

Georgia places her palms against my cheeks. 'Shut up, Dustin,' she says. 'You're doing this all on your own. It's going to be hard. And you're not a bad dad. I mean, at least you didn't leave your baby.'

I stare at her. Until today I've never heard her say a bad word about Willow. She's always been so fiercely defensive of her.

'I still don't think Willow would have left if she had a choice,' I mutter.

Georgia smiles at me in pity, the way you'd look at a puppy wanting a home. 'Yeah,' she says, but I know she doesn't believe me. And not for the first time I wonder if she's hiding something from me.

'This sort of thing … leaving, without reason. It's not the sort of thing Willow would do, is it?'

Georgia frowns. 'No. I have no clue why she's doing what she's doing.'

'Unless she was kidnapped,' I quickly say.

'Yes. Unless she was kidnapped, even though she keeps reading my Facebook messages, and had time to write a note, and block everyone on every social media. I'm so pissed off with her.'

I pause, feeling a lump in my throat. 'Was she hiding anything from me? Anything that might be linked to her leaving? If she did run away?'

Georgia shakes her head. 'Nope. She gave me no inkling, no hints, she seemed normal when I saw her last month. I have no clue. But I think you need to stop with this idea that Willow has been kidnapped or something. It's so unlikely.'

I lower my head.

'You know I got sent the blanket, that I left at the house.'

Georgia nods. 'You told me.'

'How do you explain that? What would it mean? Maybe it's her trying to give me a clue or something.'

Georgia doesn't seem enthused. 'You sure it wasn't Naomi? Trying to make you think Willow is playing games with you or something?'

'No it wasn't.'

'You sure? I never fully trusted that girl.'

'Um, OK, where did that come from? And no, Gee, she wouldn't do that, she's genuinely worried.'

'Maybe your landlord found it and passed it on?'

'But he didn't know where I used to live, and it was hand-delivered, remember?'

'OK!' she shouts and her tone is so forceful that I jump. 'OK, let's say it's Willow. Does that make you happy? If it's Willow and she's come down here and delivered that post to you, but not popped in and seen anyone, or talked to anyone, or even asked for some help, or given even the smallest explanation as to why she left, does that help you in any way? Because from my point of view, that sucks. That hurts me more.'

My stomach sinks. I know it's true, but I don't want it to be.

'Well, maybe it wasn't Willow who delivered it. Maybe it was whoever took her ...'

Georgia rolls her eyes. 'Sure, that makes loads of sense. Someone took Willow by force, but then felt a bit guilty about it so thought they'd make up for it by hand-delivering the baby blanket they didn't know Zara loves ...' She breaks off. 'Dustin, look I'm sorry. Please don't cry. It's OK.'

I didn't know I was crying. She gets up and sits next to me, pulling my head onto her shoulder. Just as I used to do to Willow.

'I just don't understand,' I say through my tears.

'I don't either.'

# Chapter 24

# Willow

Then – March 2018

We agreed that for the open day, Gran, Dustin and I would get the train up to Reading. The train journey is a lot longer than I expected. It made me realise I need to get a job when I get home, because I'm going to have to pay for driving lessons somehow. There's no way I can do this train journey twice a day. Me and Dustin have a deal: whoever learns to drive first will be gifted a full tank of petrol by the other. Dustin said the coffee shop has a Saturday vacancy, but I'm not sure I can see myself working in a coffee shop. I'm very clumsy.

I am so nervous that I can barely speak the whole way there. Gran and Dustin don't try to calm me down, instead they chatter away as if this is the most normal day in the world. Every so often one of them touches my arm or pats my hand though. I don't know why I've got myself in such a state. Is it the idea of there being a next chapter, when I'm only just getting to grips with this one? The thought of being a proper adult? I feel so far away from any of that.

I had seen pictures online, but even so I hadn't expected the campus to be so big. It's enormous and there are people everywhere. Tables have been set up at the entrance and a big sign saying 'Welcome Desk' placed next to it. People wearing blue T-shirts and huge smiles – evidently student helpers – are standing around, poised with leaflets in hand.

Further ahead I can see a giant white tent, with a stream of people moving in and out. I make a mental note to avoid that.

'Hey there,' the student helper nearest to us says brightly. 'Welcome! Have you come from far away today?'

Both Dustin and Gran look at me, obviously waiting for me to answer, and I feel my ears grow hot.

'Um, no, not too far,' I mumble.

'Great,' the student helper continues. 'Well, one of us would be happy to show you round if you like?'

Oh God, I was hoping we could just slip in unnoticed.

'Oh I'm fine, thank—'

'We'd love that,' Dustin cuts in.

So now we are trailing behind a short plump girl who is talking so quickly that I've stopped trying to follow everything she's saying. Or rather, Gran and I are trailing behind. She's walking too fast for Gran and I'm grateful for any excuse to avoid conversation. Dustin is chatting away quite happily, asking questions and nodding enthusiastically at her answers. This gives me the chance to take in the surroundings. Everything is so modern and chic – a world away from the scuffed furniture and peeling paint of college. And there's so much green space, which helps to combat the overwhelming size of everything else. I could picture myself on that lawn.

'Oh, actually, it's not me looking. It's my girlfriend.'

Dustin's words snap me out of my daydream. Both he and the girl have stopped and turned back to me.

'Oh, so sorry,' she says, clearly confused as to why I haven't been the one engaging with her. 'I asked what made you choose Reading?'

I pause.

'I don't know really … It just kind of spoke to me. Is that weird?'

She chuckles and shakes her head. 'Not weird at all, don't worry. I felt exactly the same. And what is it you want to study again?'

'It's the Graphic Communication BA?' I say quickly. I pretty much memorised the course page on their website.

'Oh cool.' The girl stops and checks the papers on her clipboard. 'There's actually a talk on that course at two p.m. in this building if you're interested. The head of the department is giving it and apparently she's amazing.'

Before I can answer she has started walking again and is eagerly picking up where she left off with Dustin. 'There is a student union which I really recommend, and there is the Mondial Café, and Mojo's Bar – I'll show you that later … Oh, and have I told you about the campus jobs …'

Two p.m. Our train home is at two-thirty. I didn't think we'd need to be this long. I turn to Gran and open my mouth to speak.

'It's fine,' she says. 'We can get a later train. It wasn't that expensive anyway.'

Gran's pension isn't huge and I know she hates to waste money. I smile at her gratefully.

'Do you want to look at our accommodation halls?' The girl has turned back to me now.

I shake my head. 'I'm fine, thank you.'

I can feel Gran's eyes on me. 'You don't want to look?'

I shake my head again. I've already told Gran I want to stay at home, like Georgia has. A big part of Reading's appeal is that it's only a forty-minute drive away.

'You sure? It might be good to loo—'

'No, Gran. I want to stay in Surrey.'

Jeez, does she want me to leave or something? I think I see a small smile from Dustin.

We go for lunch, in a little coffee shop round the corner called Marigolds. The windows are dressed with fairy lights and the menus have various book covers printed on the back. I order an almond caramel latte, as always, and eggs and avocado on toast. And Dustin starts the conversation. He's so excited and passionate, talking quickly about how well I'd do here, how he can't wait to hear all the fun things I get up to, all the cool things I learn, the person I will grow to be.

Gran nods proudly, but I feel myself quiet, for a reason I can't quite understand.

We still have an hour or so to kill after lunch so Dustin suggests we wander into the town for a bit.

'We could go to Forbury Gardens?' he suggests.

'Where?' Gran and I ask almost in unison.

'It's the park.' He pulls out his phone and brings up Google Maps. 'See, it's just here.'

Gran gives me a smile as Dustin strides off in the direction of town. I know what she's thinking. He did his research. He's taking this seriously.

In the park Gran goes to find a toilet, so Dustin and I sit on the grass, people-watching. There are kids running around, a couple with a baby, an older couple holding hands, smiling, enjoying life.

'That will be us,' Dustin says, as he holds my hand.

'Don't say that,' I mumble, squeezing his hand.

'Why?'

'Just don't jinx it.'

Dustin chuckles. 'Willow, you can't get rid of me.'

I smile, but it fades as quickly as it rose. He kisses my forehead.

After the gardens, we come back to campus and mooch around the tent until it's almost time for the talk. I want to go by myself, so Gran and Dustin go for a coffee, whilst I set off twenty minutes early to find the room the girl scrawled onto my leaflet. I need to leave plenty of time to get there. If I have to walk in late I think I might die.

I find the room remarkably quickly, which is perfect because most of the seats are free and I can grab one at the back.

The lecturer is a surprisingly young woman, given that she's the head of the department. She's tall and skinny with short cropped hair and an angular face, which gives her a slightly harsh appearance. She scans everyone in the packed room. There are people of all ages, heights and nationalities, all eyes focused at the front of the room. There's a moment when the lecturer's eye catches mine and I feel myself shrink under her gaze. I slump down in my chair as she starts talking; her voice is a lot softer, friendlier than her exterior suggests. She starts with a quote by Maya Angelou: 'You can't use up creativity. The more you use, the more you have.'

And as she speaks my nerves seep away, my body relaxes into the chair and everything else loses focus. This feels right. Finally.

# Chapter 25

# Dustin

I sit in my room, my shitty teenage room. I should have stayed in the pub longer. Zara's in the cot opposite me. As well as the posters from when I was eighteen, I still have a load of old photos Blu-tacked to the wall. Me and the gang in various iterations mostly, but there's one of me and Willow too. In the park in Reading – the day we went to look around the university there. My face is screwed up as Willow plants a kiss on my cheek. I stare at my younger self. A version of me who is head over heels in love – when love was carefree and hopeful, not the unending cycle of pain I wish I could escape from now.

Suddenly, hitting me like a wave, I feel the pressure that has been building in my body over the past week bubble up and overflow. I'm angry, I'm so so angry. I stand and quickly rip the photo off the wall. Then I'm ripping the others down too, and the posters, sick of being confronted with things that aren't any more. Then I'm pulling clothes out of drawers, sweeping things off my desk, throwing my pillows, ripping my duvet off my mattress.

And then I'm sitting on the floor, Zara looking at me through the cot. Her eyes are wide and astonished and for one terrible moment I think she's going to start bawling. But instead, she giggles. A happy, contended gargle that soon becomes a proper little chuckle.

Exhausted, I laugh in spite of myself which makes her cackle all the more. Suddenly I am overwhelmed with love for her innocence, for the way she sees the world, for her.

'What's so funny, eh?' I pick her up and bury my face into her. 'You little nutter.'

There's a cough.

I turn to see Alicia in the doorway. She's running an eye over the chaos in my room, one eyebrow arched.

Shit. How do I explain myself?

'I was um, just—'

But she holds out a hand to silence me. 'Do you smoke?' she asks calmly.

Not the question I was expecting.

'No. Do you?' I reply.

I'm shocked. Surely Mum doesn't let Alicia smoke? At least the mum I remembered would have skinned us alive if she'd so much as seen a lighter.

'No,' she says, holding up a cigarette box. 'But Elliot does.'

We sit on the wall outside our front garden. The wall that Tony sat on before puking his guts up after many double shots of vodka. The wall that Willow and I sat on after a night out trying to sober up, watching the sun rise, listening to the birds chirping beneath the trees. The wall that Joe backed into, when he tried to do a three-point turn in his car. Now it's the wall that I sit on, in my hoodie and trackies, with Alicia wearing her pjs, hair messy, make-up off, and for a short second, she looks like the sister I know.

'Zara will be OK inside, right?'

Alicia looks at me. 'It's for five minutes, Dustin. She's in her cot and anyway you've got the baby monitor.'

'I don't like leaving her,' I mutter.

Alicia has never been able to hide her expressions very well, and that hasn't changed. Every inch of her face is telling me that she thinks I'm one of these insane helicopter parents, but I ignore it. 'You know Mum's inside, the baby is fine,' she says.

Mum. Oh crap. I totally forgot about Mum. I look at her. 'Did Mum hear me ... hear me ...'

'Losing your shit?' Alicia says. 'Yes. Obviously. She was standing at her door, and I said I'd see if you were all right.'

I turn back to my cigarette, and inhale deeply.

'This is disgusting,' I splutter.

'It is,' Alicia replies, taking one last drag of hers before tossing the butt over her shoulder. 'But it's stress-relieving, apparently, so I thought it was worth a try.'

'I don't feel that much better.' I throw mine behind me onto the pavement as well, and feel only slightly guilty about it.

'It wasn't supposed to help *just* you,' Alicia says. Since when did her voice get so cold? 'You're not the only one with stress, Dustin. The whole world isn't about you.'

Jesus, does she have any other mode?

'Does Mum know about Elliot smoking?' I ask, deciding to ignore her jibe.

'Yes.'

'Does she not care?'

Alicia shrugs her shoulders. 'Probably, but even if she did she wouldn't say anything.'

I can't help but laugh. I see Alicia glare at me. 'Sorry, but are we talking about the same Mum here? Of course she'd say something.'

There's a pause before Alicia speaks again.

'She wouldn't say anything, Dustin, because she doesn't want her last remaining child leaving her too.'

Silence.

I can feel her closing off from me again, like a door slowly swinging shut when you're too far away to catch it. I need to fix this, find a way of keeping things open between us. And, for the first time, I am desperate to tell her the truth about Willow. About how I do understand her anger and her pain now, and how bitterly, bitterly sorry I am.

'Listen, I—'

She looks at me, and her expression is so cold, so unforgiving, that I feel my voice falter.

'Um ... nothing.'

She rolls her eyes, and goes back inside.

I watch her leave, the words I was so terrified she'd utter ricocheting around my head.

*Willow leaving you, Dustin? It's no more than you deserve.*

# Chapter 26

# Willow

'If you're thinking about your bloody exams, Willow, I'm going to kill you,' Georgia says, giving me a warning look in the rear-view mirror.

Gran says I am like a woman obsessed. Reading offered me a place based on the portfolio I put together, but I still need two As and a B to take it up. I can't remember ever wanting anything so badly in all my life. I barely see anyone at college any more, because I spend every single free period holed up in the library. And in the evenings too I refuse to see Dustin until I've done one extra hour of revision after school. Even weekends I can't afford to take off entirely. Gran says not to overwork myself, but secretly I think she's pleased that I've got something I'm working towards. Right now we're going shopping. Georgia is driving, blasting music through the speakers, with Dustin and me in the back. He strokes my leg slowly with one hand, the other rests on mine. It's like this a lot, the three of us, the 'fantastic three' as Georgia calls us. My two worlds colliding, my cousin and best friend, and my boyfriend. And although

126

Georgia still hasn't said anything further about me and Dustin being together, I feel like she's making peace with the idea of it.

I realise I haven't spoken in ages. For once I wasn't thinking about my exams though. Sometimes I am consumed by the fear that this will all end, that Dustin will leave me or Georgia will get sick of hanging round with us. It's a rabbit hole I can never seem to climb back out of. I imagine scenario after scenario in quick succession, each bleaker than the last. Dustin with another girl, Dustin sick, Dustin dead. And it always comes on during moments like this. Moments when I feel so high that I feel sure the only way is down.

'No, no.' I smile now and shake my head. 'Just daydreaming.' I could never tell either of them about these fears. They're both of them so happy-go-lucky they'd never understand. They're so unlike me in that respect.

'Public announcement, I love these bitches in the back,' Georgia shouts.

I shake my head and laugh.

'Public announcement, I love this bitch in the front,' Dustin says, trying to shout over the music.

'Thanks, Queen,' Georgia says.

Dustin then turns to looks at me. 'Public announcement,' he says softly, so that only I can hear. 'My heart's been taken by the girl next to me.'

I lean my head on his shoulder.

'How did you find dinner with Dustin's mum yesterday, Willow?' Georgia says after a moment. I feel Dustin stiffen next to me.

I frown and Georgia, registering my confusion, shoots Dustin a withering look in the mirror. 'You didn't ask her?'

I turn to him but he is staring pointedly out of the window, his jaw clenched. I can tell he's furious at Georgia and usually I hate it when they argue, but I am so infuriated by his evasiveness that I plough on anyway.

'Hey, what is the deal with your mum, Dustin?'

He doesn't look at me, but his knee judders up and down.

'Dustin,' Georgia says sharply.

He sighs and turns back to me. 'It's not you, Willow. It's her, she's just ...'

He breaks off and squeezes my hand.

'What? She's just what?'

'She's fine, she's just a bit of a character, isn't she?' Georgia cuts in.

'No lie there,' Dustin says, almost sadly.

'I'm telling you, Willow, when I first went round, it was like a battle of opinions between me and her.'

'Oh really?' I glance nervously at Dustin. He isn't getting offended, is he? Georgia would kick off if anyone spoke about Auntie Jayne like this.

'Yep, it was, Wills, literally. We were talking about religion and politics, it was madness.'

Dustin rolls his eyes. 'She's not a Bible basher though,' he says with a chuckle.

'Well, not that anyone would know. Honestly, you act like your mum's dead or something ...'

'Gee.' Dustin's voice is quiet.

'What?'

Dustin looks between me and her. Georgia is frowning in confusion. 'Sorry, am I missing something here?'

Shit. It suddenly dawns on me.

'Because of my parents,' I say quietly, cutting in before Dustin can say anything more.

Gee meets my gaze in the mirror. Please don't say anything, I will her. Please don't.

'Oh yeah, right, sorry, Willow,' she says eventually.

'It's OK,' I say confidently, and Dustin squeezes my hand.

Gee says nothing more until we reach the shop. She pulls into the car park but there are no other spaces and she's blocking another car. She grabs her purse from the front seat and chucks it at Dustin. 'Can you get me a bottle of wine, please?'

Dustin nods his head and smiles. We are going to have drinks and games at my house tonight, as Gran is out with friends. I go to open the door. 'Oh, Willow,' Gee says. My stomach drops. She turns around, and plasters a fake smile on her face. 'Would you be able to wait with me? I need advice about that boy I was telling you about.'

'Of course,' I mumble, letting go of the door. I look up to Dustin, hoping he'll save me.

Instead he kisses my cheek. 'I'm a big boy, I can handle going to the shops on my own,' he jokes.

I watch him carefully as he walks further and further away, feeling Gee's eyes driving into me. I finally give in, turning around to look at her. She is still turned around in her seat, glaring at me. 'So why did Dustin react like that?'

Is there a way out of this? I consider lying, but I know it's pointless. Gee seems to be able to see right through me at all times.

'I might have let Dustin believe my mum and dad aren't around any more ...'

Gee looks at me blankly.

'As in, he thinks they died.'

She sighs. 'Willow ...'

'I didn't say they were dead,' I add hastily. 'I just didn't correct him when he assumed.'

'And what if he asks how they died, what are you going to say?'

'He won't ask.'

'What if he does?'

'Then I'll tell him they died in the fire.'

There is silence. Georgia drums her fingers on the steering wheel and inhales deeply, eyes closed. When she opens them again her gaze is softer.

'Willow—'

'It wouldn't be that much of a lie really.'

'It would, it would be a very big lie.'

I avoid her eyes, starting to pick at my nails. 'It just doesn't seem worth going into all that; it's not like it has anything to do with my life now.'

Gee looks back at me, eyes wide, patronising smile. 'OK.'

'Georgia.'

'I said OK.'

'You're not going to say anything, are you?'

She turns back to the steering wheel. 'It's nothing to do with me anyway.'

I breathe a sigh of relief.

'So you won't tell him? You promise.'

'No, Willow, I won't tell him,' she snaps, clearly exasperated. 'But for the record I think this is a mistake. Lies always get found out.'

My phone pings. It's Dustin.

Forgot to ask you what you want. Red, white? Xxx

I smile, grateful for the interruption, and tap back a reply. When Georgia speaks next she's so quiet that I can pretend I haven't heard her.

'You need to let him see all of you, Willow. Not just hide the pieces you don't want anyone else to see.'

# Chapter 27

# Dustin

It's been two weeks now. Two weeks, and still nothing from Willow.

'Morning, sweetheart!'

I smile at Mum. It's five a.m., I'm only awake because Zara woke me up, as she likes to most mornings. So, just like most mornings, I've clambered downstairs, sorted her bottle and now she's on my lap, bottle in mouth, knitted blanket clutched in one little fist. And sure enough, Mum appears five minutes later, claiming she just happens to be awake at this time.

'Want me to help with that?'

'I've got it, Mum, thanks though,' I respond, as though we don't have this exact same exchange every morning.

Nodding, Mum starts making herself busy, popping the kettle on, getting out bread for the sandwiches she makes Elliot and Alicia every morning to take to work and college. I notice that they don't always take them. But Mum always makes them.

She sits down, popping a cup of tea in front of me.

'So I was talking to one of my customers from work, and

she said her baby was slow at developing and she took her to a homeopath who really helped.'

I grit my teeth, moving Zara closer to me. 'The doctor said not to rush her. And anyway she's not slow, the doctor said lots of children take longer to speak and then there's no difference between them and others when they finally do.'

'Oh I know, honey, I'm not saying she's *slow* but, you know. I just thought it might help.'

'Ok.'

There is a silence. Mum sighs, before speaking again. 'Where did you say you worked in Brighton?'

I stare at her. I never said, but good try at being subtle, Mum. 'I was an estate agent.'

'Oh yes, I remember,' she says, taking a sip of tea. 'You know there's a really nice independent one in Woking.'

I know where this is going. 'Is there?' I still haven't told her I haven't actually quit my job in Brighton. Though unless I decide to go back next week I'm probably going to have to. Despite all their messages about taking as much time as I need, I had an email from my manager yesterday asking when they could expect me back and whether working remotely might be an option.

'Yeah, where the ice cream shop used to be, they got shut down by hygiene standards or something. Shocking, that is. All the kids that used to go there, could have made them really ill.'

I nod my head, rubbing my eyes. 'I'm not thinking about a job right now, Mum.'

'I know, hon, but it's good to think about your options and plan how you're going to get your life back on track.'

'I will, Mum, when ...'

When Willow comes back.

But what if she doesn't come back? Will my life just stop? I realise I haven't pictured the future at all since she left. How can you get back on track when the path you were so sure of has suddenly reached a dead end?

'No rush, hon, I just thought it might help you to think about these things. And you know I will always look after Zara. Work would let me bring her—'

'I know, Mum, I appreciate it.' She walks over, holds her hands out to Zara and I pass her over. Mum works in an independent gift shop near town and they are very relaxed, of course they'd let her bring Zara. And of course that'd work just perfectly for Mum.

'This little one and I can catch up on missed time, can't we?' she coos. Then she pauses awkwardly and I look down, not wanting to catch her eye.

'I'm going to my friend's tonight, by the way, if that's OK?'

I look up at her in surprise. Mum never had much of a social life. 'Yeah, Mum, of course, why wouldn't it?'

'I just wanted to check you'd be OK on your own, sweetie. I'll make food so you've got something for dinner.'

'Oh no, honestly it's fine, it'll be nice to cook actu—'

'Nonsense,' Mum says firmly. 'Look at you, you're wasting away. You need some proper home cooking.'

'OK, well, thank you.'

I remember now. It's always easier to just say yes.

# Chapter 28

# Willow

Then – April 2018

'It's so nice to finally have you round, I've heard so much about you, Willow.'

After the conversation in the car, Dustin finally texted me last week with an invitation to his for dinner. And though I was relieved in a way, this quickly gave way to dread. Why the hell was I pushing for this? I was meeting Dustin's mum for the first time, and what if she hated me? What if I got there only to find I had nothing interesting to say? Conversation isn't exactly my strong suit. Would Dustin's opinion of me change as a result? And, oh dear God, dinner. I'm a really messy eater. Would she judge?

I also spent ages deciding what to wear. In the end I went for my dress with the stars and moon print. It's not too short and paired with tights and my DMs it felt like a safe choice. Nobody hates a dress and DMs, right?

So far though, so good. Dustin's mum, who tells me I should call her Carol, is all smiles and friendliness. She's a tiny bit overpowering, I guess, asking all sorts of questions and not really giving me a chance to answer, but still very nice. I don't see what all the fuss was about. She looks nothing like Dustin with her pale skin and short blonde hair.

She has made shepherd's pie for dinner and she hands a plate to me now, piled so high I don't know how I'm ever going to eat even half of it.

'Yes,' Carol says, sitting down now that everyone is served. 'He's always on about you.'

I know for a fact this is untrue because Dustin told me that asking if I could come to dinner was the first time he'd ever mentioned me to his mum. Still, she means it nicely so I smile.

'He probably doesn't talk anywhere near as much about his old mum, does he?'

I laugh and take a forkful of shepherd's pie. Only in the ensuing silence do I realise my mistake. Carol gives Dustin a tight smile and looks pointedly down at her food.

'I mean, of course he does . . .' I begin to say, but it sounds so unconvincing and Dustin gives a little shake of his head as if to say 'leave it'.

I pick at the skin on the side of my nails. My hands are raw from where I scrubbed at them earlier. I know I should address the hand-washing thing at some point.

Dustin is sitting next to me and Alicia, his sister, is sitting opposite me, which is quite comforting, because I've already met her a few times at parties. Dustin's mum is opposite him.

'So,' Carol says eventually, 'Dustin says you moved from Brighton?'

I nod my head, one too many times, relieved the silence has been broken. 'Yeah. I think.' Carol looks at me, obviously waiting for me to elaborate. 'I do miss it though,' I continue nervously.

'Not a fan of Surrey, are you, love?'

There's a definite edge to her voice. 'Um, well, no, that's not—'

'Brighton was what Willow was used to, obviously,' Dustin interrupts and I throw him a thankful smile.

'This is really nice, Carol, thanks,' I say, my voice slightly shaking, and to my relief she smiles.

'Don't worry if you can't eat it, dear, but I gave you a big serving, because it does look like you need feeding up a bit.'

'Mum,' Dustin says with a warning tone.

She looks at Dustin, her eyes wide and innocent. 'What? I'm not trying to cause offence. I'm just saying, you'd look lovely with a bit more meat on your bones. Not that you don't look lovely now.'

I feel myself stiffen in my chair. I want the ground to swallow me up. 'Thank you—' I begin to say – what else is there to say? – but Carol carries on.

'But if Dustin was that weight, I'd worry, that's all. But maybe that's just a mum thing.'

I look towards Dustin. Is she being really tactless or am I just being overly sensitive? I do have a tendency to be too sensitive.

Then Dustin puts his hand on my thigh, stroking my leg, and I instantly feel warmer. He flashes his eyes at his mum, but she continues, oblivious.

'So, Willow, you moved from Brighton with your parents, didn't you?' she says.

'Her gran,' Dustin replies stiffly.

'Oh – so did your parents stay in Brighton?'

The room is silent. Everyone has stopped eating. Dustin and Alicia exchange glances, while I try to think about the least awkward way to smooth this over. Dustin obviously hasn't told his mum – well, he probably didn't have the time, seeing as he only mentioned me last week.

136

'Umm, my parents aren't around any more,' I say, hoping that will be an end to it.

'Oh, darling – I'm so sorry. What happened?'

'Mum,' Dustin hisses. 'You can't ask people that!'

Carol looks thoroughly put out by Dustin's reprimand. 'Well, Willow doesn't have to tell me if she doesn't want to. But I happen to think it is OK to ask.'

Before Dustin leaps to my defence again I place a hand on his to let him know I'm fine. 'There . . . ' I take a deep slow breath. 'There was a fire.'

My stomach sinks as I say it, and I lower my eyes to the food I now don't have the appetite to eat. I'm praying this is enough information and there won't be any more awkward follow-up questions.

'I'm so sorry, dear,' I hear Carol say. And she does sound really sorry. For all her awkward questions, she's clearly very kind-hearted. 'You poor lamb.'

'I didn't realise that was how they died, Wills,' Dustin says quietly.

'It's OK.' My eyes are focused on my fingers; I'm now aggressively picking the loose skin around my nails. Dustin places a firm, discouraging hand on mine before squeezing it reassuringly. I give him a weak smile, trying to ignore the bubbling in my stomach.

Thanks to some excellent conversational skills from Alicia, the rest of the dinner is OK, and I happily eat one-handed, my other hand still clutched in Dustin's, while she chatters away. It seems both she and Dustin are both very good at that. They are weirdly alike in lots of ways.

'So Willow got accepted into Reading Uni, Mum,' Alicia says, winking at me.

Carol eyes open wide. 'Oh good, going this autumn?'

I nod my head, proudly. 'Hopefully.'

'Hopefully indeed, maybe that will encourage Dustin.'

Dustin's face darkens.

'I keep telling Dustin he should be thinking about the future more. Oh, I know for now he's got you and that's important, obviously, but I do say he shouldn't let himself be held back.' Dustin sighs, and I stare at her, trying to comprehend what she's just said. Is it true? Am I holding Dustin back? I have never thought of it that way.

Carol carries on talking. 'After all, you're both so young. You can't miss out on opportunities in life at your ages, can you?'

'No,' I reply quietly.

'Mum,' Dustin says sharply. 'Not now.'

She glares at Dustin. 'I know you don't want to hear it, Dustin, but—'

'Mum . . .' Dustin practically shouts.

Carol shakes her head, her face suddenly compressing. Alicia, Dustin and I clear away the plates, and I can't help but steal glances at Carol. I can't tell if she's furious, or if she's on the verge of tears.

'I really like your nose piercing, Willow,' Alicia says, taking the plates from my hand.

'Thanks,' I say, moving my hand to my nose self-consciously.

'I really want to get mine done,' she says, and she and Dustin disappear into the kitchen.

'Oh no you don't,' Carol calls after her. 'It can look a bit chavvy.' She looks at me. We are alone in the living room. 'Not saying it looks that way on you, Willow. I'm just saying, it can give the wrong idea, you know?'

I don't know. And I don't know what to say in response to that. Later, after dinner, Dustin and I go up to his room and I'm grateful to escape his mum for even a few minutes. Dustin's room has album posters all over the wall, and magazines and old vinyl records are strewn everywhere. But my favourite thing is the knitted blanket lying on his pillow, the one he discovered half finished the first time he came to dinner with Gran and me.

Dustin flops down on the bed, looking up as I stand in his room uncomfortably. He leaps up, grabs me, and pulls me down on the bed with him, so that I'm forced to laugh. As the laughter fades, Dustin starts apologising for his mum's comments.

'It's OK,' I say, gently tracing patterns across his chest with my finger.

'No, it's not, she's always like this these days. It's like she doesn't know social boundaries any more.'

'She means well,' I say, which I do think is true, though she made me so uncomfortable. At least, she means well when it comes to Dustin. I feel like she'd quite happily push me – the foil to all her son's potential, apparently – under a bus given half a chance. But I don't want Dustin to think I have a bad impression of his mum, especially as he's only just let me meet her. I pause and prop myself up to look at Dustin. 'Why didn't you tell your mum about us until now?'

Dustin lets out a heavy sigh. 'Wasn't it obvious from tonight? I love my mum, but she's overprotective. It gets intense.'

'Has she always been like that?'

Dustin frowns. 'Um, well, sort of. She got a lot worse after my dad left. And she's not as bad with Alicia. Sometimes I worry that ...'

'What?'

'Well, that she thinks I'm like him. That I'm just going to take off and leave her one day.'

I am quiet. Under my hand Dustin's chest rises and falls sharply.

'But I'm not my dad. I just wish she would see that.'

'Of course you're not.'

'And she can be so bloody judgemental sometimes, it drives me insane.'

I stare at him. 'Judgemental of me?'

'No. Not at all. I don't mean that. She's just got an opinion on everything. She just likes to be involved, I guess. Anyway, I wanted to wait to introduce you to her until we were more settled, so it wasn't overwhelming.'

I look at him carefully for a few seconds. It wasn't because he was embarrassed by me, it was because he was thinking of me. He always seems to be thinking of me. I smile, before planting a kiss on his nose. 'What would I do without you?'

'You would carry on living your life,' he says as I lie down on his chest.

'No, I couldn't. Not any more.'

'Don't be stupid,' he says, stroking my hair.

He doesn't get it, does he? He doesn't get how he came at the right time. How much I needed him. 'I think I've only started living properly now I'm with you.' I sit up. 'I have never felt this before.'

He smiles, wrapping his arms around me, pulling me on top of him again. 'Neither have I, Willow.'

# Chapter 29

# Dustin

'Mum said to tell you a letter came for you.'

I have just returned from one of my regular walks with Zara (we are limited in our range of activities here) and Alicia is slouched in front of the TV. Elliott and Mum are, I assume, both at work. I am so focused on wrestling a grizzly Zara out of her pram that it takes me a moment to register what Alicia has said. We've barely spoken since our failed bonding smoke.

'What did you say?'

'Letter for you.'

'For me?'

'That's what I said, wasn't it? It's on the kitchen table apparently.'

Alicia turns her attention back to the TV and, placing Zara securely on the sofa, I go into the kitchen. Sure enough, there's the letter. A small white envelope, with my name and address on the front and a stamp stuck at a wonky angle in the top right-hand corner. I recognise the scratchy block capitals at once though. I go back through to the living room and perch next to Zara on the sofa. Part of me wants to tear it open, and part of me never wants to see what's inside. What if it's a letter from Willow? What if she's writing to tell me she's never coming back? In the end I decide the plaster option is best. Rip it off, get it over and done with. So I do, I rip open the envelope and empty the contents onto my lap.

'Oh that's pretty,' Alicia says, obviously forgetting she's supposed to be stroppy with me as I hold the necklace up to the light.

'Yeah,' I breathe.

'Let's have a look. I feel like I recognise that necklace.' Alicia holds out her hand to take it and I quickly move it out of her reach. She can't touch it.

'Fine,' she says moodily and slumps back into her chair. But for once I don't care about upsetting Alicia. I'm too focused on the necklace in my hand, the delicate chain and, secured at the end, a tiny silver angel.

Willow's necklace.

I check the envelope for a slip of paper, a scrawled message, anything. But there's nothing.

I exhale and flop back against the sofa.

Why, Willow? Why?

# Chapter 30

## Willow

Then – May 2018

Dustin stayed round again last night. He stays over most Saturday nights after we've been out, and then we spend Sunday mornings lazing around before making a Sunday roast with Gran. This has become a routine now. He likes it, I like it, Gran likes it. I do go round to Dustin's, just . . . not as much. It's a bit more stressful for both of us. After one drink too many last night, Dustin decided to open up about how his mum is giving him a hard time about him staying over mine so much, which makes me feel great.

Right now Dustin is still crashed out, dead to the world. I prop myself up on my elbow, watching the gentle rise and fall of his chest. He looks so relaxed. I can't imagine I'm ever that relaxed, even when I'm sleeping.

Dustin's phone pings with a new message, and quickly I grab it to silence it. But then I see the message. It's from his mum.

Are you going to apologise yet?

I sneak a glance back at Dustin, and he's still asleep. My fingers hover over his screen. This is a bad thing to do, Willow. It's a breach of privacy.

But still I type in his passcode. I read the message.

And I don't seem to stop there, I scroll up.

Are you eating dinner at home?

> Not tonight Mum, eating at Willow's.

Of course you are.

> What do you mean by that?

There's a half-hour gap between that and the next message.

I think you know, Dustin.

I scroll back up again, past the first message to those from the last few weeks. There are masses of them.

Ever since you met her you've lost all your drive. You're throwing your life away.
She's letting you waste your time in that coffee shop whilst she's off studying. But would she do the same for you? Mark my words, she'll go off to university and live her life and you'll be stuck with nothing.
I don't trust her, Dustin. You're the one giving all your time to this relationship, what are you getting out of it?

And then I find myself lingering on one conversation, a month ago.

No, I'm being honest Dustin. I'm telling you this
because I love you.

                                    She loves me.

Not as much as I do.

I put the phone down. I don't want to read any more. I'm
disgusted with myself for looking at his phone, but what
I've read makes me feel physically sick. I wish I could unsee
those messages.

But I can't, so I crawl back into bed with Dustin, my heart
pounding in my chest.

She hates me.

What if Dustin starts hating me too?

Somehow I manage to put the messages out of my mind and the
day passes as normal. Over lunch I tell Gran and Dustin about
my plans to learn to drive, and they make jokes about the poor
drivers on the road, and how they will need to make crash hel-
mets a legal requirement, etc, etc, and I roll my eyes and ignore
them. This has become our MO, Gran and Dustin teasing me
and me pretending to get cross. It's amazing how easily we slip
into it. But then Dustin's phone pings a few more times, and he
says he needs to leave now, and I know the reason, and a pit of
sadness whirls in my stomach. But I kiss him, hug him, and say
I will see him tomorrow. I guess it isn't an awful thing, it gives
me more time to revise anyway.

As we are clearing the table, Gran keeps pausing and looking
at me; she wants to tell me something. I take the plates into the

kitchen, pop them in the dishwasher and come back, and she's still staring at me.

'What?' I ask.

Gran sighs, her face dropping. 'It's not working, hon ... I was going to wait and tell you.'

I frown at her. 'Sorry?'

She sighs. 'I miss Brighton.'

'So do I, Gran, Brighton is special,' I say, wrapping my arms around her, embracing her in a hug. I notice she is tense, she doesn't hug back. I pull back, watching her.

'Oh,' I say, as I watch her guilty expression. 'You want to move back?'

Gran sighs again. 'We are moving back.'

I step away again. 'What?'

'After your exams. I've given notice with the landlord.'

'Without asking me? Gran, I have a life here, finally. Finally I fit in. I have friends, I have a boyfriend, I nearly have a job. And you're taking me away from that.'

'I don't have the life here I had at home. And Auntie Jayne has had her operation, she doesn't need us any more. And I thought because you'll be at uni it wouldn't matter as much. I actually did some research and the halls are supposed to be really nice. I'd pay the extra money for you!'

'But I wasn't going to stay there! I never was going to go to halls. Do you realise how far Reading is from Brighton? And I don't drive. How would I afford to see Dustin, how would I afford to see my friends?'

'But the halls ... '

'I don't want to stay at halls, Gran.'

'Ah, Willow,' she says, taking a step closer to me. 'I thought you'd have wanted to stay there! What about if I look into buying you some driving lessons? I just thought ... that it was a money thing, that's why you were adamant about staying at home. I thought—'

'No, Gran, you didn't think. I wanted to stay at home so I was with you and Dustin.'

'I'm sorry.'

I back away. 'You're not, or you wouldn't have done it.'

# Chapter 31

# Dustin

I am still crying when Mum comes home from work in the early afternoon. Slumped at the kitchen table, Willow's necklace clutched in my hand, I haven't been able to stop since the envelope arrived. Alicia tried to ask me what was wrong, but I couldn't get the words out. After a while she slipped away awkwardly, taking Zara with her, and for the first time I didn't mind that my daughter wasn't glued to my side. It was probably better for her not to see me like this.

'Oh, sweetheart, what's happened?' Mum drops the bags of shopping in each hand and rushes to throw her arms around me.

For what feels like hours we stay like that, her cradling my head in her arms, stroking my hair slowly and rhythmically, telling me over and over that everything will be OK, I'm not to worry, she's there. Just like she would when I was eight and had woken up from a nightmare.

I need to tell her now, I need to tell my mum everything because I can't deal with any of this any more. Any minute now I'm going to fall apart, break into a million tiny pieces, and I'm not sure I'll be able to put them together again.

'She's left me, Mum.'

'Who, darling?'

'Willow,' I sniff. 'We didn't break up, at least, if we did I didn't know about it. I just came home from work and she had gone. There was just this letter and ...' My breath is so jagged it's a wonder Mum can understand any of what I'm saying. 'And I have no clue where she is, or why she ... why she went or if she's OK and she won't answer any of my messages or Georgia's ... and ... and she's also been sending me stuff and I don't know what it means and my head is such a mess and I just don't think I can ...'

I lapse back into sobs and Mum says nothing, still stroking my hair, until my breathing slows again.

'I needed to tell you,' I whisper into her shoulder.

'It's OK, Dustin,' she says, squeezing me tighter. 'It's OK.'

I hug her back. For the first time in over two weeks, I feel something like calm. Why didn't I just tell Mum everything straight away?

'My poor baby boy,' Mum mutters. 'I don't know what she thinks she's playing at. Still, it was only a matter of time, really, wasn't it, darling?'

I freeze, and pull back, looking at her. 'Mum ...'

'What, hon?'

I shake my head slowly. 'Please don't.'

'Well you know what my thoughts were, I made that quite clear at the time. I always thought she was very selfish, keeping you waiting around for her like that.'

I get up angrily. 'Mum, don't talk shit about her, I'm worried about her. I love her.'

'Oh, for God's sake!' Now Mum is on her feet too. 'Don't tell me you still haven't seen the light? She obviously doesn't love you, otherwise she'd never have left you like this. Left her own child. Honestly, I wouldn't be surprised if that girl was incapable of real love . . . what kind of mother abandons her own daughter, for Christ's sake?'

I am trembling with rage, all tears banished. 'What is your problem? What have you got against Willow? You've always hated her and—'

'Is it any wonder?' Mum is really shouting now. 'When this is the kind of thing she does? But you've always been blind to it, Dustin, you've always been so stupid in that way. Tunnel vision for a girl who doesn't care . . .'

'You've always been jealous of her,' I yell. 'Jealous of your own son's girlfriend. It's pathetic. You were so scared she'd take me away but in the end she didn't need to, did she? You drove me away yourself.'

The words are out of my mouth before I can take them back. Silence echoes around our kitchen and I can see Mum's jaw twitch.

'You're just like your bloody father,' she said quietly. 'Pissing off and abandoning your family then acting like it's everyone's fault but yours. Well, maybe it's only right you've had a taste of your own medicine.'

I stare at her for a moment. Then I turn and leave the kitchen and keep going out through the front door, slamming it shut behind me.

# Chapter 32

# Willow

I can drink at the pub now. Yay to being eighteen, not so yay to the situation I'm in. I wait till I'm a few drinks down, I need the confidence.

I wonder what Dustin will think about Gran. He adores her. He calls her his fashion icon, Beautiful Mary, the Lady with Silver Hair Whose Earrings Always Match Her Clothes. She always giggles when Dustin says she's his favourite. And she always says he's a charmer.

'Dustin, I have something to tell you.'

He sips his beer and grins at me. 'If you're asking to finish my pint, then yes, I guess you can. See, this is how much I love you.'

I watch him, feeling sadness creep over me. He's doing the classic Dustin thing, of finding fun in every second of life, but he won't be laughing in a minute. I want to dive inside his head, find out what he sees in me, what he thinks about when we're together. I remember when living used to feel like just existing, but then I met him and everything changed. He gave my life purpose and meaning, he gave *me* meaning. What happens when I move away? Is that all going to fall apart? I take a deep breath.

'Gran is moving back to Brighton,' I blurt out.

It takes a second for Dustin's grin to fall.

'Wait ... what?'

My heart is pounding in my ribcage.

'Willow, what did you say?' he says again, sliding his pint glass onto the table and taking me by the shoulders.

I close my eyes. 'She's ... she's moving back to Brighton,' I mumble.

'And does that mean you're going ... you're going too?'

When I force myself to look at him again his eyes are filled with horror.

Neither of us has jobs – Dustin got fired from the coffee shop, he took too many 'sick' days on a Saturday, after we'd been to the White Hart the previous evening; he has applied for a few part-time retail jobs, and hasn't heard anything back – and neither of us drives. We don't have the money to pay for train tickets.

But maybe I'm overestimating how he's feeling. Maybe he just throws the word love around, whereas I now realise that my love is all-consuming, overwhelming. I can't control my love. Don't cry, Willow, don't cry.

'Willow, does that mean you are moving too?' he asks again, his eyes burrowing into mine.

Unable to look away from him, I nod slowly.

'Shit.' Dustin's jaw clenches. 'Why does Mary want to move back?' he says.

'This isn't her home,' I say, though I don't really understand her myself. 'I guess she misses Brighton. She didn't think about how it would affect me. I was pretty annoyed at her, but I guess eventually she has to do things for her, rather than thinking about me, which she has done the last eighteen years.'

Dustin wipes his eyes angrily. Is he crying?

'Dustin, please,' I say, and can hear the tremor in my voice. 'Don't get upset.'

'You're going to break up with me?' he says.

I take his hands in mine. 'No, of course not, I don't want to go.'

'But I thought—'

'It's not my choice. I don't want to go. I don't want to leave you. Leave the first group of friends I've ever had in my life. I don't know what I'm going to do about uni, I don't know if I will be able to commute. My life is down here. But I've got nowhere else to stay. And I want my gran to be happy. As much as Gran pretends she doesn't, she feels lonely here. Loneliness can do bad things to people. She needs to go home. She needs to think about herself.'

He looks up to me, squeezing my hands. 'I can be your home.'

'I know, one day, but this is about Gran.'

'Live with me.'

I sigh, letting go of his hands. 'Your mum doesn't like me, she's only just started letting me come round again, after the weed thing.'

About a month ago, Dustin and I had come back to his late at night to find his mum waiting for us in the living room, holding the bag of cannabis Dustin keeps in his bedside drawer. It didn't matter how much Dustin argued with her, she was insistent that he would never have been smoking that stuff before he met me. Which shows how little she knows me. I don't touch it.

'Mum just overreacts. You know she worries about losing me or whatever . . . but if we lived at mine we'd see her more, she'd be more relaxed and she wouldn't be worried about that stuff any more.' He takes my face in his hands, forcing me to look at him. 'Would you feel comfortable staying there?'

'If it means I get to stay with you,' I say. He kisses my forehead, before encasing me in a hug. 'I know she's not all bad,' I whisper into his chest. 'She just cares about you.'

'Yeah,' he says, planting another kiss on my head. 'She cares a lot, and this will be a good thing. I'll talk to her tomorrow. Don't worry, Willow, it will all be fine. I promise.'

✤

He looks at me. Even in the darkness I can see him smiling at me, as he sips from his beer bottle. It was his idea to walk back from the pub, which is usually a ten-minute drive, and it has taken ages, but I don't mind. I have his coat on, and his hand in my hand. We are just approaching the park when suddenly his legs buckle beneath him, and he falls to the ground.

Oh my God.

'Dustin! Dustin?' I shout, dropping to the ground next to him. He doesn't reply, his eyes fixed on the sky above him.

'Dustin, are you OK? Oh my God. Are you all right?'

'It's crippling . . .'

My heart is pounding. 'What is? What's crippling?'

'Wills,' he whispers faintly. 'It's overwhelming . . .'

I bring my face towards his so that I can hear him better, my breath coming in sharp pants.

'I just . . .' he mumbles.

'What?! Shall I call an ambulance?'

'I just . . . I just love you so . . . so . . . much.'

I pause.

He turns his head, a cheeky grin forming on his face.

Oh my God.

He starts laughing. I scowl at him.

'For God's sake, Dustin, I thought something was wrong with you.'

'It is, I'm in love with you, that's what's wrong with me.'

'You're a ... a Di ... a D bag!'

He smirks. 'Oh, have you just made that up? I like that.'

I sigh and roll my eyes. He keeps laughing as he grabs me, pulling me onto the ground next to him. He wraps his arms around mine, as I try my hardest to stay annoyed. Why is he like this?

'One day I'm going to shout and scream about my love for you in front of a crowd. I'll stand on a bench.'

'A bench?'

'Yes, a beautiful bench.'

A smile forms on my lips; I try to bite it away. I can't believe I've fallen for this trick again. Every single time, Willow, every single time.

'I dropped my beer for you.'

'Whoa, now that is love.'

After lying in the middle of the road for a while, by some miracle not getting run over, we walk back to Dustin's house. I could have stayed out there with him for ever. But it's getting late. We get to the house, and the door is locked. Dustin tries calling Alicia, but she doesn't answer. He is just resigning himself to calling his mum, when Carol opens the door, her face contorted with fury. She doesn't stand back to let us in.

'Why are you back so late?' she says.

'Mum, it's a weekend. I don't think we need to be—'

'How much have you had to drink?' she hisses.

'I don't know, a few? It doesn't matter.' Dustin grabs onto my hand, trying to pass by her, but she moves forward to block our way.

'You both stink of alcohol,' she says, eyes flicking between me and Dustin. Even with all the alcohol in my system, butterflies start nervously fluttering in my tummy. As if he can tell, Dustin wraps his arm around me, pulling me closer to him.

'Well, we've been at the pub. Now it's cold, I'm sorry if we woke you up, but next time can you not lock the door?' Dustin says, lightly pushing past her and into the house, pulling me behind him.

'You're being rude now, Dustin.'

'I'm not being rude, Mum.' He disappears into the kitchen leaving me and his mum alone. Why did he leave me? Did he think I was behind him? Don't leave me alone. Why am I not following him?

Carol sniffs the air, and glares at me. 'Willow, I can smell it.'

My stomach drops further, as I feel heat rise to my cheeks.

Keep it together. I'm too scared to look in Carol's eyes. 'Sorry?'

'You smell of smoke, and frankly it's disgusting.'

'I . . . I haven't been—'

'You better not get my son into that dirty habit.'

'Mum, what the fuck?' Dustin has reappeared and is standing in front of me.

'All both of you do now is get drunk, waste your money on dinners out and the pub, when you know money is tight for me, and that really upsets me. I have no issue with enjoying things when you're young, but you two are just plain profligate.'

'But for us, those things aren't a waste of money. That's what we want to spend it on – having fun with our friends and with each other.'

Wait, did I just say that? Where did that come from?

There's a silence after I finish speaking.

Carol gapes at me, and I feel immediate regret for opening my mouth. 'Sorry?'

'Well ... I was just saying, just because you may think it's a waste it doesn't mean—'

'Willow, don't be rude to me, please.'

'The only one that is being rude is you, Mum.'

But Carol hasn't taken her eyes off me. 'I have to say you won't be welcome here if you turn up drunk on my doorstep again.'

'Mum, maybe you're the drunk one,' Dustin mutters, as he starts dragging us both up the stairs.

'Before you were with *her*, you'd never talk to me like that. What's all that about?' She's shouting now and I can't get up the stairs fast enough.

Once we're safely in Dustin's room, I try desperately to hold my tears in.

There's a knock and Alicia appears at the door, dressed in pyjamas, her tired eyes peering at us. 'You all right?' she says.

Dustin shakes his head. 'Mum,' he says.

# Chapter 33

# Dustin

I find myself at the college. I don't know what made me come this way. I was barely even aware of where I was going until suddenly I rounded a corner, and there it was. I guess classes are still going on, because the gates are deserted.

I lean against the fence like I used to, waiting for Willow to finish her classes. She would come out of the gates, dwarfed by an enormous backpack, a book or two under one arm, and then she'd see me, and her tired eyes would light up and she'd be running to hug me. Every single time.

That was in the awkward stage where we were dating, but unsure of how to progress from there. I agonised over how to get to the next step with her. How did people go from dating to a relationship? I couldn't figure it out. And yes, everyone was surprised because I was Dustin, the guy who never seemed to have trouble in that department, the guy with all the experience. But the truth was I didn't have a clue what I was doing for so much of those early stages with Willow. I had zero experience with a proper relationship, and I wanted a relationship with Willow. She was going to be my forever girl.

Mum is wrong about Willow, she always has been wrong about Willow. She was the best thing to come into my life. She gave me purpose and meaning, she's what kept me moving forwards.

So how the hell have I ended up back here?

Slumped against the fence, I pull out my phone absent-mindedly, open up Instagram and search, as I do hundreds of times every day, for Willow's handle. Nothing.

Then it hits me. Were her accounts private? I had assumed so because Willow is inherently such a private person, but it dawns on me that I never actually checked. Hands trembling slightly, I log out of my account, and tap 'Create new account' on the home screen. I need a new email address. I bring up gmail and do the same thing. I choose the first thing that comes to mind for the email name: Findingwillow2020@gmail.com

Once the email account is created, it's a matter of minutes to set up a new Instagram account. Feeling my breath catch in my throat, I type Willow's handle into the search bar.

She comes up instantly. I tap her profile. A grid of images flashes before me. Her account isn't private. I don't know how I long I spend like that, scrolling through her old photos, intently studying each one. Three weeks ago, only a week before she disappeared, she posted a photo of the three of us – Willow, Zara and me at the weekend. She captioned it: 'The Three Musketeers'. We're walking to our favourite café, Zara on Willow's hip. I'm holding the camera, grinning like an idiot. I stare at my own face, almost unrecognisable in its easy, confident contentment. Willow is smiling. I remember that day so clearly – it was a happy one. I pinch to zoom in on Willow's face. Was that a real smile? Before that she posted a photo of Zara asleep, captioned it: 'Mummy's gorgeous angel'. But how did Mummy manage to leave her gorgeous angel behind? Before that she posted a photo of the view of Brighton beach, caption: 'Home is where the heart is'.

'Well, where the hell is that then, Willow?' I don't mean to say it out loud but I do and the bitterness in my own voice surprises me. The more I look at the happy little life we had, the life she documented on social media, the more I struggle to understand what went wrong. What am I missing?

I scroll through the grid of her posts. Perfect squares of bright, sunny happiness. Where are the cracks? Then my thumb knocks the tab at the top of the screen and a new grid pops up. Her tagged photos. I sit up. I've never seen these before. Why have I never looked at her tagged photos?

She hasn't been tagged in many, most are from my account: Zara's first birthday, Liam's house party years ago, a picture of her and Gran cooking in the flat in New Haw. Wow, times change. Then there's a few tagged photos from Gee's, and one posted by my old work friends, when she went to my Christmas do a couple of years back. All pretty standard ...

I pause.

There's one photo I don't recognise. It's Willow, and when I peer at the caption I can see the date is from three months ago. She's sitting with Zara in her lap at a coffee shop. She is smiling at the camera but I notice her eyes straight away. They're wide and red and her face is slightly puffy. She's been crying. She has a cappuccino on the table and I recognise from the mug that she's in the independent coffee shop we used to go to when we first moved to Brighton. The one with the books on the shelves, the recycled menus, the chalkboard on which I'd draw bad self-portraits of us both. Then over time these turned to bad self-portraits with a little baby in the tummy, then self-portraits with a baby in a pram. We haven't been to that café in ages. I can't remember why now. I guess we just drifted to new places.

So who was she with? And why was she crying?

I peer at the username: Jake Woods.

My brain desperately racks its library for some sort of explanation, any piece of obscure knowledge connected with this person. But nothing.

Who the hell is Jake Woods?

Willow never mentioned him. I'm sure Willow never said his name, let alone mentioned that they went out for a coffee. What is this part of her life I know nothing about?

I click onto his account. Private.

Of course it bloody is.

I'm suddenly aware of a prickling sensation on the back of my neck. Instinctively I turn around to see a man across the road. He's just standing there in the middle of the pavement and he's watching me. He's tall and stocky, wearing a scruffy overcoat pulled right up to his scruffy salt and pepper beard. He looks familiar.

Wait, he *is* familiar. It's the man I hit with the pram, outside my house that first morning back.

'Hey.' I walk towards him. 'Hey!'

But he turns around and walks away. And for some reason I can't explain, I don't follow.

## Chapter 34

# Dustin

I go back inside the house grudgingly.

I can see straight away Mum isn't there because her coat isn't hanging up in the hall, but when I go into the kitchen I find Alicia sitting at the kitchen table, surrounded by a Pot Noodle, a bottle of wine and a smaller bottle of Fanta. I know without looking into her glass that she will have mixed the red wine with the Fanta. It all started after a boy she went on a date with recommended it. The guy didn't last but her love for Fanta and wine did.

'Where's Zara?' I ask. I can hear the exhaustion in my voice.

'Upstairs, asleep,' Alicia says, taking a sip of her wine-Fanta cocktail. 'I gave her a bath and she nodded straight off.'

That sounds very unlike Zara. Why doesn't she ever nod straight off with me? I go to the fridge to get a beer – it is Friday, after all – and I find a Tupperware with a sticky note on it.

*Dear Dustin, here's some shepherd's pie for your dinner. Let's forget about earlier. Love you, Mum x*

I sigh. I wish I hadn't argued with Mum. What did I expect her reaction was going to be? She wasn't going to side with Willow was she? I think of Jake's Instagram photo, the picture of Willow on his feed. And what if, at the end of the day, she was a little bit right about Willow? I slam the fridge door shut.

'So you came back then,' Alicia says, arching an eyebrow, as I sit down at the table with the Tupperware and the beer.

'Where else was I going to go?' I reply, with a half smile that quickly dissolves.

Alicia doesn't reply. I struggle to think of a way to keep the conversation going. 'Didn't want Mum's shepherd's pie, then?'

Alicia shakes her head. 'I'm in the mood for crap.'

'Where is she?'

Alicia looks at me. 'Her friend's house.'

I frown. 'I've never known Mum to have friends.'

'Well she does now,' she says, prodding her Pot Noodle.

I wonder if Mum told her why we argued. Alicia isn't exactly forthcoming, but she hasn't completely shut me down either, which is something.

'Seems like you're having a wild Friday night,' I say.

'Elliot is out with friends.'

'You're not friends with his friends?'

Alicia shakes her head. 'You know you and Willow were an anomaly. It's rare for couples to share friends like you did.'

We didn't share all of our friends though, did we, Willow? Some we decided to keep secret ...

'Anyway,' Alicia continues. 'Elliot's friends are so much older. They act like middle-aged men.' She gestures to the bottle. 'Do you want some wine?'

I leap at the sign of some generosity from my sister. 'Yeah, I'd love some, thanks.' I push my unopened bottle of beer further down the table.

Alicia stands and returns it to the fridge for me, then grabs a wine glass from the cupboard.

'What about your friends?' I ask. 'Didn't you want to see them tonight?'

She sits back down, placing the wine glass in front of me. 'I don't really have friends.' She shrugs. 'My school friends are all at uni now, and the people in my year are younger than me, and you can really tell, you know? So, I don't really see many people at the moment.'

I smile sadly at her. 'Join the club.' I pause. 'Well, I do have Zara, but she's not very good on the conversation front, you know.'

I see the briefest of smiles on Alicia's face as she pours wine into my glass.

'Yeah, it's the same with me and Elliot. I just spend all my time with him.' She opens the Fanta bottle. 'But you've always had lots of friends, Dustin. Here you had loads of friends, and it seemed from photos in Brighton you did too. You want Fanta, too?'

'Yeah, go ahead.'

We sip on our Fanta and wine concoctions in silence, and I'm surprised by how weirdly nice it is.

'Alicia ...' She's waiting for me to complete the sentence but now it feels like the words are lodged in my throat. 'I ... I'm sorry for leaving home.'

She frowns. 'Dustin, I'm not hurt at you for leaving home. I was there for that, remember? I know why you left. I know you had to. I'm hurt because you left my *life*. I needed you.'

I don't have anything to say to this and so she continues. 'I needed my brother, and you left me. I was being punished for yours and Mum's problem. It wasn't fair. I hated Willow for a long time. It helped me to believe that it was her, rather than

164

you. But she messaged me. She was the one who let me know about the baby, she was the one who said she tried, she was the one who said sorry, and I realised I couldn't blame her. I had to be honest to myself that it was you. You made those choices, you cut me off.'

I stare at her. I never knew that Willow had messaged Alicia.

But then again, I'm starting to realise there were many things I never knew about Willow.

I think about it. I guess I did just cut my sister out. She had sent me so many messages in the early days – fearful at first, and then angry – and I didn't know what to do with them. Then she sent me that drunken voice note. She called me all sorts of names, told me she hated me and yeah, I was annoyed by that. She had been there, had seen the situation Mum had put me in. Why did she think sending me bitter, offensive messages would help? And I couldn't see what I could say to make the situation better. So I didn't say anything. Saying nothing, cutting yourself off from your feelings somehow seemed better for me.

'I'm sorry ... if I had known everything would go so wrong when I left then maybe I wouldn't have actually left for real,' I say, rubbing a hand through my hair.

Alicia stares at me. 'What do you mean?'

'With you still at school, and Mum ... being the way she is being – she will barely let me out of her sight now, she obviously struggled, and I just feel so guilty ...'

'Dustin, it hasn't been easy at all, yeah – but it's not like we've fallen apart without you. I might be retaking school but I'm really happy with Elliot – I like my life – I just would have preferred you to be in it for the past couple of years. And yeah, Mum didn't deal well at all. She had a proper breakdown. She had to go to therapy.'

'Oh ...'

'But the point is, we're OK now. There was a time when it didn't feel possible, but our lives have kept on going without you. After you get over the hard bit it gets easier. People adapt.'

And will this be the same for me? Can I keep my life going without Willow in it? Does it mean it's possible?

'But Mum is OK, she is even seeing someone. She dates her therapist. That's the "friend" she is seeing.'

I think my mouth drops to the table. '*Dating?* Mum has never ... dated.'

Alicia shrugs, tracing the rim of her glass. 'Yeah, I know, but after you went, I think the fact Mum had someone who made her feel like she mattered was important to her.'

'Is that allowed though? A therapist dating one of their clients?'

'Well, she isn't Mum's therapist any more.'

'Wait – she?' I say.

Alicia nods her head.

'Wow, who knew.'

'It's just a bit of a weird one, like we've never met her and they've been dating for a year now.'

'Oh.'

'It's fine, Mum seems happier. That's all that matters. She's easier to deal with. But I will say that half the shit that she says and does around you is an act. She's scared of losing you again. She's still Mum, deep down. She still worries, and she still seems terrified of losing me. Like I said, why do you think Elliot was invited to move in? So I don't move out and leave her.'

There's a pause. Alicia quietly wipes her eyes, and my stomach sinks further. I don't know what to say. It suddenly seems insane to me that I would have done those things, that I would have turned my back on the sister I cared about so much.

'I don't know, it was shit for me, Dustin. I really needed you.

I missed you. I kept thinking, what did I do wrong, for him to not care about me? To just cut me off like that.'

'I never even thought of that, I didn't think how you might have felt,' I mumble.

'I think that's the problem, you didn't think of me. You had Willow, and Zara, and Willow's gran, who replaced us all. Your little life was complete. But our life wasn't. I would be reminded of you every day, just leaving my room and walking past yours. Every day I thought of you. And all because you and Mum were both too stubborn to sort it out. And now you come back, and Mum is all "Dustin this, Dustin that". When you were the one who left us. You were the one who broke the family.'

'Lis ... I'm sorry.'

She exhales heavily. 'I know you are, but sorry is just a word, isn't it. It's pretty easy to say.' She pauses. 'It was just hard, seeing you on Instagram living a perfect life, while it wasn't so perfect here.'

'Apparently we weren't living a perfect life,' I say quietly.

'Well, I guess so, if you broke up. But whatever your problems were, they didn't show in your pictures online.'

I think about the pictures she means, and suddenly feel butterflies in my stomach. They did capture happy memories. They were real happy memories.

'No. How it was online, that was how it actually was. I mean – at least for me it was. It really was perfect, I thought I was living the dream.'

Alicia frowns. 'So what happened?'

'I don't know. I came home one day and she was gone.'

Alicia's mouth twists. I know she heard the argument earlier with Mum, but I don't know how much she knows.

'I can't contact her, no one can. She's just gone. She left me, and she left her baby. She was the one I was going to marry, have more babies with, live out my entire future with, and she's just gone.' I can feel my throat starting to tighten. 'And it really, really hurts. And I realise it's a taste of my own medicine for what I did to you and I know it seems like you guys are my second option now. I was young and stupid, I did cut you off, and now I know how that feels. I'm sorry, Alicia. I'm really, *really* sorry. And I'm sorry it took me until now to *say* sorry. Until now to realise it. I guess sometimes you need to feel your actions, to realise they were wrong.'

I can feel her shoulder grow damp with my tears as she wraps her arms around me. I am so angry at Willow for putting me through this. I am so bloody angry. I cry into my sister's shoulder, and pretty soon she's crying too.

# Chapter 35

# Willow

'No.'

Dustin looks at his mum, I look down at the floor. Why did we think this would be a good idea again?

We didn't ask her the day after the pub in the end. Dustin thought we should wait a little while to get his mum on side, and that she would handle it better if I was the one to ask about moving in – that she might even see it as a compliment. We waited until we thought it was the right time. I've been round loads recently and have been trying my hardest to be the kind of girlfriend she wants for Dustin – I brought her flowers last week, I helped her cook dinner tonight, me and Dustin cleaned the bathroom on Saturday.

We were having dinner and it all seemed to be going well, apart from the fact I didn't have much of an appetite, which I put down to nerves. I've been feeling sick a lot recently, ever since that night we came home late from the pub. I could sense Dustin's anticipation next to me, waiting for me to say something. I have barely stammered my way through 'And Dustin and I were wondering if perhaps I—' when she cuts through me.

'No.'

'No?' Dustin says, dropping his fork on his plate. 'Why?'

'She can't live here, I can't afford it.'

'I'll pay rent,' I offer, feeling my voice crack. This is humiliating. 'I already do with Gran.'

'Don't argue with me, love. This is my house. My decision.'

I shrink back in my chair, my stomach sinking.

'Mum, her gran is moving away,' Dustin says. Suddenly, I wish he would just leave it. I want more than anything for this conversation to be over, for us to be anywhere but here in this kitchen.

'Yes, and you can see each other at weekends, like all the other couples your age.'

'What do you mean "all the other couples our age"?' Dustin snaps back. 'What are you saying?'

My face is burning whilst at the other end of the table, Alicia's has turned white.

'You know exactly what I'm saying, Dustin. I'm asking you both not to be so melodramatic and to see this for what it is – it's a teenage relationship, for God's sake. Nobody moves in together at seventeen.'

'Eighteen, Mum.'

'Whatever.' Carol brings another spoonful of curry to her mouth. 'It's your first relationship, it's not like you're getting married.'

I take a deep breath. Don't cry, Willow, don't cry.

Dustin squeezes my hand again as he stares at his mum. 'Why are you being like this?'

I can't keep the tears in any more, I know they're about to

170

spill over and flood down my face. I stand up, eyes focused on the ground. 'Sorry,' I say quickly and dash to the door. Nobody tries to follow me. In the living room I sit on the sofa, and I start to cry. Hiccoughing, wracking sobs. But not loud enough to drown out the shouting from the dining room.

'Things have gone far enough, Dustin. I'm not going to stand back any more and watch you throw your life away.'

'She IS my life.'

'She's a bad influence. She's very often rude to me and it's rubbed off on you.'

'She's never been rude to you. She brought flowers round last week!'

'Getting you into drugs and God only knows what else.'

'It was my weed! Jesus Christ, how many more times do you need to hear it?'

'Funny how I never found weed in your room before her, and you've lost all motivation since you've been with her,' Carol continues as though Dustin hasn't spoken. 'You lost that coffee shop job, and now you just go out all the time. Well I won't stand for it. I'm not prepared to let you waste your life on some girl who's just using you until she can go off to university and forget all about you.'

I hear a chair screech, and then someone slamming their hands on the table. 'What are you talking about? You don't know anything! You don't have a fucking clue how I feel.'

At this point Alicia appears at the door to the kitchen, holding a tissue in her hand. She walks over and hands it to me with a sad, apologetic smile, still standing awkwardly opposite me. I take it, trying to wipe the tears from my face as I tune into the conversation again.

'Mum,' Dustin says. 'I love Willow, and if you won't let her stay, I'll go stay with her.'

I can hear the plates being stacked, before Carol gives a short, unpleasant laugh. 'No, you won't. I won't let you.'

Now Dustin is the one laughing, though nothing about this situation is funny. 'I can do what I want. I'm an adult.'

I hear footsteps and Dustin walks into the living room, his mum following him. Her eyes are red, mouth trembling. He is walking away, coming towards me with a hand out as if to say, 'Let's go', but then she grabs his arm. He sighs, pulls his arm out of her grip and turns around to look at her.

'Can't you understand how this feels for me?' Carol says.

Dustin grits his teeth. 'That's the problem – I do understand. I know you're sad. I know me and Alicia are your whole world, but I can't be responsible for that. I have a life too, Mum, and Willow is part of that now. But you don't even make an effort with her.' Something about Dustin's voice has changed. Alicia has obviously noticed it too because she puts a hand on his arm, but Dustin continues anyway. 'And I'm sick of it. I'm sick of hearing you talk to my girlfriend like this. You're acting like a crazy person. To be honest, I'm starting to see why Dad left.'

She slaps him. I must have let out some kind of noise because Dustin looks towards me, holding his cheek. He stares at me for what feels like ages, before he moves towards me, takes my hand again, and leads us to the door. I turn to look at Alicia who has her hand over her mouth, tears streaming down her face. She looks completely helpless. Dustin picks up the overnight bag he hadn't unpacked since staying at my house. Carol follows us, and I think maybe Alicia as well. I'm not really focusing on them, I'm focusing on Dustin. I've never seen him like this, his eyes bloodshot red, glossy, a single tear running down his cheek.

We are halfway out of the door when Carol shouts behind us. 'Don't come running back to me when it all goes wrong.'

# Chapter 36

# Dustin

I sit on the wall outside the house. I'm trying to find anything about this Jake guy. Jake Woods. Could he have a more common name? I don't know how many Jake Woods I've already scrolled through on Facebook. I'm going down, and down, and down, and then, eventually, I find him. It's the same profile picture as his Instagram. I tap into the photo to enlarge it. He's the surfer type – shaggy golden hair, partly covered by a beanie. Strong jawline. But he wears glasses too, which gives him a more intellectual appearance. He doesn't look like the kind of person Willow would be friends with. Her friends look like ... well, like me and Georgia.

I start searching through his friends, trying to find Willow, go onto his friends list.

I find her straight away.

What have you been hiding from me, Willow?

I open WhatsApp and start typing.

Who is Jake Woods?

I send it to Willow.

It doesn't even deliver.

# Chapter 37

# Willow

Then – June 2018

Dustin and I are sitting on a bench in the park, tears streaming down my face. He has his arm around me, pulling me into his chest.

'It's OK,' he says, kissing my hair.

'I should be saying that to you,' I sniff.

'It's fine,' he says, his hand rubbing my back.

'I'm so sorry, Dustin, I'm so, so, sorry.'

'Hey,' Dustin says, gently taking my chin, forcing me to look at him. 'You have nothing to be sorry about, we will work this thing out. We will work out the uni thing. We will work out living in Brighton. It's all going to be OK, I promise. It's you and me for ever, right?'

I stare at him, my hand slipping into my coat pocket. I stroke the package of the pregnancy test, the pregnancy test I haven't yet told him about.

'Yeah,' I say. 'You and me together.'

# PART II

# Chapter 38

# Willow

**Then – August 2018**

'So, what did you get?'

Dustin is sitting across from me on the sofa, next to Gran. Both of them are looking at me with wide excited eyes. I lower the letter, and swallow heavily.

'I ... umm,' I mumble. There are simultaneous shouts of protest from Dustin and Gran.

'Oh, Wills, we're not breathing over here.'

'Come on, love, out with it.'

'I got three As,' I exhale quickly.

I got three As for my A-levels. I never thought I would. It doesn't feel real. And it doesn't feel fair.

'You what? YEEESS!' Dustin punches the air and throws his arms around Gran, who is grinning from ear to ear.

'My girlfriend's a genius, my girlfriend's a genius,' Dustin chants, getting up and doing some ridiculous dance around the room.

'Oh, Willow.' Gran comes over to me, her eyes glassy. 'I'm so proud of you. More proud than you can possibly know.'

Then she's pulling me into a hug, and I feel Dustin's strong arms around me too. And all I want to do is cry.

'Right,' says Gran, pulling away and brushing a tear from her eye. 'I'm off to bingo but let's celebrate properly tonight.'

'I'll get the Prosecco, Mary!' says Dustin.

Gran smiles at him, and blows a kiss to me, before shrugging on her coat and leaving. Dustin goes into the kitchen, and I sigh, staring back at the results with shaking hands. We've been here two months. Brighton. We moved back into the flat Gran and I used to rent. By a stroke of luck, the family who'd rented it in the interim had found the commute to London too much and decided to move back to the city, and the landlord was only too pleased to have us back. Dustin hasn't spoken to his family. I know his mum was texting him, then he blocked her. He refuses to speak to me about it and I can't help but feel it's all my fault, though Dustin insists he doesn't blame me at all. I hope one day things get better.

Dustin comes back in, two wine glasses filled to the brim with the pale bubbly liquid. I feel a tightness at the back of my throat looking at it. I shake my head. 'I'm OK, thank you.'

'Willow, you haven't had a drink for ages and we need to celebrate. You're going to uni!'

I have to tell him.

'No I'm not.'

'What?' Dustin frowns. 'What are you talking about? You smashed your offer!'

'Dustin, I'm not going to uni, I can't.'

'Why not?'

I close my eyes, take a deep breath. 'I'm pregnant.'

Silence.

I open my eyes and look at him; he's watching me, saying nothing.

Shit.

I count to ten in my head, he still hasn't said anything.

'Dustin, please say something.'

He blinks, and sits down slowly next to me. He takes his hand and wraps it around mine.

'This is amazing.'

'What?'

'This is amazing, this is perfect!' He smiles. 'Our life is just getting better and better.'

I frown at him. 'But we're so young.'

'So? We know we'd want this eventually anyway.'

'But uni ...'

He holds both my hands now, and smiles at me. 'Hey, we'll work it out. Maybe you can go part-time, or once the baby is old enough you can go. We can still do everything, we might just have to change the order of things.'

'But what about money?'

'Willow, we will work it out. I've got loads of job interviews lined up, this will give me even more motivation to ace it, and then maybe we can try and move out to our own little place eventually.'

I throw my arms round him in relief. He's right, we can figure it all out. Reading can wait. 'You and me, D-bag.'

Then a thought hits my mind.

'Are you going to talk to your family?' I ask.

'You're my family now,' he whispers, his breath hot on my cheek. 'This is the best gift you could give me, a baby that's fifty per cent me, and fifty per cent you.'

And though I feel happier than I have done in weeks, I feel a small flicker of – what, anxiety, fear? – at his words.

A baby that's fifty per cent me. Is that definitely a good thing?

# Chapter 39

# Willow

**Then – August 2018**

Alicia didn't reply to my message, but it's OK, I don't blame her. I decide to do the same thing with Gran, quick and fast, get it over and done with.

'I'm pregnant.'

Gran drops her knitting needles.

It's been two weeks since I told Dustin, and somehow in that time he managed to find a job as an estate agent down the road. The salary is basic, but Dustin said he can make a lot from commission. He even came home with a ring last week, a slender silver thing from a proper jeweller's. It's not an engagement ring – neither of us feel that's necessary right now – but it's got an infinity sign. I haven't taken it off since. I'm still doubtful he can afford it, but he told me that soon he'll have enough to buy all the rings we could want.

So once that worry was over, I decided to tackle my next. Gran. She is going to be disappointed. She wanted more for me than this. My mum got pregnant at seventeen, I'm only one year older. I waited till we were deep into a knitting session, *Coronation Street* on the TV, water bottles on our bellies.

I look at Gran, tears are now forming in her eyes. Oh, man.

'Gran, please don't be upset ...' I put my knitting aside and tentatively put my arms round her.

'I'm so happy,' she says.

I pull away. 'What?'

'I'm going to be a great-grandma.'

She's beaming from ear to ear. Am I the crazy one? Why am I the only one scared shitless about this?

'But, Gran, what about—'

She holds onto my cheeks, forcing me to look down at her. 'I will help you out, with whatever you need.'

I nod my head slowly. 'I'm just scared, that I'm going to turn out like—'

'I'm going to stop you there, because you won't. We know you won't.'

Then I ask her the question that has been weighing on my mind since I told Dustin the news.

'Should I tell Mum?'

# Chapter 40

# Dustin

In the end, I message Jake. I don't care about my self-respect any more.

> I don't know who you are but you seemed to know my girlfriend Willow. If you know her whereabouts please let me know. Please.

No response.

He hasn't even read it.

I'm aware of how Facebook works. If someone you don't know messages you, it goes into your 'other' folder, and you have to actively check that to read your messages. Let's just hope he's in the one per cent of the population that actually does look at their 'other' folder.

I minimise the Facebook app and my phone screen shows me the picture of Willow and Zara again. In the picture she's wearing the necklace, the one she always wore. The necklace now sitting on my bedside table, because Willow apparently enjoys tormenting me. The more I stare at the picture of her, the more angry I can feel myself becoming.

Opening up my photos I find one of just Zara, and change my phone background to this one instead. She's all I need. I need to be a dad for her. I need to actually live for our future together, not for the past, not for her mum who didn't care about us. How could I have spent so long with a girl that just left us like that? My hands are shaking.

Zara is my now. Zara is my future.

There's no way I can go back to Brighton, not when it would remind me of her. So, Surrey is my now. My family is my now.

You know what? Everything will be OK. I don't need her.

# Chapter 41

# Willow

Here's the plan: get a job, have the baby, look after the baby, then when I feel ready, Gran will look after the baby, I will reapply to courses, and I will go to uni. We haven't talked yet about whether or not it'll be Reading, but I'm trying not to think about that. I'm focusing on the here and now, and the future of our new family. And I'm actually really excited. Dustin is doing well in his job, we have managed to move out to a one-bed flat, just round the corner from Gran's. Things are tight, but it's OK, we've got each other. Gran is helping out, scouring charity shops for a second-hand pram, and a crib. Meanwhile, I'm trying to get a job, and it's not quite as straightforward as I had hoped. I'm not exactly being choosy – I'll work in a shop, a café, I'll be a receptionist, anything. I just want to have something to do.

I tried to do freelance jobs, put my graphic design skills to the test, but sadly no one wants to pay a girl with no experience. I would usually happily work for free, build my CV up, but money comes first at the moment. I'm four months now and I'm showing, and it seems hard to get a job, maybe people don't want to hire someone who will be leaving in a few months.

Dustin walks through the door, planting a kiss on my cheek, then my belly. 'How was today?' he asks.

I sigh, rubbing my head. 'Not successful, no one will reply to me.'

'Have you tried not telling them you're pregnant?'

'Yes, obviously. Then I get to interview, and they ask my longer-term plan, and I tell them because it's obvious and then I don't hear back. Is that legal?'

Dustin shrugs. He sits down next to me, taking my hands in his. 'Maybe you don't need to work? I think I can make ends meet.'

'But I want to work, Dustin. You know me, I like keeping myself busy. Maybe I can look for some freelance design work or something.'

Dustin smiles, and nods his head. 'OK, just don't feel like you have to. Last month you've been really struggling, and having a job and feeling so ill, it worries me.'

'It's OK, the morning sickness is getting better,' I reply, squeezing his hands, trying to convince him and myself. I do love being back here. But it's weird. My situation now is so different from the life I envisaged for myself when I was in Brighton. For some reason, being pregnant and settling down made more sense back in Surrey. It felt more like the person I became later, not the person I'd been in Brighton. The shy, anxious girl who hardly spoke to anyone, who only ever felt properly at peace with a pencil or knitting needles in hand.

I see people I know sometimes, people I went to school with. And, apart from the odd awkward wave or half smile, they blank me. I mean, it's not like we were ever friends at school or anything, but I just feel like a stranger in the place that in other ways feels so much like home.

'Well, good,' Dustin says, nuzzling into my neck. 'You know I just—'

My phone rings and I put my finger to his lips.

'Hello?'

'Hello, is this Willow?'

'Yes?'

'Thank you for coming in last week, it was great to meet you. I'm calling because we would like to offer you the part-time receptionist role. It will only be on a temporary basis though.'

'Oh, no, that's totally fine . . . That's great. Thank you. Thank you so much!'

# Chapter 42

# Dustin

I'm moving on.

I'm seeing my friends, going to the pub. Some semblance of routine is starting to form.

And I'm officially an estate agent again. I got a new job. I gave in my notice at Brighton, they knew it was coming. Mum offered to arrange a couple of interviews but, as I tried to tell her, a twenty-one-year-old guy having an interview organised by his mum doesn't give off the best impression. So, for the first time in weeks, I sat down and did something productive. I wrote some applications and the third interview, at the estate agent round the corner from the coffee shop where I used to work, came good.

Mum is thrilled.

I've been at this job for two weeks. The people I work with seem nice, and I can walk to work. The walk to work means I pass the college, which brings a host of accompanying complicated feelings, but I've got to get over it. This job is for me, and for Zara, so that she has a future. Because I'm a dad. I need to remember that. Zara needs her dad. Mum is happy to look after

Zara to start with, and then we're going to look into nursery for a couple of days a week. I'm starting part-time at work. They might offer me a full-time contract if everything goes well.

Putting Dad mode first has worked pretty well for the past couple of weeks, but you can't just ignore your other thoughts. They stay in the back of your brain, stewing and soaking, until eventually they swell, pushing their way forward.

That's what they've done today. I'm sat at my desk and it's like a dark blanket has been thrown on top of me, and I can't get it off.

It's hard not to compare this job to Brighton – the people there, how comfortable I felt, how I just knew how to do everything. And thinking about Brighton sparks a spiral of negative thoughts. The Brighton lot were apparently really sad that I'm not coming back. Naomi texted me the day after I handed in my notice, asking if I wanted to meet for a coffee. I didn't reply, but then she asked me for a postal address and I gave her one. Her envelope arrived a few days later.

The note was on one of the official 'with compliments' slips, written in Naomi's elegant, looping handwriting.

*Miss you D and hope to see you soon. I know things are tough right now, but I'm always there. Love, Nom x*

And tucked in alongside the note was the picture of Willow I'd had stuck next to my monitor since my first day. I scrunched it up and stuffed it into my wallet. At my new desk, I have a photograph of Zara Alicia took last week. She printed it for me and framed it.

'Good morning, Dustin,' Darren, my manager, says, sliding past me, popping a coffee on my desk and perching on the one opposite mine.

Darren is a friendly guy, in his late twenties, I reckon, and very confident. It turns out his mum works with mine, and I am not entirely sure that didn't play a role in getting me the job. What I am sure about, though, is he has been fully informed about my situation and that's why he's being so nice to me.

I look down at the coffee, and back at Darren. 'Is this a Friday thing?'

Darren smiles, twirling round on his chair. 'No, this is a "I saw you walking in looking like death, get some caffeine juice down you" thing.'

I chuckle. 'Thanks, Darren.'

He twirls his pen between his fingers. This is something I've noticed about Darren, he never keeps still. 'Late night, huh? Pub?'

I shake my head. 'I didn't get much sleep. Dad life, I guess.'

Darren looks disgusted. 'Ergh, Dad life is not for me,' he says, grinning, and then instantly looking serious. 'God, no offence or anything.'

'None taken, seriously.'

'Well good, let's finish this second viewing if we can. I think your lady is looking very serious.'

I sigh. 'I don't like to be too hopeful these days.'

'Well that attitude won't get you a sale,' he says, before his phone starts ringing and he swivels to answer it. I deflate again. I sip my coffee, surveying my desk. There's a cactus that Georgia bought me; it has two googly eyes. She left a very Georgia-style Post-it note attached to it. 'Don't be a prick and blow your first day on the job, good luck D!'

Safe to say I kept the note in my drawer. Next to the cactus is the water bottle my mum bought me, and the reusable coffee cup Alicia got. Nobody got me gifts when I got my first job. Maybe this is what happens when people feel sorry for you.

The sound of my phone ringing brings me out of my thoughts with a jolt.

'Lucie Slates Estate Agents, Dustin speaking,' I say, a little dazed. 'How may I help you?'

The voice at the other end is breathy, excitable.

'Hello, Dustin, it's me, Lesley. I'd love to book another viewing of 66 Grandly Road if I can?'

I smile. 'Hey, Lesley, happy Friday. Of course, I can get that booked in for you, I had a feeling you liked it.'

I can hear her giggle. 'What gave it away? Deciding where my potted plants were going to go?'

'I think it was more the fluffy rugs.' She laughs again, and I force myself to laugh back in response. Darren turns around. He sticks his thumb up in the air and I try to force another smile now he's watching me. 'So give me a time and date and I'll see what I can do for you, and let's hope the second viewing is as good as the first.'

Fake it till you make it, Dustin.

# Chapter 43

# Willow

'It's just a few hours, Wills, I won't be long.'

I look at him, breathing heavily in pain.

I'm huge. I'm heavy. I'm uncomfortable.

My back hurts daily, my skin is stretching, I didn't even know my boobs could get this big, and no, they aren't the perky happy boobs I always dreamed of.

'I have just finished my last day at work, Dustin,' I say, slowly, as my back pain gets deeper.

'Yeah, and now you don't work for the foreseeable future' he says. His mouth turns into a smirk. 'I wish I had that luxury.'

I glare at him.

'I'm joking, Wills,' he says, raising his hands. 'Look, I'm sorry, but it's important, this guy is an important client – he owns a lot of properties and rents almost all of them through us, and my boss will be annoyed if I don't go.'

I rub my hand through my hair, shaking my head. I'm feeling so uncomfortable, I just want to crawl out of this pregnancy suit that's weighing down my body. 'Can you not do it another day? I just really feel like grabbing a takeaway and doing nothing.'

'OK, well how about I order you one? And by the time you watch a film or something I'll probably be back.'

I agree, sulkily. When, after Dustin has fetched pillows and a duvet, ordered me a pizza and kissed me on the forehead, I hear the front door slam, I wonder if I am being a tad unreasonable.

I guess it isn't fair to expect him to stay in all the time just because I'm too big to feel like going out now. And we'll have a whole two weeks together once the baby is born. We'll be a proper family.

And I am excited by the prospect. It wasn't exactly the plan, but then again when has anything turned out like I planned?

The pain in my belly is growing stronger. As I stroke it absent-mindedly I think back to the conversation Gran and I had about Mum, and about whether I should tell her. I'm still not convinced I made the right choice.

Ow.

The baby kicks me hard, and suddenly a wave of acute pain washes over me. It intensifies, burrowing deep into my belly.

Oh God, it's so painful. I try to breathe but I can feel panic rising. I reach for my phone, but just before my fingers clasp it another stab of pain hits me.

I need to call Dustin.

# Chapter 44

# Dustin

The picnic in the park is Alicia's suggestion. If the truth be told I am a bit hungover and would rather spend the morning mooching in front of the TV, but it's the first time Alicia has suggested we go out just us and I'm not about to turn that down. Things have been so much better between us since I talked to her about Willow but still not as they were before.

We stop in the middle of the park. Alicia retrieves a worn and scratchy picnic blanket and the two meal deals from her tote bag, and sets the blanket out on the grass. Zara sits happily on the picnic blanket, and when Alicia hands her a fruit pouch she takes it eagerly.

She's made a lot more effort since I told her about Willow, and I wonder if it's pity, or if she's faking having forgiven me. I wonder a lot of things, but I won't take it for granted. I smile a thanks as I open the pasta pot.

She went for a BLT, a surprising choice for someone who was vegetarian when I left. Things change, Dustin, you know this now.

I take a look around the park. It's quiet here. A long stretch of green to all sides and there's hardly a person in sight.

'So Elliot did something really stupid the other day,' Alicia says, shovelling sandwich into her mouth.

She tells me about Elliot messing up at work, and she's laughing so much as she tells it that she half chokes on her sandwich. Then she tells me about college and how afterwards she's thinking of getting into PR, because it seems like the kind of job you'd never be bored in and she reckons she's good at talking to people. I am just about to respond encouragingly when I catch sight of him.

Near the entrance we came through, a man is leaning against the railings, smoking a cigarette. He is heavily tattooed, and he has a thick beard.

What the hell?

Is it him? The salt and pepper guy. I scramble to my feet, squinting at him. I can't see clearly in the dappled sunlight, but I'm almost certain.

'Dustin? Dustin, where are you going?'

I can hear Alicia calling me but I ignore her. I'm getting closer now. It's definitely him, and he's staring right at me.

'DUSTIN!'

I turn back to Alicia. She's on her feet now, Zara in her arms, staring at me in open-mouthed confusion.

'It's nothing,' I say, 'I just want to talk to someone.'

But when I turn back to where the guy was standing just seconds before, he's not there. I scan the whole line of trees, the benches, the play area to the right, my head whipping wildly between each point. But he's nowhere.

'Dustin, what the hell is wrong with you?'

When I reach Alicia, her expression is full of anxiety.

'Nothing,' I stammer. 'Just this man, I've seen him a few times recently.'

'Well, I couldn't see anyone. But anyway, New Haw's a pretty small place. You see the same people ...'

'Yeah.' I cast another eye over the park. He has definitely gone. Hasn't he?

Was he even there to start with?

Or am I going crazy?

# Chapter 45

# Willow

She's beautiful.

Her name is Zara and she was born on 2nd February 2019. I had a really short labour, just three hours, and then she was there. The midwife said she clearly couldn't wait to be here. A healthy girl, seven pounds. And she's wonderful. Dustin was there for the birth, and so was Gran. And now our first two weeks together have flown past, and it's been surreal.

I'm not saying it has all been plain sailing – she cries almost constantly some nights, and I couldn't get her to latch on to breastfeed for a few days even though she did it the first time in the hospital fine. Then there was Dustin. Me and Gran both tried to have conversations about the fact he should tell his family, but he wouldn't even hear us out. He said we are all the family he needs and I felt guilty about the warm feeling in my stomach when he said that.

But Gran has been amazing and has stayed for the whole time, sleeping on the sofa-bed in the living room, even though it's probably not good for her back at her age. She didn't inter-fere too much with me and Zara, but things magically got done around us. The washing up, the laundry, the dusting. And meanwhile I was totally transfixed by the new little human I had made. I would sit on the sofa, Zara asleep in my arms, studying every inch of her face, breathing her in. I can't get enough of her. Neither of us can.

But we agreed that Gran would go back to her flat today, and that she'll just stop by every day. So now it's just the three of us. Dustin and I are on the sofa. Zara is bundled up in his arms, fast asleep for the first time all afternoon, and even though I'm more tired than I've been in my life (in fact I didn't know it was possible to be this tired) I just can't stop smiling. I don't know when I last washed my hair, I can't remember the last time I put make-up on, and I haven't showered for days. It sounds gross but I think I haven't even brushed my teeth today.

Dustin has been great – being a dad seems to come naturally to him. Except those moments when he's watching her, and I recognise the flicker of fear in his eyes. The fear that she's too good to be true, the fear that any moment she could just snap in half or fade away in front of you.

'I can't get over how much she looks like you,' he whispers.

'What? I think she looks like her dad.'

'No,' he says firmly, looking deep into my eyes. 'She's all you. That's why she's so perfect.'

Dustin looks back towards Zara. I can see the love he feels when he watches her, because I recognise it in myself. It's a different type of love, it's protective, and I'm fascinated by the feeling.

'I'm so jealous that I have to go back to work tomorrow,' Dustin says, eyes still on Zara. 'And you get to be with this beautiful girl all day.'

I smile, watching them both proudly. 'I know, I'm pretty lucky,' I say. 'I'll send you photos every single day.'

'FaceTime too, please.'

I chuckle. 'OK, FaceTime on your lunch breaks.'

'Deal.'

I exhale, happily sinking into the sofa, my eyes heavy, head tight, but heart warm and full to the brim.

'I feel so complete, Dustin,' I mumble, as my eyelids begin to droop, weighed down by two weeks of sleepless nights. 'I don't think I've ever felt this whole.'

# Chapter 46

# Willow

It sounds like a terrible thing to say. It sounds so awful I haven't been able to bring myself to admit it for the last three weeks. But today the truth was there, staring me in the face.

I don't like being alone with the baby. In fact I can't stand it.

Between Dustin rushing home from work in the evenings, and lunchtimes if he can, and then Gran popping by every day, it's not for very long that I am alone with her, a few hours at the most. But still, I've come to dread them. I am tense when I'm with her and I swear she can sense it because she cries all the time. She cries relentlessly. It's as if she's screaming for help, for someone to come and take her away from this anxious, incompetent imposter pretending to be her mother. Not a single day has gone by since Dustin went back to work when there hasn't been half an hour of Zara howling, purple-faced and angry in her cot, with me crouched against the wall, sobbing into my knees.

Gran is here again right now, in the act of bundling Zara into a clean, freshly ironed Babygro. She tried to coax me out of the house again today but I can't face it yet, so we stayed inside. She offered to cook me and Dustin dinner tonight, but she's always helping out and I know I can't get too dependent on this. So I say no, but thank you, I've got it. I want her to cook, I want her to stay, and put the baby to bed, but even more than that I want to be like all the mums all over the world and do it on my own, like I should be able to.

If I believe I've got it, at some point maybe I will have it.

I say goodbye to Gran, put a snoozing Zara down in her crib, put the kettle on to make a cup of tea and sink onto the sofa. OK, I'll take twenty minutes now to recharge and then I will start preparing dinner. It's a Friday, it's the weekend tomorrow, which means Dustin will be here for two whole days. Him and me together, the three of us a family. I close my eyes. I've never appreciated silence as I do right now. This snippet of time just for myself.

I wake up to Zara crying. Shit. I fell asleep. Shit. You idiot, why did you fall asleep? I clamber towards our bedroom, my head foggy, eyes squinty with sleep as I pick up Zara, and start feeding her. I hiss in pain as she latches on, rubbing my eye with my other hand, trying to force myself awake. I can't believe I fell asleep, what's wrong with me? I sit down on the bed as she continues to feed; she's very hungry. I grit my teeth, closing my eyes, trying to remember what Gran and the midwife told me. That it will get easier. And I'm feeding my daughter, some women can't do that at all ... But they said it'd get less painful, and it hasn't. They said the pain would last only a couple of weeks, but it has been more than five now. Is she doing it wrong? Am I doing it wrong?

It's OK, Willow, I tell myself. Pain is worth your baby being fed. I grab a pen and start doodling with one hand, the other supporting Zara's head. It's my coping mechanism, I've found. Doodle through the feeding pain. Anything to distract myself from the sensation that someone is holding a lit match to my nipples every time my daughter feeds.

I sigh, letting go of the pen, using both hands to support my daughter. I was so much better at designing, doing work, revising at school, than I am at being a mum. How does that work? Shouldn't this be natural? Isn't this what I was meant to do?

Zara stops feeding and pulls away, looking up at me with her big eyes. My heart opens, I do love her so much. I really do love her.

Then she starts crying again.

Here we go.

Just at that moment I hear the front door slam.

'I'm home, where are my girls?' Dustin's voice is booming and exuberant.

'In the bedroom,' I call, and my voice cracks with the exertion.

Within seconds, Dustin comes through the door, a smile illuminating his face. He comes towards us both, kissing my forehead, then Zara's.

'You can take her,' I say, already feeling conscious of the bags under my eyes. 'She's done feeding.'

He smiles even wider. 'Are you?' he says, in a high-pitched tone, as he carefully takes Zara into his arms. Were you a hungry baby?' He strokes the end of her nose with his finger.

Dustin's a natural.

# Chapter 47

# Dustin

Time to move out of my previous life.

I stand at the door of the flat, what used to be our flat, where I used to open the door to Willow and Zara, sweeping them both into my arms. I exhale, then I open it sharply.

And I'm met with ... boxes.

Boxes, bags, bin bags, suitcases. Everything piled in the living room.

Maybe it's good. If it looked exactly the same, it would have hurt. It would have been a gloating replica of my previous life. My landlord called and said my contract had run out, which was no surprise, but also that he had people moving in next week, which was. Elliot hired a van, and he and Alicia drove me here. They said they would help me pack everything up, but I didn't want that. So Mum has Zara, and those two are at the breakfast club down the road, the one Willow and I used to go to, while I pick through the worn-out pieces of our old life.

I am just clambering over the boxes towards the kitchen when the bathroom door opens and I turn to see Naomi coming out, a large box in her arms. She stops and stares at me for a moment, then without hesitation she carefully places the box on the floor, walks over to me and wraps her arm around me. I hug her back, feeling my face sinking into her shoulders, taking in the familiar scent of her perfume, the coconutty smell of her hair.

'Thank you for doing this,' I mumble.

'It's nothing, seriously, it's nothing.'

I pull away, a little awkward. 'It is, thanks, Naomi.'

She smiles. 'I'm happy to help, I've told you that.'

Suddenly I feel so overwhelmed by the task ahead of me. How can I pack up the life we had? How can I box and label and sort the two happiest years of my life? I sink down onto the floor, and Naomi does the same, a concerned hand on my shoulder.

'Hey, are you OK?'

'It's just ...' Oh God, am I going to cry? 'It's just so weird being back here.'

She laughs slightly. 'Well God, yeah, I can imagine! I think anyone would find it strange.'

Except there's nobody to compare with, is there? Because nobody we know has had their girlfriends run off and leave them literally overnight.

'We all miss you at work, Dustin,' she says quietly.

I take my hands away from my face and look at her, properly. She looks sad. Why is she so sad?

'Yeah,' I mumble.

'Are you sure moving back to your mum's is the right decision?' she asks gently. 'You know they haven't replaced you yet at the office? You could still come back if you wanted to?'

I shake my head. 'This is the right thing for me, Nom. I've got to move on and I can't do that here. My focus is Zara now.' Then I stand up, clapping my hands, before any more mopey conversation can happen. 'Well, the rest of these boxes aren't going to pack themselves.'

Naomi stands up too. 'You better start with your room then, I haven't been in there since you left. I didn't want to ... you know, I didn't want to intrude.'

'Thanks,' I say.

I try the same tactic with my bedroom, opening my door quick, and this time it's not boxes I'm greeted with. It's our room, it's our bed, our bedside tables, our rug, our photos on the cabinet, our Post-it notes on the mirror, our photos on the wa—

Wait. There are no photos on the wall.

We had had a ton printed last year, and Willow had stuck them all over the far wall of our bedroom. She had called it our mosaic. It was a pretty incoherent mosaic, I had said. Black and white, matt, gloss, many different types, pictures of us at the pub, pictures of us by the beach, bed selfies, group selfies, standing on the pier, eating breakfast, Zara in our arms, so many different photos ...

But now all I can see are the remains of the Blu-tack on the wall.

'Naomi!'

She's there in an instant. 'What is it?'

'Where are the photos?'

'What?'

'Where are the photos that were on this wall? Did you already pack them away?'

She frowns. 'I haven't touched them. I told you, I haven't been in here.'

Well, I think, someone has been.

# Chapter 48

# Willow

Then – April 2019

People are staring. All around me I can feel their eyes burrowing into me and my ears are growing hot. Terrible mother, they're thinking.

I cannot get Zara to stop screaming. We are at the checkout aisle and there's an enormous queue behind us, but I can't wrestle her into her pram. My basket of shopping stands abandoned next to me. I'm trying to gesture to people that they should go ahead of me to the empty till, but I can't do two things at once and nobody is moving. And even if I could I doubt I could make myself heard over Zara's wails. She's like a siren.

An old lady passes me, and I swear I see her shake her head disapprovingly.

I blow my hair away from my clammy face and try gently hushing her again. But it won't work.

'You might want to try feeding her love,' someone calls from behind me. 'She's hungry.'

I ignore them.

I've tried feeding her. I've burped her. I've changed her. I was in the toilet for half an hour hoping she'd stop crying. Nothing is working. Zara is screaming with the full force of her lungs, and suddenly I feel like I can't get enough air into mine. Oh God, I haven't had a panic attack in almost two years. But I recognise the warning signs instantly. I abandon the shopping basket and, clutching Zara in one hand and desperately trying to steer the pram with the other, I make for the exit.

Once outside I lean against the glass pane of the shop window, trying to force oxygen into my lungs. Keep it together, Willow, deep breaths. Deep breaths.

I fumble in my pocket for my phone and call Dustin.

One ring.

Two rings.

He doesn't answer.

I try his office line, but that rings out too. A familiar cheery tone at the end tells me I've reached Dustin at James Milton Estate Agents, he's away from his desk right now but if I leave him a message he'll get back to me just as soon as he can. Alternatively I can reach him on email.

I groan. Zara hasn't let up for even a second. How does she have the stamina? How can something so small make that much noise?

I call Gran. Two rings, and she picks up the phone.

Fifteen minutes later, Gran is walking towards me, folding me and Zara into a hug.

'You all right, petal?' she says with a frown.

I try to nod, but realise it comes out a firm shake of the head.

'Do you want me to hold her?'

Passing Zara to Gran feels like handing over a searing hot

plate that has been burning into my flesh for the last half hour. I breathe a heavy sigh of relief. And as soon as she is snuggled in Gran's arms, Zara's wails subside. And apart from a few snuffles and the odd hiccough, she's quiet.

Why?

# Chapter 49

# Dustin

'What, even the photos of me?' Georgia says.

She is sitting opposite me on my bed in my room back in New Haw, standing Zara up, as she makes guided steps on the bed in Georgia's arms.

I'm pacing back and forth, as I have been for the last twenty minutes.

I roll my eyes. 'All the photos, Georgia, literally all of them.'

She shrugs her shoulders. 'That is weird.'

I grit my teeth. Why is she not more freaked out about this? Her lack of reaction is really pissing me off.

'Georgia, do you know something?'

She finally looks up. 'What?'

'Do you know something? Because you never seem anywhere near as stressed, panicked, or worried as I do.'

She glares at me. 'Dustin, I'm offended.'

'I'm serious, Georgia. If there's something you're not telling me ...'

'Dustin, just cos I don't freak out all the time like you do, doesn't mean I'm any less worried or confused. But honestly, I really don't see the point in us both acting like this.' She makes a disdainful gesture towards me. 'Are you sure you didn't take the photos down before you left? You were really upset and anxious, maybe you got angry and ...'

'And what?' I say furiously. 'Went on some psycho rampage tearing down things in the flat? I think I'd remember that.'

She's quiet for a moment.

'Alicia mentioned she's been a bit worried about you when she let me in earlier. She mentioned something in the park ...'

I groan. I knew Alicia wouldn't let that go so easily.

'Yes, well, there's this guy I'm seeing ...'

Georgia frowns. 'As in ... dating?'

'What? No! I keep seeing him randomly. Like he was on this street once when I was coming back from a walk, then I saw him watching outside college, then in the park. I feel like he's following me.'

'Alicia said she couldn't see anyone.'

'Well yeah, every time I try to speak to him, he disappears. And I don't know what's going on, but what if he's got something to do with Willow disappearing?'

I'm speaking so quickly I run out of breath. I steal a glance at Georgia who is stroking the top of Zara's head, watching me carefully.

'Well say something, Georgia.'

'I don't think you're crazy, Dustin.'

I breathe a sigh of relief. 'So I'm being stalked then.'

'Well no, I'm not saying that either, I just think maybe you should look into talking to someone.'

'Well that's what I'm doing here.'

'No, I mean a professional.'

'So you *do* think I'm crazy.'

'Dustin, talking to someone doesn't mean you're crazy, not at all.'

Yeah, whatever. I know what she means.

# Chapter 50

## Willow

Then – May 2019

Gran spent all day with me today, we knitted when Zara had naps. Then she left, and I decided I would do some housework, get the house spic and span for when Dustin comes home. But Zara isn't having any of it. Once I finally get her settled I glance at the clock. Shoot. It's nearly five. Right, sorry, Dustin. I was going to make tuna steaks but it'll have to be pasta. Dustin is really good with the housework and he doesn't like me to cook, telling me to wait till he gets home so we can do it together, but it's Friday. He's been working all week and I want to surprise him. At least I can do a nice sauce, instead of our usual pesto from a jar. I am halfway through dicing the vegetables when there's a wail from the bedroom. I don't believe it.

I burp her and she throws up all over me. It's in my hair and I think about showering but I really don't have time, so I just run my head under the tap and go back to the kitchen.

Dustin will be home in about forty minutes, and though I wanted to have everything ready for him, now I just want him to be here. An order to the chaos, a light in the dusky dimness of our flat. Just then my phone, on silent as it almost always is these days for fear the slightest noise will disturb Zara, vibrates with a message. It's Dustin.

Is it ok if I go out for a few drinks with the boys tonight? Be back later, order a takeaway or something?

I stare at the message, my stomach sinks.

I've already started cooking dinner x

Oh, shoot. ok, don't worry. I'll come home.

Now I feel guilty. I start texting back.

No, honestly it's fine, go out. I'll just leave the leftovers in the fridge for you. It's only pasta.

Ok Willow, love you.

Love you too. So much.

I can feel my bottom lip starting to quiver. Don't be pathetic, Willow. I text Gee.

You don't fancy coming round this night? Keep me company? I'll pay for your petrol.

She replies straight away.

Sorry babe, I'm out with friends. See you soon, sorry it's been a little while since I last came, I've just been busy. I'm missing Zara!

I put the phone down. Turn off the hob, leaning against the worktop. Though I've longed for it all day, the silence in our flat suddenly feels deafening.

# Chapter 51

# Dustin

Dear Miss Church,
    I'm delighted to say your offer has been accepted.

I smile at my email as I type it. Good news to start a good morning. And things *are* good, honest. I'm not just saying that.

Work is decent.

Money is coming in.

I'm getting more and more commission.

I got myself noise-cancelling headphones, that I listen to on my walk on my way to work. Nice, upbeat, happy music, that I sometimes even find myself skipping along to.

I am not crazy.

I haven't seen that guy since my chat with Georgia.

I just had a little slip-up, a little moment, that's all. But I will not let Willow destroy everything.

Me and Zara are totally bossing this thing called life. Did I mention, the other day when I was bathing her, she reached her arms out to me and said, 'Want Dada'? Well, man, that made me warm inside. That was important to me. She's making progress, I tell you that. Yes she wants Dada, cause all she needs is Dada. And Dada won't leave her like Mama did.

All I need is her.

I am totally fine, as long as I have her, and she has me.

Everything's fine.

Honest.

# Chapter 52

## Willow

Popcorn, TV, Zara asleep. This is perfect. We have decided on making movie night a monthly thing, and this month I chose the David Bowie documentary, *Bowie: The Man Who Changed the World*.

Dustin comes in, our duvet in his hands. He places it on the sofa, leaning forward and tucking it around me, so that warmth instantly hits my body. He smiles at me.

'You snug?' he asks.

I smile, nodding my head. 'There's room for two,' I say, patting the side of the sofa.

Dustin grins. 'Thought you'd never ask,' he says, and jumps in next to me, pushing the duvet around his legs. He wraps an arm around me, and I lean into his chest, breathing in the lingering scent of aftershave on his T-shirt. It's the same one he wore when I first met him.

'Are you smelling me, you weirdo?'

I look up at Dustin, straight-faced. 'Yes, yes I am.'

He shakes his head, laughing, and points at the cup of tea he made me when we first sat down. 'Oi, that'll be cold now.'

'Oh yeah,' I say, leaning forward, grabbing the cup, and taking a huge sip. It takes me a second. At first I think it's the lukewarm milk that tastes so bad. But no, it's like a wave of seawater has just entered my mouth. It's almost suffocating, and then I'm spitting it all out on the floor. I'm gasping, running to the kitchen to get some clean water into my dehydrated mouth. I glug from the tap, and from the living room I can hear Dustin cackling. Wiping my mouth on my pyjama sleeve, I take a glass, fill it with water, and go slowly back into the living room. Dustin's face is bright red, tears streaming down his cheeks.

'Sorry,' he says, in between breathy laughs. 'But it was a perfect opportunity. I had to. I just had to.'

'Oh,' I say, walking forward, a sly smile forming on my lips. 'We playing these games again, D-bag?' I stop, standing over him on the sofa as he looks up at me. I hold my glass of water so it's hovering over his head. 'Be a shame if I dropped it.'

Dustin's eyes widen. 'You wouldn't.'

I cock my head slightly. 'Wouldn't I?' I say, just as I let it tip, the water flowing from the glass straight onto his head.

He stands up, wiping his now wet hair away from his face and picking up a half-empty glass from the table. 'Game on, Wills,' he says before running towards the kitchen and turning the tap on. A year ago I would have screamed, but I'm so conscious of waking Zara now that I don't say anything, I just pelt to the bathroom. I fill the glass up, then stand in the bath, pull the shower curtain across, and wait like a naughty kid, finding it hard to contain my excitement. Waiting for Dustin to find me.

I stay there for what feels like hours. What's he doing? He's taking ages.

Then I hear talking.

I step out the bath, open the door, and see Dustin sat on the sofa, the glass of water in his hand, phone in the other as he chats to the person on the other end of the phone. Laughing.

'No, Nom, don't be stupid,' he says, before his eyes catch mine. He pulls the phone away from his ear. 'Sorry, work,' he whispers. 'Won't be long.' I nod my head, as he goes back to the phone. 'Naomi, you there? Yeah, no, that's cool. Well done, I'm happy for you. Sorry I'm not there tonight.'

I sit down next to him, and he continues chatting to Naomi. I've never met her, but he's mentioned her a few times. I rest my head on his chest, but this time his arm doesn't wrap around me. I close my eyes, enjoying the sensation of his voice humming in his chest.

Then Zara starts crying.

✦

Social media is my enemy.

I now know what Naomi looks like. She's tagged Dustin on Facebook with the wink emoji, in a screenshot of Dwight from *The Office* talking about bears. It must be some kind of inside joke because it makes no sense to me.

I click on her profile and the first picture that comes up is her in a bikini. I hear myself gasp. My eyes focus on her toned, flat stomach immediately, she has actual visible abs. I instantly put a hand on my own stomach, which is better described as a belly now. It's just one of the things that have changed since I had Zara. I used to worry about being too skinny, and now it's another story entirely. I have stretch marks everywhere, but my tummy is the worst. It doesn't feel like my stomach. It's spongey, heavy, saggy. Dustin says he loves me for me. And he loves my belly, he tells me to stop covering it with my arms, to stop changing in the bathroom. He says he loves the stretch marks, the tiny little tiger stripes that decorate my skin. He says they are beautiful tattoos that I'm lucky to have. When I complain about the spongey stomach, he says it's lovely, a reminder every day of the beautiful miracle that we made. But I wonder how he'd feel if it was his body that had changed. He hasn't changed. He looks the same. I have no doubt that Dustin loves me, I have no doubt that he truly means what he says. What I just can't understand is *why* he does. Especially when there is someone looking like that, who he sees every day at work. Someone who seems to like him a lot, judging by how much she tags him on Facebook.

There are quite a few photos of the two of them together. At the work meal last week, then another few from when they went to the pub before Zara was born. Mostly they are in a group with the rest of the work lot, but there's one of them on their own. It looks like a candid picture that someone has snapped without them knowing. She's grinning at Dustin and he has one hand clamped to his mouth, his eyes screwed up with laughter. I wonder what she said. When was the last time I made him laugh like that?

He looks so happy.

He has no reason to be that happy when he's around me. I'm tired when he comes home. I'm groggy. Some days I don't even shower. I go a week without washing my hair, instead of every other day like I used to, taking special time to comb it through when wet, adding coconut oil to the ends. Instead of shampoo, I smell of sick, and steriliser. Why would that make anyone happy?

The door opens and Gran comes in, Zara in her arms. We leave the pram in the hallway downstairs.

I shut my laptop, and smile at them.

'How was the walk?'

Gran smiles at Zara, who is calm and nestled into her chest. 'It was fun, wasn't it, Zara?'

Zara giggles. Gran looks back at me pointedly. 'And you should have come.'

'I told you, Gran, I don't feel very well.'

'Because you've been cooped up indoors. It's no wonder, is it?'

I yawn. This again. 'No, that's not it. I'm just really tired.'

Gran doesn't look convinced. 'I worry about you, you know. You need a hobby, something to get you outdoors.'

I stand up, taking Zara from her. 'You never need to worry about me, Gran,' I say, leaning forward and kissing her cheek. 'I'm doing just fine.'

Once Zara is asleep and Gran leaves, my laptop is open again. Social media time. When I'm this tired, it's the only thing I feel like doing. It's like an addiction. Some people are hooked on smoking, drinking, drugs, caffeine. Mine is scrolling.

There are so many news photos, even since I last checked this afternoon. Georgia on another night out, some shots from her girls' holiday to Ibiza a couple of weeks ago. Various members of the New Haw gang, living their separate lives with new uni friends. Parties, clubs, drinking.

I don't post stories on Instagram, because I have nothing to post. I can't remember the last time I dressed up and didn't wear sweatshirts and leggings. I can't remember when I last went to the pub, or when I last saw a friend. I get up, I look after Zara, I clean, I cook, and I try to manage things, until I go back to bed. It's a big achievement if I make it outside for even half an hour, and that's usually because Gran has dragged me out.

But my baby is amazing, my baby girl is beautiful, so why do I feel so sad?

I've talked to Gran about it ever so slightly, just saying I'm finding it hard, I'm finding it exhausting, but I'm careful to keep from her quite how bleak I feel most days. She'd worry, and at her age stress is dangerous. She says I'm just adjusting, and she says all new mums feel like this too. But do they actually? Because I see photos from people from school that have had kids, and they are happy, and fresh-faced. They don't have the eye bags I do. And they get out, they go places, they post pictures of their kid every single day. And I want to post pictures of Zara, but I go to do it and I notice she has sick on her top, and then what if they think I'm a bad mum? Or they might notice the dry skin on her forehead, or the fact one of her little socks has a hole in it.

Suddenly my phone comes to life in my hand, and it's Gran, sending me a link to baby yoga. 'A class would help,' she'd said earlier. 'A chance to meet other mums, get out the house.'

I don't tell her that I know it won't work.

The same reason I don't tell Dustin how I've been feeling.

I don't want Dustin to know I'm like this. I don't want Dustin to know I feel sad, when he seems to be on cloud nine every single day. I don't want Dustin to think that he's had a baby with the wrong girl.

# Chapter 53

# Dustin

Alicia looks at me, then at the brown envelope on the floor between us, then back at me.

'Well? Are you going to open it?'

I shake my head. 'I don't know.'

'Well ... do you want me to open it?'

I rub my eyes. 'I don't know, Alicia.' I look at the envelope, groaning. 'Why is she doing this to me?'

Alicia sighs, picking it up. 'Dustin, you don't even know what it is yet.' I can see her fingers are itching to open it.

It's the same handwriting. Those bloody block capitals.

'Fine,' I say, defeated. 'Open it then.'

She rips open the envelope and I close my eyes. I can hear Zara gurgling, rustling. Then quiet.

'Dustin,' Alicia finally says quietly.

I look at her, to see her holding a white rectangle of card in her hands. 'What is it?'

She frowns. 'Photos.'

'What?'

I snatch the bundle in her outstretched hand.

They're photographs, printed cheaply from a disposable camera, like the ones that are missing from our bedroom wall.

In fact, two of them are definitely from our bedroom. I recognise them instantly.

The first one is just of Willow. It's a head and shoulder shot and Willow is looking upwards, the traces of a dorky grin just visible on her upturned face. Her necklace with the angel pendant, now sitting on my bedside table, is captured in intricate detail. She's in Georgia's room. I think it was just after Willow moved to New Haw.

The second is of the two of us, and it was the day we went to the Reading open day. We went to the park after lunch and had sat there in the sunlight for a while. Willow had asked Gran to take the photo. You can tell, because the angle is wonky.

But I don't recognise the next two. I've never seen them before and when I look closely, I can see the third is not from a disposable camera at all. It's much older, possibly from a digital camera and is of three people I don't know and a baby. Except when I peer closer I realise I do. That's Willow's gran, standing to one side. Albeit a younger gran, with cropped red hair. And the woman holding the baby has Willow's bone structure – the same elfin ears and pointed chin. I guess the baby in her arms must be Willow. I stare at the man in the photograph. I feel like I know him from somewhere, but maybe it's just a familiar glint of Willow I see in him. Where did this come from?

When I get to the last photograph, I gasp.

'What?' I hear Alicia say.

I look up at her. 'Don't tell Mum about the photos, she'll just give more of her opinion.'

'So you think Willow sent them?'

'I know she sent them,' I say, looking back at the photo again. A selfie of her and Jake. Why send that to me, Willow? What a bitch.

# Chapter 54

# Willow

**Then – August 2019**

I have my bag ready. Zara in the pushchair. Yoga mat. I'm showered, hair brushed, and dressed.

But.

I.

Can't.

I'm just staring at the door, and I can't go.

I can feel the flutter in my stomach, my chest tightening. What if Zara cries, and I can't get her to stop? What if I leak milk through my top again, like I did yesterday? What if the age group is different to me? What if they all know each other? What if they get me to speak? I run to the toilet, hovering my head over the bowl. Breathe, Willow. Breathe. Just. Bloody. Breathe.

It took me half an hour to sort myself out, and in that time I came to the realisation that if baby yoga is going to make me feel like that, it's obvious I shouldn't be going.

When I come back into the kitchen Zara is screaming blue murder in her pram. My head is pounding.

'Zara, please,' I say desperately, 'just calm down.' I pop a dummy into her mouth. She spits it out.

I pick it off the floor, rinse it under the tap, pop it in again. She spits it out. I put her in the high chair, somehow get a bib around her neck, and try to spoon baby food into her mouth. She pushes her face away, moaning. 'Zara, please,' I say, voice monotone. She thrashes from side to side angrily, her cries drilling into my ears, each one like a knife twisting into my brain. Then one of her flailing arms catches the jar in my hand and knocks it straight onto the floor. It smashes, and the orange puree sprays everywhere – the high-chair legs, the table, the rug in the middle of the kitchen. Everything is spattered with orange and there's glass everywhere. For a moment Zara is shocked into silence by the commotion.

Stay calm, Willow. Stay c—

She starts screaming.

Breathe.

'Can you not,' I hear myself shout, 'can you just give me a fucking break? Please just give me a fucking break and shut up!'

I stare at her, my chest pumping. Zara stares back, her eyes full of hurt and bewilderment.

I want to comfort her, tell her I'm sorry, but the words won't come.

I rush out of the kitchen, not really sure of where I'm going, but I pass by the mirror in the corridor and for a second I catch sight of my reflection. Pale, blank eyes stare back at me.

I recognise the person in the mirror.

But it's not me.

It's Mum.

# Chapter 55

# Dustin

Willow, if you're going to send me things please just talk to me. Please Willow. This isn't fair on me or Zara. Or come round. We can talk. Please. Just talk to me. I need something.

It doesn't even deliver. It doesn't even send. I know she has blocked me, I don't know why I keep sending them really.

Hey mate, I know I don't know you. But it seems Willow did. I need answers Jake, I'm struggling right now. I just really need to understand what's going on.

He hasn't read it.
He hasn't read any of my messages.
I put my phone down and sigh. Darren walks in, a smile on his face, placing a coffee on my desk.
'Everything good, D?'
I plaster a smile. 'Yes, always. I think we'll get a sale today,' I say.

He winks at me. 'This is why I like you.'

He clinks his mug with mine, and I just pretend, pretend I'm enjoying the coffee, pretend I'm enjoying my life, pretend my mind isn't occupied, pretend that I'm not going crazy.

# Chapter 56

# Willow

Then – October 2019

This is repeated every single day. It gets harder. I barely leave the house. Then Dustin went on a work trip for two nights to Manchester. I didn't want him to go. But he said he had to, and that meant forty-eight hours alone. So when he left, I poured myself a glass of wine.

When I wake I'm groggy. What time is it? My head is pounding, and I am confused as to why for a moment. Then I remember the glass of wine last night. And the one after that. And the one after that.

And the one after that.

I fumble for my phone. Oh God, it's nine a.m. Shit. Why isn't Zara screaming the place down? She's usually awake hours before this.

I throw myself out of bed and dash into the living room.

And there's Gran, holding Zara in her arms.

She's washed Zara, changed her, is now feeding her, and she

looks great. Wearing her blue earrings, with that royal blue shirt, trousers. Pink lipstick on, hair pinned back.

'Dustin called me,' she said. 'You weren't picking up early this morning and so he asked me to stop by.'

I feel shame flood through me. 'Yeah, I . . . I had a bit to drink.'

Gran doesn't say anything for a moment. She just nods. Then she says: 'Go and shower, you and I are going out. And maybe run a brush through that hair, eh? You look like you've been dragged through a bush backwards.'

'You might find something for Dustin,' Gran says, pushing Zara through the busy streets of Brighton. I'm plodding behind her.

I had been very unenthusiastic when Gran told me about the fete one of her book-club friends is holding in her back garden. I had started to protest but then Gran said how excited her friend was to see me and the baby, and she'd been so lonely since her husband died, so then I felt bad.

'Remember that I need to go food shopping though.'

'Yes, yes, we will only be an hour.'

'Very precise, Gran.'

She stops walking, smiling at me.

'Precise for a reason,' she says, her grin spreading further. She then nods her head to the side of the door. We're standing outside the gym Dustin joined for a little bit, but stopped going. Is Gran making me go to the gym? Is she telling me I'm putting on too much weight?

'Baby yoga starts in ten,' she says.

'What?'

'Yep, in you go.'

'But I'm not dressed for it!'

Gran presses a carrier bag into my hands. 'I packed your leggings and a T-shirt for you. You don't need anything else.'

'What the actual . . .'

'There you are,' she says firmly.

'Gran,' I say, 'this is ridiculous. You can't make me go.'

But, as it turned out, she can. 'If you really don't like it, you don't have to go again,' she said, bundling me inside the gym and wheeling Zara in after me.

'Come with me at least then!' I whined, but she refused. She said it was best just Zara and me. Some bonding time.

Isn't that what we do every day?

So I waited until the class was just about to start, then I slunk in. The lady holding the class, dressed in the kind of outfit I can only describe as 'floaty', wasn't having any of that though, and asked me for my name and Zara's and whether I'd done yoga before. The whole class turned to look at me and I felt my face grow hot. God, how I wanted to just shrivel up on the floor.

But after that, it was OK. It might even have been more than OK.

I just kept my eyes focused on Zara. Now and then when everyone was distracted I analysed the room. It was a mix of people, mostly mums, some grandparents – see, Gran could have come! They were mostly women, but there was one guy and he looked young. My age or just a few years older. Although, unlike me, he seemed to know what he was doing.

As we were leaving, he held the door open for me. Which made me all kinds of awkward.

'You're new, right?' he said to me, as we walked out, push-chairs moving parallel to each other.

'Yeah, was it that obvious?'

He chuckles. 'Well, I mean, only a bit. Don't worry though, this is a nice class. Did you enjoy it?'

I nod. 'Yeah, I did, actually.'

'Well that's good, hopefully, see you next week ... er ...?' He holds his hand out.

'Oh.' I shake his hand. 'I'm Willow.'

'Well, nice to meet you, Willow.' He indicates to his baby boy he's carrying. 'This is Theo, and I'm Jake.'

# Chapter 57

# Dustin

I get home from work and Mum is cooking dinner – spag bol tonight. It's like this most evenings, unless she is out with her *friend*. She has already picked Zara up from the nursery who is now settled happily in her high chair and banging a wooden spoon against the little plastic table.

'How was your day?' Mum asks over the racket.

'Yeah, it was OK,' I answer, stroking Zara's hair. 'Is there anything I can do to help?'

She shakes her head. 'You'll just do it wrong.' I roll my eyes. I am not in the mood for her to be like this today. I go to the cupboard to grab some plates. 'Dustin, it's fine,' she snaps. 'I said leave it.'

'Well I'm here now, Mum.'

I move away, and start placing the plates down. But I find myself pausing as I notice a little postcard on the table. I leave the plates to one side and pick it up.

It's a photograph of a park. A green lawn, trees, brightly coloured flower beds, and a giant statute of a lion. At the bottom, in orange looping letters, is written: *We welcome you to Forbury Gardens.*

I turn it over, looking for a message on the back. But it's blank. 'Mum, what is this?'

'Dustin, I'm a bit busy right now,' Mum says, her voice strained as she loads the dishwasher.

I storm up to her, holding up the postcard in front of her. 'Mum, what is this?'

She frowns, swiping it away. 'Ergh, I don't know, it came with the post. Probably came with a magazine or something. I thought it looked pretty.'

I stare at it again, my mouth trembling, exhaling through my nose, and I can feel my fists clenching. Yes, it is very pretty. I know, because I've been there. With Willow and her gran. When she went to visit Reading Uni. The place Gran took that photo of us.

Later in my room, I am so angry I can barely jab the letters into my phone.

Leave me alone, Willow. Yes OK you've left us, maybe that was a good thing. So just leave me alone. Leave us both alone. You're crazy.

# Chapter 58

# Willow

**Then – January 2020**

I joined baby yoga three months ago. It was the meanest thing Gran ever did to me, and possibly the best. I have been so much calmer since, and I swear Zara has too. Dustin says it's just that she's getting older but she definitely cries less.

It's a new year, and I have decided I'm going to have a new attitude. We had our first Christmas as a family of three, and Gran of course – it was lovely. It was so special. We are a proper family, I forget that sometimes, I forget how lucky I am. And then New Year. Zara was so agitated that night, constantly crying as we tried to put her to bed, and me and Dustin were so exhausted we ended up falling asleep on the sofa before the fireworks, but it was perfect. 2020. This year will be different. I will be happier, I will stop taking things for granted, I will appreciate life, and my little family. It's going to be good. I'm excited.

Gran's book club has moved to Wednesday, she's going to join me. Lunchtime classes, every Tuesday. I deliberately got to the studio fifteen minutes early so that we could get ready together. But it's five to twelve now and there's still no sign of her.

'Where's Gran, eh?' I say to Zara in my arms, who gurgles as if in answer.

'You're right,' I mutter. 'She probably just lost track of time. Or maybe she popped back to that gift shop down the road. The one she dragged me round whilst you had a massive hissy fit, remember?'

Zara blows a spit bubble, as if to present herself as the picture of innocence, far removed from the screaming, thrashing nightmare of that trip to the gift shop on Monday.

'Hey, Willow!'

Jake is heading towards the door and I instantly feel revived. Even if Gran has forgotten, I won't totally be on my own.

'Didn't think you were going to make it today,' I say, leaning by the door.

Jake sighs, smiling, as he holds Theo on his hip. He nods his head towards him. 'Someone decided to have a poo explosion this morning.'

I can't help but snigger. 'Don't worry, I've been there.'

'You still down for a coffee today?'

I look at Zara, squishing my cheek next to hers. 'We are both looking forward to it!'

Jake smiles. 'So are we.' He holds the door open for me, and then pauses, standing awkwardly. 'You coming in?'

'Oh . . . I will be a minute, but my gran's coming along today, so I'm just waiting for her.'

Jake's face lights up. 'Ah, the famous Gran, can't wait to meet her.'

'I'll see you in there, Jake,' I say.

I wait five more minutes before calling her to tell her I'll meet her inside. She doesn't answer, but she rarely answers her phone anyway. An hour later I emerge back into the sunlight, both Zara and I feeling much more relaxed. Jake says he's got to pop to the shops, and then will meet me at the coffee shop. I nod, and say I'll grab us a seat, before looking at my phone. Weirdly, Gran hasn't even tried to call me back. Even weirder, I have multiple missed calls from an unknown number. I call Gran. She doesn't answer again. I'm starting to get worried now. I call Dustin.

'Have you heard from Gran?'

'I'm at work, I can't talk.'

'I know, sorry, but have you heard from Gran?'

'What? No.'

'She was supposed to meet me, but she hasn't.'

'Look, I really can't talk at work, but I'm sure she just forgot.'

'But—'

'Willow, I'll call you at lunch. Stop overthinking it.'

'OK, bye.'

He hangs up.

I guess he's right. Gran isn't getting younger, and neither is her memory. I'm just being silly. I pop Zara in her pushchair, and start walking towards the coffee shop. I bet she's probably on her balcony sorting out her flower pots. She does get carried away with them.

Then my phone starts ringing. It's the unknown number again. I hate answering the phone at the best of times, but when I don't know who it is it's even worse. I probably should answer it though: what if it's Gran calling on a landline somewhere?

'Hello, is this Willow?'

'Yes . . .'

'Hi, I'm calling from the Royal Sussex County Hospital. You are listed as your grandma's next of kin.'

# Chapter 59

# Dustin

'London?'

I have to shout to check I've heard Lucy right. The pub is so noisy and I am, admittedly, quite drunk. She nods and grins.

Lucy is a regular at this pub. She's nice to me. She doesn't delight in torturing me, she's kind. She's everything Willow isn't. And I'm going to kiss her tonight.

I don't feel guilty. I know Joe has been staring at me the whole night, Georgia has been giving me dagger eyes and trying to lead me away. But fuck that. I'm having a nice time. Lucy lifts her shot up to me, clinks it against mine and we drink, slam on the table, and I feel the fire slither down my throat.

I try to focus on her, smiling again, but the alcohol blurs my vision.

'Dustin,' she shouts. I'm not sure why she's shouting, I'm right in front of her. 'Dustin.'

Wait, her lips aren't moving.

'Dustin.' I feel a hand on my shoulder and I turn around to see Georgia standing in front of me, wobbling. I put a hand on her shoulder to steady her. Or steady me. I'm not sure.

'Come on,' she says, firmly. 'It's time to go.'

'I'm not going,' I say, grinning at her.

Georgia sighs. 'Come on, Dustin, you're drunk.'

'Yeah, and? I'm not ready to leave yet.'

'The pub's closing, so you kind of have to, mate.'

I cast a glance back at Lucy, who smiles and nods her head. I look back to Georgia. 'Me and Lucy are going to London.'

From Georgia's expression you'd think I had just announced I was going to Mozambique. 'You're what? Sorry?'

I shrug. 'Going to a club. She has friends there.'

Then I feel another pair of hands on me, and I turn to see Joe.

'Come on, dude,' he says softly. 'You barely know this girl.'

'I've seen her a few times at the pub.'

'Yep, so you barely know her.'

I wriggle out of Joe and Georgia's grasp. 'So? Do we ever know anyone truly?'

'Dustin, you can't just go to London with a stranger. Not when you're this drunk,' Georgia snaps.

I'm started to get annoyed now. Why am I the one in trouble? 'I had a baby with a stranger. I didn't even know my own girlfriend. So I don't think I need to worry about that.'

Georgia closes her eyes, as if she's trying to weigh her words very carefully before speaking. 'Dustin, you can't do this, you have a daughter at home. You need to be responsible.'

'Oh, what, like Willow was, you mean? Your cousin? I know what being responsible is, Georgia, but I deserve a night off, don't you think? After all the crap she has put me through.'

My heart is pumping. Chest heaving. I'm angry. I'm fuming. I was having such a nice night until this.

'I know, Dustin, I'm just saying—'

I step away, glaring at them both. 'Leave me alone.'

'Dustin, just let us take you home.'

'I said leave me alone.'

# Chapter 60

# Willow

Then – January 2020

He holds my hand, squeezing it tightly. I pull away from him and sit down on the sofa, feeling . . . numb. Dustin stands awkwardly in the doorway to the living room. We have barely spoken the whole drive home.

I'm aware that I smell of hospital. I feel dirty.

'Georgia and her mum are going to look after Zara overnight,' Dustin says.

I nod my head slowly.

He stands there for what feels like hours. Or maybe seconds. I can't tell.

Then he comes and sits next to me on the sofa, wrapping an arm around me. I sink my head onto his shoulder.

'I can't believe she's gone,' I whisper. And then I feel myself crumble. I sob into Dustin as he pulls me onto his lap. I just never thought this day would come. I never actually considered living a life without Gran. I never planned or prepared myself for it. I didn't consider the fact she was getting older, that something like a fall could be fatal. I got to the hospital and she was already gone. She was healthy. She was so active for her age. But she tripped on a loose bit of pavement, hit her head and …

I feel guilty, I should have met her before baby yoga, I should have phoned her before I left. I should have walked with her, it would have all gone so differently. I didn't get to say goodbye.

Gran wasn't just my gran. She was the one who made my packed lunches for school, she helped me when I first started my period. She was my mum, she was my dad, my fun auntie, my best friend, she was my everything. And now my everything has gone.

We're not going to have a funeral. We should, but I can't bring myself to organise it. Auntie Jayne offered, but I just don't want it, I just keep thinking about the two empty spaces there would be in the church: my parents. My parents should be there, for everything she had done for them, everything she had done for me. Especially Dad – she was his mother, he should be there for his own mum. But they won't be there, so I don't want a funeral. Auntie Jayne said she will be sorting everything out legally, when it comes to the will, and things like that. But I don't care. I don't bloody care about anything.

Dustin took the next week off work. He has been great. Georgia and her mum looked after Zara and Dustin looked after me. He just let me stay in bed and be sad. He didn't ask me if I'm OK, because he knows I'm not. He didn't say everything was all right because he knew it wasn't. He didn't tell me to go out, he didn't try and make me feel better, or talk to me, he just hugged me, and stayed near. And I clung to him, overcome by the fear that he would slip away from me too. Nauseous and feverish with the need for him.

Then Zara came home, and I managed to crawl out of bed. We bathed her together, put her to sleep, and went to sleep ourselves. I've enjoyed sleeping, because that's what I like to imagine that Gran is doing right now, I imagine she is sleeping. And when I'm sleeping I don't miss her, my heart doesn't ache, my brain doesn't freak out at the idea that I can't physically touch her again, that I will never hear her voice, I will never taste her apple pies. We will never watch *Coronation Street* together. Never have a cup of tea with her three sugars, extra milky, and my one sugar, extra strong. I can't drink a cup of tea now. It doesn't feel right. How do people deal with this? How do people accept that a person is gone from their life for ever?

'Morning,' Dustin says. I open my eyes groggily to see him holding a cup of tea in his hand. He places it next to my bed. I find myself sitting up. Staring at it, feeling my eyes start to burn. Why did he make me a cup of tea? 'Is Zara still asleep?' I ask.

Dustin smiles. 'I've fed her, we had a little play, and now she's downstairs in her playpen. She's fine.'

I lean back into the pillow staring at him. He looks refreshed, healthy. He's dressed in a shirt, tie, trousers, his hair still slightly wet from the shower, and the smell of aftershave wafting from his skin. When I do the morning routine with Zara I look exhausted, I usually haven't got dressed yet, let alone showered, and there might be sick in my hair, or a bit of wee on my clothes.

'OK, we have lots of food in the house, I stocked up yesterday—'

'Wait.' I pause. I look at him again. He's in his work clothes. 'Are you going back to work?'

Dustin's smile falls, he nods his head. 'You're going to be OK, right?'

'Why didn't you tell me yesterday?'

'I thought you knew. I always said I wouldn't be able to take much more than a week.'

I feel tears prick at the corner of my eyes. 'I can't manage on my own.'

Dustin sighs. 'Willow, I have to go back.'

'But it hasn't even been that long since—'

'You'll be OK, you can call me whenever, you can call Georgia, but I have to go back to work. I don't want to use any more of my holiday up, because I think we should go away, the three of us, at some point. Make sure we have something to look forward to.'

I stare at him, trying to blink away my tears. I can't even think that far into the future. 'OK,' I say quietly.

Dustin smiles, kissing my forehead before walking towards the door. 'I love you,' he says.

'I love you too,' I mumble, but he's already left the room. I get up to follow him, go into the living room, but then I hear the front door shut. He's gone.

I slowly sink towards the floor and sit down, in a daze. I'm all alone now.

With trembling hands I go onto my phone. I've had it turned off, it's easier that way. I turn it on, and filter my way through numerous sympathy messages from all the New Haw lot. Georgia clearly hasn't kept her mouth shut.

Then I stop at Jake.

I read his last messages.

You coming?
Hey? We are here.
Have you forgotten?

Tears drizzle down my face, as I start typing.

Hey, can you come over? We live opposite Grundys Bakery.

My fingers hover on the send button. Then I delete the message, pick myself up off the floor and go to tend to my daughter.

# Chapter 61

# Dustin

Now we're in a club called Heaven, and the music is pounding in my ears. I have actual sweat running down my forehead and I'm struggling to focus on Lucy as she dances in front of me. She's smiling, bopping her head to the music, holding my hand, pulling me closer.

She sees me as a normal person. She doesn't look at me in pity, she doesn't tread on eggshells around me. Around her, I'm just Dustin, a normal guy in his early twenties. Not a dad. Not a heartbroken idiot. Not a guy who feels like control of his life is slipping further and further from his grasp every day.

She pulls me closer still, her lips inches away from mine. Her hand strokes my jaw. 'You're lovely, Dustin,' she whispers, sending shivers down my ear.

'I'm really not,' I reply, practically shouting to make myself heard over the pumping music.

She doesn't say anything else, she just looks at me, smiling, before her lips are on mine.

And I kiss her back, feeling amazing, feeling free, happy, warm. A deep contented heat runs through my body until she pulls away. She holds my hand and leads me through the throng, the people dancing, the people kissing, the people jumping up in the air screaming, until we get outside into the smoking area.

The quietness is almost painful on my ears, the difference in volume disorientating. I look at Lucy, confused. 'I don't smoke,' I say.

Lucy smiles, that mysterious smile she's been giving me again and again all night. 'Neither do I,' she says. 'Do you still feel drunk?'

I shake my head. 'Do you?'

She shakes her head, stepping closer. Her face reaches mine, and I think she's going to kiss me again but instead she moves her mouth to my ear. 'Are you up for a bit of fun?' she says, as I feel pressure in my hand. I look down to see the small white pill she's placed into my palm. I look at her, eyes wide.

'I don't do that sort of stuff,' I say.

Lucy smiles at me. 'I thought you wanted to forget who you were, isn't that what you said at the pub?' I look down at the pill in my hand. It feels stuck to my sweaty palm. 'It's just a bit of fun.'

I wake up, my head heavy. Mouth dry. I turn over to see a girl, passed out asleep next to me. I rub my sore temples. How many days has it been since I went to London?

I've lost track. On the first night I had so many missed calls and texts from Georgia, it was driving me crazy. So after sending her an 'I'm fine, stop worrying' message, I switched my phone off. And then I think the battery must have been flat, because I haven't managed to switch it back on again.

If I'm honest, I haven't given it too much thought. For the first time in weeks, I have been thinking about something other than Willow and my grief.

I lost Lucy somewhere around day two, but somewhere along the way I managed to latch onto some new friends.

I don't know the girl in bed next to me. In fact, I literally can't remember last night at all. She is pretty, with a small sort of pixie face and a mane of red hair trailing down her shoulders. She looks peaceful, relaxed. I envy her. Where even am I? I rub my eyes, hoist myself onto one elbow and survey the room. It has fairy lights, polaroid pictures, and many art prints in white plastic frames. It looks like a snapshot straight off the Urban Outfitters website. White-painted 3D letters on her desk spell out the name Jess. At least that awkwardness has been avoided.

I sniff my armpits. Jesus. I need a shower. As soon as I sit up, Jess groans, her eyes open, and she stares at me groggily. 'Dustin?' she says, her voice husky. 'Thanks for staying, I thought you might have left by the time I woke up.'

'I wouldn't go,' I say, lying back down next to her. I don't have anywhere to go anyway, except I probably shouldn't tell her that. I put my arm around her, scooping her closer to me. I feel totally numb.

She smiles, cuddling into my chest. But I stare upright, as thoughts start flooding into my head. What are you doing, Dustin?

Me and Jess go out for breakfast, to a little café round the corner from her flat. She orders us both avocado and eggs on toast. That's what Willow used to order. I feel bad to leave it, but with every bite I feel worse. Is it the hangover or the memories? Jess is also a student. I swear everyone I've met so far is a student.

Jess is chattering away, and I'm trying to listen but I can't seem to focus on what she's saying. She doesn't seem the slightest bit hungover. Is this because she's a student? Are their livers used to this life? From what Joe and the New Haw lot have said about their own university experience, that would make a lot of sense. Jess had a shower, put make-up on and now seems to be fresher than a daisy. We're sat outside, and the heat of the sun is hitting my neck, making me feel more uncomfortable, and then Jess decides to light a cigarette. I have to subtly cover my mouth, because as the smoke hits my nostrils, my stomach lurches again.

'So you're going to come tonight then?'

I close my eyes, hoping that'll make me feel better, and nod my head. Why do I keep getting invited to all these things? Is it not a bit weird, inviting a stranger to all of your nights with friends? Maybe they just feel sorry for me. But then why would they? They don't know that my girlfriend has left me, and I've got a baby I don't know how to take care of. They just think I'm a guy who needs some time away from home. Which, to be fair, isn't a lie. I just didn't mention that the last time this happened I didn't come back for two years.

'You sure it's OK for me to tag along?'

Jess smiles. 'Of course. Last night was pretty fun. My group of friends are all so chill,' she says, blowing smoke into my face. 'Party with us as long as you like, Surrey boy.'

'Thanks, Jess,' I say, giving her a weak smile. 'So where are we going tonight?'

Her eyes light up. 'A warehouse rave.'

My liver screams in horror.

'Sounds fun,' I lie.

And Jess decides to tell me how fun it is going to be, and I let her natter on. It's safe to say I'm going to get ruined again, but that's the aim, isn't it?

'Zara, Zara, come here.'

Zara. Sorry, what? My stomach drops. My head whips around as I try to identify the owner of the voice. Jess is totally unaware of my distraction as I hear her voice drone on in my ear.

'Sara, come to Mummy, Sara,' a lady with a magnificent head of curly hair says from the opposite side of the seating area. She is standing at the entrance, holding a pushchair, and there's a little bit of panic in her voice. Oh. Sara. Not Zara.

A plump little girl with almost identical hair weaves herself through the chairs and runs up to the lady. From looking at her she must be about two years older than Zara. The lady crouches down and scoops her up. 'You've got to stay with Mummy,' she says, a look of relief on her face. 'Mummy doesn't know what she'd do if she lost you.'

My stomach lurches further than it has before, and I move my hand to my mouth again. I feel sick, sicker than I was. Worse than I thought I could. And it's not the messy nights, it's not the stupid things I've done in these past couple of days, it's not any of that. I feel a shiver run through my body as I look back up at Jess. She's still blathering on. Does she seriously still think I'm listening? I look over to see that the girl and her mum have walked away now.

'I need to go, Jess,' I say, cutting her off.

She looks at me for a few seconds, before nodding her head. 'Yeah, that's fine. To be honest I have a lecture in forty minutes, I should go soon. But see you tonight, yeah, I have your number right? I'll text you the details.'

I shake my head, feeling my brow scrunch.

'No, no. I need to go home. I need to go now.'

# Chapter 62

## Willow

Then – February 2020

I barely leave the house now. Gran was the one that forced me outside, encouraged me to do things. When I can face it, I try to sort through some of her things. Dustin keeps telling me I need to decide what I'm keeping and what to throw away.

But how can I make a decision like that? This is Gran's whole life. How can I judge some of that life to be worth keeping, and other parts of it fine to discard?

I take out my phone and open up our WhatsApp conversation. She left me a voice note once, by accident. It's ten minutes long and it's just her watching *Coronation Street*, muttering to herself or yelling at the screen when one of the characters does something stupid. I must have listened to it a hundred times over the last few weeks.

It makes me smile to hear her voice again. But it also means I can't watch *Corrie* any more. Why should I get to watch it, when Gran can't?

I don't recognise the majority of these photos. I didn't realise

Gran had kept so many. I flick through the photos of Dad when he was younger. As a child he looked so innocent and happy – chubby-cheeked with a toothy grin and freckles that faded with age. To see the later ones you'd never think it was the same boy. He filled out a lot in his teenage years. Muscly, yes, but there's a flabbiness in places too. Extra skin under the chin and around the cheekbones. In later pictures Mum is there too – skinny and sallow with black hair. There are fewer photographs as time goes on. Only a couple of Mum pregnant, then a few more of me as a baby and young child.

There's one photo that I focus on. It's us in Disneyland. Gran, Mum, Dad and me, a tiny toddler, dressed in a Minnie Mouse costume. I don't remember the trip, but I remember Gran talking to me about it, how she surprised Mum and Dad with the tickets, how we all had so much fun, how we went on It's a Small World ten times because I loved it so much. I wish I remembered it. I'm sitting on Dad's lap, Mum is next to us and Gran stands behind them both, beaming from ear to ear. Dad is looking down at me, planting a kiss on my head, and Mum is staring straight at the camera but she's not smiling. The expression on her face isn't sad exactly, more ... vacant. Absent. Like her mind is somewhere completely different. I wonder if Gran lied to me, and just made me believe it was a happy trip. I don't look happy either. I look like I'm on the verge of tears. I stroke my fingers along the picture of Dad, holding me, kissing me on the forehead.

Where is he now? I feel my eyes starting to water, my lips trembling. 'I need you, Dad,' I whisper, my fingers going automatically to the chain around my neck.

The necklace he gave me the last time I saw him. The night Gran announced we were leaving Brighton.

I wipe a tear from my eye as I push my earbuds further into my ears, trying to block out the sound of the traffic, the shouts of pedestrians, the coming and going of the world. I'm taking the long route home. I'll go past the pier, walk on the pebbled beach, and hopefully the air will make me feel better so Gran won't know I've been crying. I can lie and tell her I met up with a friend for a coffee. I can't help but laugh at the idea that Gran actually thinks I have friends. I thought college was going to be different. A new set of people, a new environment. But it turns out it's just more of the same. Cliques, conversations broken off quickly whenever I approach. Right now the group of girls I thought were my friends are all at Lucy's house. An early birthday party. I only found out because Jenna accidentally let it slip this morning and asked me what I was wearing. Alice next to her turned bright red and muttered something about Lucy's mum only letting her have a limited number of people.

So whilst they all took the bus together after college, I'm walking home listening to Keaton Henson. Joke's on me, quite literally. The whole group. Apart from me. I don't know why I ever thought I was part of the group anyw—

Suddenly I feel two hands grab me, and pull me into the alleyway. Fuck. I try to cry out but the scream gets caught in my throat, I thrash my arms wildly.

'Hey, calm down,' a voice says. It's a male voice, gruff, older.

Finally I find my voice and I scream, a shrill piercing noise that ricochets off the cold stones walls. A heavy hand clamps over my mouth. I can't see him, which makes it even worse.

Then I feel myself being pinned against the wall and I am

suddenly face to face with my attacker.

'Ssh, Willow,' he says. How ...? I stare at his small green eyes, dwarfed by his bushy black eyebrows. The hair on his head is thick too, though losing its colour, just like his salt and pepper beard, and he has a small heart tattoo on the side of his cheek. I stop screaming and the hand is lowered from my mouth.

'Hey, Angel,' my dad says.

✛

He is not supposed to see me, I learn. It's one of the conditions of his parole. The others – staying on the right side of the law and checking in with a supervisor every week – he intends on keeping, apparently. And he's sober, clean, and looking for a job.

I haven't seen my dad in over six years. Not since he first went to prison. With his beard and the extra weight around his middle, I wouldn't have known him if I'd passed him in the street. But now that I look closely, I can see he's still the same dad I remember. A few more wrinkles, a crookedness to his nose I don't remember from before, but fundamentally the same. The weirder thing is how on earth he recognised me. Given that I was eleven that last time he saw me.

'Your gran sent me pictures. With her letters,' he explains.

I didn't even know Gran had been writing to him, but now that I think about it, of course it makes sense. He's her son, after all.

'You've grown so much, Angel.' He puts a hand gently on my cheek. 'I can't get over how grown-up you look. And I can't believe I wasn't there to see it all happen.'

'I can't believe you're here,' I whisper, smiling at him.

He looks down sadly. 'I'm sorry I wasn't a good dad to you.'

I stare at him, blinking a few times to check it's still him. 'You're still my dad though.'

'No, that's not an excuse, just because someone's family doesn't mean they get a pass for being horrible.'

'You weren't horrible, it wasn't your fault you were ill. You had an addiction.'

'Yeah, and I put my addiction before you, Angel. And you suffered the consequences. I missed you growing up.' He frowns again. 'I'm not allowed to be in your life till you're eighteen, and even then that's your choice to make whether you want to see me.'

'I'm old enough now, Dad.'

'Not in the eyes of the law, hon,' he says sadly.

I stare at him, trying to work out how I'm feeling.

'Does Gran know you're out?'

Dad smiles slightly. 'Since one of the conditions of my parole is not seeing you, I reckon they'll have to tell her.' He pauses. 'Don't tell her you saw me, it'll get me in trouble.'

Dad starts to stand up, and my stomach drops. 'It was good seeing you, kiddo, but now I have to go.'

I scrabble to my feet. 'Wait, Dad.'

He tries not to look at me. 'I have to, I can't get in trouble again, sweetheart.'

'But I want my dad,' I say, my voice cracking, and I grab onto his arm.

'I'll be looking after you, I'll always be with you, just not physically.' He holds out a small silver chain. A necklace, with a charm at the end. An angel.

'See?' he says. 'I'll always be with you. Looking after you like an angel.'

I take it carefully, staring at it. 'You make it sound like you're dead.'

254

He chuckles. 'Hey, please don't be one of those kids that say your parents are dead. A few of my mates from inside, their kids used to tell their friends their parents were dead. I guess it was easier than saying they were in prison, but it broke their hearts.'

'I'd never do that.'

I put the necklace in my pocket and look up to him, but by that point he's already left.

✛

When I arrive home, Gran is sitting on the floor, packing books into boxes.

'What are you doing?' I ask.

'Your Auntie Jayne needs a hip replacement,' she says. 'And she's going to need a bit of help. So I've said we'll go and help. Going to move to Surrey.'

But the way she looks at me, her eyes so sad and serious, I can tell.

She knows.

Once I turned eighteen, I tried all I could do look up Dad. I found nothing.

Absolutely nothing.

Every month I'd search his name, and eventually I accepted you can't find someone when they don't want to be found.

# Chapter 63

# Dustin

Georgia picked me up from the station. I had been gone four days. After that one text to her, I didn't let anyone know I was safe. I didn't tell anyone my plans. I spent the majority of the time drunk, while everyone was stressing out. I called Georgia from Jess's phone, as she didn't have her charger with her. Georgia was the only person's number I could remember. When I got into the car, Georgia said Mum and Alicia and everyone at the pub had been worried sick. She didn't say much else other than that.

Then I get home, and Mum immediately wraps her arms around me. 'I thought you had left again,' she whispers, with a shaking voice.

'Sorry, Mum,' I mumble. I stand frozen, not hugging her back.

She pulls away, her hands on my face as her eyes scan me intently. 'What the hell have you been doing?'

She's definitely angry, but she's trying to keep it under wraps. Back in the day, she would have shouted, probably chucked me out of the house temporarily. But somehow I can't imagine her doing that any more.

I avoid her eyes.

'Oh, um, I got a bit waylaid, and then my phone kind of ran out of battery.'

'Are you OK?'

I force myself to nod my head as I step away from her in the direction of the stairs. I briefly glance inside the living room and see Alicia standing in the doorway, Zara in her arms and Elliot behind her. Her eyes are cold and blank. Zara is giggling happily. I cast my eyes down, move away from everyone and go upstairs. I'm totally aware that I should stay down and talk, hold the daughter I haven't seen for four days, apologise to my family for having been so selfish and stupid and putting them through such anxiety. But I can't do that.

I have a shower, and then I sit in my room, head in my hands, eyes closed, wishing more than anything that I could just disappear. Wish I could turn back time. Wish I was a different person.

I put my phone on to charge, and go downstairs. Mum is in the kitchen, Alicia is holding Zara on her lap. I don't know where Elliot is.

'Georgia left,' Mum says.

I shrug my shoulders and stand awkwardly.

'I'm sorry I left,' I mumble, leaning forward to pick up Zara.

'At least it wasn't for two years this time,' she says.

I don't know how to respond, so I nod and walk back upstairs.

I pause outside my room, and stare at Zara.

There it is: Willow's eyes, Willow's face. My heart aches and swells with love at the same time. It hurts me every time I look at her, but I know as well that she's the best thing in my life. I can't neglect my daughter, she deserves better. We both deserve better. I tickle her nose and she giggles. 'I'm sorry I left you,' I whisper, before cuddling her into me. 'Daddy will never leave you again, I promise.'

Back in my room, my phone has come back to life. And it has pretty much exploded with messages and missed calls. From Mum, Georgia, Joe and Alicia primarily.

Dustin pick up the phone.
Where are you?
Please, Dustin. Are you ok?
Please don't ignore me … Dustin, for Zara. Please.
Dustin, talk to me.
Dustin, let me know you're ok.
Dustin, please, this isn't fair.

There's a familiar desperation to the messages.
I'm such a dick.
And then I see it. The notification on Facebook messenger, and the floor feels like it has just dropped away beneath me.

Hey Dustin, sorry, your messages went to the 'other' folder. I didn't see them. Shall we meet for a coffee?

Oh my God.
Jake.

258

# PART III

# Chapter 64

## Willow

In the wise words of ... someone: 'Fake it till you make it.'

That's what I'm doing. I'm faking being happy. I'm faking getting over Gran. I'm faking being a great girlfriend, a great mum, a happy, young, got-it-together Willow.

It's hard faking it all the time though.

It's been just over three months since Gran died, and I swear I feel worse rather than better. Zara has started speaking, kind of. It's about time, she's a little behind. She can't walk yet, and can only just stand. But she started saying 'Mama', and although I could have cried with relief that she wasn't incapable of speech after all, I didn't feel completely happy at her choice. It felt accusatory. Like she was the one taking the major steps in our relationship. Then she said 'blankie' and that made more sense to me, her blanket is special to her. It was the one I knitted for Dustin back in New Haw. How times have changed since then. I don't knit now, not since Gran, that wouldn't be fair.

I'm so worried that I'm the reason she's slow at developing, that it's my inability to bond with her. Of course I haven't said that to Dustin, but I did mention that I was concerned so a few weeks ago we took her to the doctor's together. When the doctor said it was nothing to be too worried about, I burst into tears. Was it relief? Or was it because I didn't believe him?

Thankfully it's Friday, which means Dustin will be home to help with Zara. And we'll be able to spend some time together, even if I'm not exactly up for going out and having fun at the moment.

When Dustin comes home about half six, he rushes in, lifts Zara out of my arms, twirls her around and kisses her, before placing her back in my hands, and going into the bedroom. 'Hey, Wills?' he calls across the hallway.

'Yes?' I reply quietly, following him into the room. He's laid a T-shirt and jeans on the bed and is looking in the mirror, checking his hair. 'What are you doing?' I ask, but I already know the answer.

'Going to the pub with the work guys for a quick drink,' he says as he sprays aftershave on. 'I was sweaty, I had to get changed.'

My stomach sinks, my heart pounding as my limbs almost start to feel weak. This feeling is happening too often, and I can't seem to get away from it. I stare at him silently, holding a stirring Zara in my arms.

Dustin smiles in the mirror, before looking back at me. 'Did I not tell you?'

I shake my head. If I speak I might cry, and I might never stop.

'Oh, I'm sorry, Wills. I won't be late tonight though,' he says, with a wink.

He walks past me and out of the door. I follow him almost in a daze, placing Zara in her high chair. I take a deep breath.

I have to tell him. I can't be alone tonight again. I'm struggling. He's drinking orange juice from the carton in our tiny kitchen area.

'Dustin, I really want you to stay here tonight.' Dustin turns his head towards me, carton still in his hand, his brow furrowed. 'I . . . I think it's unfair you didn't tell me you were going out, and I'd really appreciate it if you'd stay. I'm feeling really . . . tired.'

Dustin puts the carton back in the fridge, closes the door, and walks over to me. He holds my hands, and I feel proud of myself for being honest. For saying what I think for once, and he actually listened.

'I'm sorry, Willow, I'll make more of a conscious effort to tell you next time. I just didn't think.'

I smile. 'Thank you, I really appreciate it,' I say. But then Dustin walks over to the coat rack, and starts putting his coat on, and my smile disappears. 'Wait . . . you're still going?'

Dustin pauses. 'What, you really don't want to me to go for a quick drink?'

I nod my head, feeling so embarrassed, pathetic. 'I just really want you with me tonight.'

'But, Wills, I'm with you nearly every night. And if I don't go, I'll let the work lot down. You know I hate doing that.'

I feel my lip start to tremble. 'But . . . you're letting me down.'

I instantly feel Dustin's arms around me.

'I'm sorry, Willow,' he mumbles in my ear, his hand stroking my hair. He pulls away, so he's looking at me. 'I won't be long at all, and we have the whole weekend together. Why don't you put some Netflix on, there's a chocolate bar in the fridge, pour yourself a glass of wine, and before you know it, I'll be back. OK?'

I look at him, feeling my heart deflate. 'OK.'

When he leaves, I find myself leaning against the door, slowly sliding onto the floor. I pull my phone from the pocket of my sweatpants. I hover over Gran's number, my heart deflating even more. 'I miss you, Gran,' I hear myself say, as a tear spills down my cheek. 'Why aren't you here? You'd make everything better. I need you. I really really need you.'

I open up Gee's contact details and start typing a message.

*Gee I think there's something wrong with me*

I pause. I look at the last message she sent to me, when I asked if she was around to FaceTime a few days ago.

Sorry, I can't talk right now. I'm on a date. Hoooooot guy! Luv ya.

I delete the message.

I open up my last conversation with Jake. I haven't seen him ... since ... the thing happened.

Hey Willow, haven't seen you at the class in a while? I hope it's not because of me. Just want to check we are cool. Hope you are ok! Send me a message, we can chat.

Then I look at the message above.

Hey Willow, I know we talked about it, but I just want to say sorry again for ... what happened. Totally my fault. I would really like us to stay friends! Please come back to class, it would be great to see you again. I hate the fact we don't talk any more. Let's do that coffee date we were going to do?

I miss him. But I ruined it. It was my own fault. I place my phone on the floor and close my eyes, trying not to let the ripple

264

of sadness that seems such a part of me turn into a tidal wave. Piece by piece, my life has fallen apart.

I hear a soft grizzle.

I look at my daughter, her bottom lip trembling. 'Why do you cry so much around me?' I whisper. Can she see the real me? The heavy weight pressing down on me so that most of the time I feel I can barely breathe? Does she know that I suck at being a mum? Can she tell I have felt miserable ever since I had her? Does she know that? But then I love her. I love her so much, so why do I feel so sad? Why do I find it all so hard?

What is the future going to be like? Will she have a childhood like mine? Will I do that to her? She doesn't have a gran to save the day, to take her to her school plays, to cook dinner, to tuck her in at night. But she has a Dustin.

This empty feeling isn't going to go away, is it?

I wipe another tear off my face, my shaking fingers playing with the loose threads on the carpet. I need to get up, give Zara a bath, but I like it here, on the floor, by the door.

I need to fix myself.

But sometimes things are too broken to fix, aren't they?

And there's nobody I can talk to about any of this. Nobody who understands how hard being a parent is.

Except . . .

*2 days later . . .*

When I get back to the flat, I don't even take off my coat. I unpack, take Zara out of her pushchair; she's sleepy. I put her in her high chair and look at her again. My beautiful daughter. She doesn't deserve to have a mother who can't cope. And won't it just get harder, as she gets older and she begins to resent me? Wouldn't it be better for everyone if . . .

I stand up. For the first time in months, everything feels clear.

I take a pen from the mug on the kitchen worktop, and I start to write.

# Chapter 65

# Dustin

'Right, no rush, take your time, I'll wait for you, just text me when you're done,' Georgia says, as we stand outside the coffee shop.

'Thanks, Georgia,' I mumble.

She nods her head. 'You sure you don't want me to take her?' she asks, nodding to Zara who I'm clutching to the side of my hip. I stroke Zara's head protectively.

'Yeah, I'm sure,' I reply.

Jake suggested we meet in Brighton, which is a pain, but I guess it makes sense. He's not going to traipse to New Haw, is he? It's not like there's much in it for him.

He isn't there when I go in, so I grab a two-seat table and a high chair and pop Zara into it.

'Dustin?'

I jump, turning around to see a man standing awkwardly

behind me. He has shaggy golden hair, and is carrying a baby boy in his arms, just a little bigger than Zara.

'Jake?' I ask.

He nods his head, reaching out to shake my hand. I pretend I didn't see it. I look around and quickly move a spare high chair next to him, in which he places his baby boy. I stare at the kid. I didn't know he had a kid.

'How old is he?' I ask.

'Theo is nineteen months. Two months older than Zara,' he says proudly.

Like I need you to tell me how old my daughter is, mate, I think defensively. But I say, 'You've met Zara a few times?'

'Well, yeah, at least once a week.'

'OK.'

'Well, I'd see her at baby yoga. That's how Willow and I knew each other.'

Sorry ... baby what?

'Baby yoga? Is that really a thing?'

Jake raises his eyebrows. 'That's how Willow and I met. Did you not know that?'

For a second I think about lying, pretending I knew all about it all along, but this is my chance to find out the truth. It's time to be honest.

'No ... I didn't,' I say quietly. 'I think there were a few things I didn't know.'

# Chapter 66

# Willow

Now

Life surprises you, huh?

Sometimes people win the lottery.

Sometimes it's a surprise party.

Sometimes you get the dream job you wanted.

Or maybe sometimes you find yourself here, no partner, no child, lost. But I have a job, at least. I make coffees. And I'm actually pretty good at it. So much for me thinking I would be too clumsy for it.

When I came to Reading, it was the first place I saw a job listing at the window. A cute little coffee shop, so I went in, asked, got the job that day.

I do like the job. I mean I wouldn't say it's my passion, but it keeps me busy. The five a.m. wake-up time is perfect because I don't really sleep much, and when I do it's only for a few hours a night. The girls who work here are nice. A lot of them are students. One is a mum. When she told me I said I couldn't imagine how difficult it must be to have a child.

And the manager is a nice friendly lady in her thirties, who moved here from France. But I swear her English is better than mine.

They always ask me questions about myself, and where I've come from, what I did before here, and there's only so long you can avoid questions. So it became easier to invent answers instead. I've come up with an alter ego. My name is Willow and I'm a creative design graduate, straight out of Brighton Uni. I've now moved back home with my family in Reading, got this job while I take a gap year and figure out what I'm doing for the future.

That's probably the biggest lie of all. I don't ever think about the future.

'Ergh, I'm so tired,' Libby says, slamming her head on the till.

The shop opened at seven today, it's now twelve. She looks at me, squinting. 'How are you not tired?'

I shrug my shoulders. 'I don't really get tired any more.' Which is a lie. Physically I'm always tired. But my mind isn't, my mind is always awake. But there's no point trying to explain that to Libby.

She looks at me, and it makes me nervous, like she's trying to work me out. 'You sure you don't want to do the tills for once?'

I smile, shaking my head. 'I'm good, but thanks.'

I like doing the coffees, it gets busy, and stressful, and that's good. That's what I need. A never-ending to-do list. Constant activities. Like right now, it's too quiet for me. But at least I can change the filters, I can clean the surfaces, I can do the dishwasher, I can do so much. Standing at the till you have time to think. Also you have to interact with the customers. Who wants that?

I stroke the spot where my necklace used to hang. I lost it a couple of weeks ago. I had noticed the clasp had come loose, but hadn't got round to fixing it. By the time I got to work, it was gone. I scoured the pavements, traced my route. But I guess someone must have taken it.

# Chapter 67

# Dustin

Jake buys us both a coffee. I get an almond caramel latte, which is what Willow would always order. I want to see if Jake will say something about it, but he doesn't. So now I have to drink this super-sweet drink for nothing. He just sits down with the drinks and asks me if I want sugar or anything.

'Nah, I'm good, cheers,' I say. There's an awkward silence, and I think about breaking the ice by asking him more about his baby, but then I remember he's not a friend, and I'm here for a reason. So I go straight in.

'So, Willow didn't tell you that she was going to leave?'

Jake shakes his head. 'I mean ...' He pauses, thinking better of what he was about to say. 'Nah, it's silly.'

I stare at him. Is he playing with me? Is he an actual arsehole? 'What? Don't do that. Tell me what you were going to say.'

He looks at me thoughtfully. 'Well, it was just that she once asked me if I ever felt like I wanted to disappear. I thought she meant it metaphorically.'

My stomach feels like it's twisting, as I clench my jaw. 'Why would she ask *you* that?' I manage to spit out.

Jake shrugs. 'Like I said, I didn't think she meant anything by it. But we talked about a lot of things, so it wasn't weird.'

Stay calm, Dustin, Georgia had said. My legs are starting to shake. I'm not sure I'm doing a good job of that.

'I just don't get it. Willow really wasn't one to jump into conversations with strangers.'

Jake runs a hand through his hair, before looking back at me. 'Well we weren't strangers, Dustin.'

'Or even to make friends on her own,' I protest.

'She and I were the only ones there our age.'

'Well, she didn't even tell me about it. I would have gone if I'd known,' I cut in defensively.

Jake looks at me evenly before continuing. 'I went up to her that first day, I thought she must be a single parent too.' *Yeah, I bet you did*, I think. 'So I held the door open to her, and then we just started talking. And I guess we had quite a bit in common. Both young parents. Both like design.'

I look quickly at Zara, who's happily playing with a bit of fruit on the high chair. OK, I'm going to cut to the chase here.

'Did you and Willow have an affair?' I say it quietly.

Jake frowns. 'No, we were just friends.'

'You sure? You're not lying to me? Did you fancy her or anything?'

Jake looks uncomfortable, pushing a hand through his hair again. 'I mean … well, at the beginning, yeah, a little bit, but once I found out she was with you … I was just happy to be her friend. I was just happy we got on so well.'

I let out the breath I didn't realise I'd been holding. 'If that's the case I can't understand why she didn't tell me about you.'

'Maybe because she thought you wouldn't be interested.'

Excuse me?

'Sorry, what?'

'Well, it was just that she mentioned that sometimes you didn't listen when she tried to talk to you about things. Like feeling lonely.'

'Willow was never lonely. She had me.'

Jake calmly sips his coffee. 'Of course she did, but I think sometimes Willow felt like she had no social life. You know what it's like, when the baby comes, that's the first thing to go. Willow felt like she didn't go out any more, she didn't see anyone. I think she felt stuck, trapped.'

'But she always liked staying at home. And there were always opportunities for her to come out to see our friends.'

'It's not that easy though, is it? Who was going to look after Zara?'

'Her gran could have. At least before, well ...'

'Was she ever actually invited?'

'Yes! Well, most of the time. I mean, she didn't need an invitation, she knew she was welcome. I don't think it's fair for you to say anything when you don't—'

'I'm not judging you, Dustin, I just—'

'Hey,' I say cutting him off. My chest is starting to feel tight. 'I loved her. I know how she felt, I know her better than you.'

Jake is still so annoyingly calm as he looks at me. He nods his head. 'I know you loved her, and she loved you, so much. I'm just telling you what she told me. That's why you wanted to see me, right?'

I avoid his eyes. I'm aware I'm acting like a sulky teenager, especially when Jake is being so adult about everything.

The tosser.

'I never knew she was feeling like that,' I say.

Jake takes another sip of his coffee. 'Maybe you should have asked.'

I glare at him. Thinking of all the swear words I would say if my daughter wasn't sat next to me right now. 'It's easy for you to sit on your high horse, but you don't get it.'

'No, Dustin, I do. And I know that probably whenever she was with you, she was happy, so it wasn't easy for you to see. But it was when you weren't there she felt herself struggling. That's why we got on; as a single dad I could relate to that.'

Is it true? How didn't I see it?

I chew on my lip. 'So, you think she left because of everything she was telling you?'

Jake shakes her head. 'I really don't know, she never actually talked about going away, she was so scared of losing you and Zara, that was something she talked about a lot, so I don't know why she would have left.'

'When did you last see her?'

For the first time, Jake looks perturbed.

'Um,' he runs a hand through his hair. 'I dunno, it must have been about six months ago? It was two or three weeks after her gran died. We met up for a coffee.'

'And you didn't hear from her after that?'

'No, we ... Willow stopped responding to my messages. I didn't want to push her, I thought she probably just needed some space after her gran.'

There's something he's not telling me.

'She just stopped responding?'

'Yeah.'

I push my coffee away. I'm starting to feel sick.

'I should have been better,' I mumble. I look up at Jake, who doesn't say anything. 'I bet you thought I was a right prick from what Willow was saying.'

Jake smiles. 'I never thought that. And neither did Willow. I just thought maybe you could have appreciated her more.'

'I did,' I snap back. But then I look down awkwardly. 'But

maybe I should have shown it. What's the point in appreciating her, if she doesn't even know it?'

I wish I'd never even met up with Jake.

I feel worse, rather than better.

'You all right, Dustin?'

I look up at Jake, nodding my head. 'Sorry. I was just thinking about it all.'

'You want another coffee?' Jake asks.

I shake my head. 'Am I allowed to ask why you're a single dad?' I say. I'd never normally ask something that personal, but it's not like this conversation hasn't been pretty personal already.

'It's totally fine,' Jake says, moving his hand to hold Theo's. 'His mother and I, we weren't together. We just had sex sometimes. It was a big accident. She wanted to give him up for adoption, but I said I'd look after them both, but she knew she wasn't ready to be a mum. So I decided to take full custody. It worked out best for both of us.'

Wow. He did it all on his own, fair play to him. 'Does she ever see him?' I ask.

Jake shakes his head. 'She hasn't yet, but I message her every three months and keep her updated. I told her she is always welcome to see him. She will always be the one who gave birth to him, that door is always open. But I make it clear that if she wants to be in his life as a mum, she needs to act like one.'

How has he been doing this on his own for this long? I've only been doing it for a month and a half or so and it's been the hardest time of my life. 'Is it not really hard being a single parent, though? Like doing it on your own?'

'Oh, yeah, it is,' Jake says. 'I don't think I've ever done anything harder. It can be lonely, and to begin with I always had the constant fear of doing something wrong, that I wasn't able to give him enough. That he needed two parents, not one. But then I remembered I was trying my best, I love him, I'm learning, and that love from one parent is better than no love from any parents.'

I watch Zara, she looks at me, and smiles. 'Yeah, I get that.'

'That's why I loved talking to Willow so much, we could really relate on some things,' Jake says.

My smile falls and I sigh. How did I make her feel like that, when she wasn't even a single parent? How did I not even realise it? 'Has the stress ever got so much that you just wanted to walk away?'

'Never,' Jake answers seriously. 'Never. I am so scared of losing him. I would never walk away. Becoming a dad was the best and hardest thing that has ever happened to me, but I wouldn't change it for the world. I could never walk away. The thought that I wouldn't see him again kills me.'

So how was Willow able do it? Even if that's how she felt. How could she leave her child?

'I'm super lucky, my parents are amazing, my mum looks after Theo while I work. I couldn't do it without them. Obviously Willow didn't have that.'

I feel my mouth suddenly going dry.

'Jake,' I say, my voice quiet. 'Did Willow ever tell you anything about her parents?'

# Chapter 68

# Willow

I get back from my shift at the coffee house, and dump my bag on my bed. It's getting heavy. I really need to empty it. I open it up and spread all the contents in my bed. God, what a mess. Spare coins, water bottles, stupid amount of leaflets and paper, these can all go in the bi—

I pause.

In amongst them all is the lilac sheet of paper.

Visitor Form.

HM Prison.

From the day I left Brighton. The day I went to visit Mum.

I debated whether it was a good idea to bring Zara or not, I eventually decided I would. I took the train. I felt sick the whole way there. Maybe she wouldn't even see me. When I was about fourteen I had gone with Gran and she just refused to come out of her cell. I had been so upset and Gran said she wasn't putting me through it again. I don't think she and Gran ever saw each other again; I saw her only once after that – it was when I first moved back to Brighton, before I told anyone

278

about being pregnant. The only time in years I had spoken to my mother.

⚜

*May 2020*

*There were about eight people waiting in the visitors' room. We avoided each other's eyes, not wanting to acknowledge our presence there.*

*Her expression, when we were finally seated in the booth, was hard to read. Blank.*

*'Hello, Mum,' I whispered, with a nervous smile.*

*I didn't get a hello back. She just stared at Zara.*

*'Um, this is Zara.'*

*'Huh,' she sniggered. 'Well, I guess there go all your grand plans of university. I knew it was only a matter of time.'*

*I felt tears spring to my eyes, but I brushed them away.*

*'She's one and a bit. And I'm still with her dad.'*

*She didn't say anything, but there was a victorious smirk on her face. Like she didn't believe a word of what I was saying. I took a deep breath and continued.*

*'I'm here because—'*

*'If you're going to mention your father, don't bother. I won't talk about him. And if you're going to ask where he is, I wouldn't know, because I've been stuck in here. But we know what your father is like – he's probably dead now, isn't he?'*

*I blink heavily, take a deep breath and try to talk again.*

*'I wanted to talk to you because I'm struggling and I know you ... I wanted to ask how you felt in the early days.'*

*'How I felt? Now there's a question nobody ever asked me.' She leans back in her chair. 'You were such a pretty baby,*

Willow. I'd take you out in your pram, and people would stop me to look at you. Isn't she gorgeous, they'd say. And I was so proud of you. God, this is easy, I thought.'

She tapped her fingers on the table in front of her and my eyes were drawn to the scratch on her hand. I couldn't look away from the wound, the skin red and raw around it.

'But then as you got older, you were so demanding. Oh, not in a screaming and crying way. I guess you learned pretty quickly where that got you. No, you were so quiet. You'd give me this look, this look of . . . ' She struggled to find the word, and when she finally did, she practically spat it. 'Superiority. Like you couldn't believe life had landed you with someone so shit.'

I looked up at her and the look in her eyes terrified me. It was anger, and something else. Pure hatred.

And all the way home, I couldn't get that expression out of my head.

# Chapter 69

# Dustin

Georgia raises her eyebrows as I get into the car. 'Well, what did he say?'

'I'll tell you in a minute. Firstly, I need you to answer me something. Why didn't you tell me about Willow's parents?'

She's silent and for one horrible moment I think she's going to deny it. And I don't know how I'll react if she does. But instead she sighs.

'I promised Willow I wouldn't. It was her story to tell.'

'Bullshit, Georgia. Even after she went missing? It was relevant! All this trauma in her life and I never knew anything about it. I never knew how she felt about it.'

Her next sentence stumps me.

'Yeah, well, maybe you should have asked.'

The silence is so sharp I think it's going to cut one of us.

'But I was also afraid to tell you,' Georgia says. 'I knew you'd be mad that I hadn't told you earlier and I didn't know how you'd react. People get freaked out by stuff like this. I worried it would make you not want to have anything to do with Willow.'

I breathe deeply.

'Georgia, of all people, I should know that a person isn't their parents. I shouldn't be finding out her parents aren't dead from some guy I don't know.'

She looks at me for a moment, then nods. 'Yep, OK. Sorry.'

'So what happened? I need to know everything.'

And she tells me. She tells me about Willow's parents, their tempestuous marriage and the car-crash of their lives. They were both addicts – drugs, alcohol, whatever they could get their hands on. Most of the time they were so stoned out of their minds they barely noticed. Her gran looked after her a lot, but not all the time. She hadn't realised quite how bad things were.

Her dad had other problems too. Gambling. He owed money everywhere, had debts piling up around his ears. He owed money to the wrong sort of people. But they owned their house – Willow's gran had helped them with the money left from her granddad's life insurance and pension payout. So Willow's parents hatched a plan. They'd burn down the house, claim the insurance, and make a run for it. They got drunk, doused the lower floor in petrol, went outside and threw a lit match into the open living room window. Then they ran.

What they didn't realise was that Willow was still inside. That evening, she was supposed to stay at her gran's, who would have picked her up from school. Except her gran had come down with flu and had to cancel. Neither of them noticed Willow creep home from school and up to her room.

The firemen got her out, but only just. When they finally tracked down Willow's parents, they were looking at arson, child neglect and attempted murder, though they were cleared of that last charge when it became clear how devastated they were. At least, how devastated Willow's dad was. Apparently her mum said next to nothing all the way through the trial.

And Willow's gran never forgave herself for not being there. Nor her son and daughter-in-law.

I listen to Georgia in silence. I can't imagine Willow going through that. The fear as the flames licked her bedroom door. Her confusion in the dark as she called out for her parents and received no reply. How could I not have known any of this?

'We need to go home,' I say. 'I need to find her.'

# Chapter 70

## Willow

I stand outside the gates of Reading University, shivering in the cool air. I watch students pile in and pile out, a pang of jealousy hitting me. I remember coming here with Gran and Dustin, the thrill of excitement at what lay ahead. I was happy back then, I was unaware of what was to come. How different my life would be if I hadn't ... hadn't what? Had a baby?

I was going to ask about re-enrolling.

I stare at the gate again, feeling my lips start to tremble.

You're evil, Willow, you don't deserve that.

I turn around before tears start to form in my eyes.

You don't deserve Dustin.

You don't deserve Zara.

You don't deserve anything.

# Chapter 71

# Dustin

Georgia drops me at home and I race inside. I don't know what my plan is exactly, but I need to find Willow. 'Hi, love,' Mum calls. 'Where've you been? I've got tea on.'

I follow her voice into the kitchen. 'Mum,' I pant, breathless, 'I can't stop. I need to find Willow, she ... I never knew ... I need to tell her ...'

Mum turns to me, a strange expression on her face. Then she points at the kitchen table.

'That came for you.'

I stare at the thin envelope, with its shaky block capitals.

This time, I'm not afraid. I'm desperate for information. I tear it open.

When the object falls out of it, it takes me a while to work out what it is.

I turn the coffee shop loyalty card over and over between my fingers. And then eventually I spot it. The writing scrawled in the bottom right-hand corner.

An address.

# Chapter 72

# Willow

Another day, another coffee made by me. I'm getting good at this coffee malarkey. After rush hour it goes quiet, then lunchtime comes and it gets busy again. It's order after order, after order. Libby calls out the order, gives me the cup, I make it, call out the name. Then do it all over again.

'Almond caramel latte,' Libby calls out.

I smile to myself, a person after my own heart. I grab the cup and place it under the coffee machine, make it. It's all a natural routine. The next step, pop the lid on the cup, look at the name and call it out.

But when I read the name on the cup, I fall silent.

It says Willow.

Surely that can't be a coincidence.

And then I see him.

He's standing in front of me, his arms crossed, brow lowered, jaw clenched tight.

Dustin.

'I have forty minutes left of my shift,' I told him quickly. He said he would wait.

So then I had to carry on. It was getting busier, and I couldn't focus. Every time I'd look up, I could see Dustin, sitting on a table by the door, staring at me. Then I kept messing up my orders, my hands would be shaking, I'd forget to add coconut milk, I'd add cream when they said no cream. I couldn't focus. Libby started to catch on, her eyes narrowing at me then following my gaze to Dustin.

'Hey,' she asks me. 'What's the deal with the moody dude?' I deliberately don't look at Dustin.

'Oh ... it's just an old friend, haven't seen him for a while,' I say, popping the lid on the soy flat white that took me three attempts to make.

'Soy flat white, Martin!' I shout, placing the coffee on the surface. I turn back to Libby. 'What's the next order?'

Libby just watches me. 'You can finish now,' she says with a smile. 'Carol's joining in ten.'

I glance at Dustin. He's now looking down at his phone. He looks exactly the same, and yet so different he could be a stranger. Does that make sense? I force a smile at Libby.

'Thanks, but it's fine, he can wait,' I say. It's easier to say that rather than say I'm not ready yet. So I carry on working until Carol comes along, and I know I have no choice but to leave. I go to the cloakroom, and try to take as long as possible, spending ages taking my apron off, slowly closing and locking my locker. I go to the toilet, wash my hands three times, splash water on my face, wash my hands once more. Then, I finally accept, I have to face him.

When I approach him, Dustin looks at me, his eyes scanning

every inch of my face, and then he looks down again. 'Shall we go somewhere and talk?'

I look at him, swallowing a lump in my throat, before nodding my head. 'I'll take you to where I'm staying?'

# Chapter 73

# Dustin

Mum said she would drive me. Georgia and Elliot offered too. But I needed to do this on my own.

So I got the train up to Reading.

Then I stood outside the coffee shop for half an hour, fighting all instincts to run. Eventually I forced my feet inside, and I saw her immediately.

Willow.

Behind the coffee bar, apron round her waist, a black T-shirt underneath. She has cut her hair off, so that it barely reaches the bottom of her ears, there are dark bags around her eyes, and she looks skinny. Very skinny. She smiles at the customer she gives the drink to, as she looks at the cup for the next order. She looks happy. She is chatting to her co-worker, laughing, smiling at each new order that comes in.

I slink into a seat in the corner so I can watch without her spotting me. She has no idea I'm here. I wonder if she thinks about me at all, if she knows that she has snapped my heart in two. And just like that, all the sympathy and understanding I thought I had ebbs away. How could she have done this to me? All the time I felt like I was being torn in a million pieces, she was happily here, playing at this new life. A life without me and Zara.

Once I finally get up the confidence I order my drink from the other barista, a friendly girl with bright pink hair, who frowns as I state my name is Willow. I see her throw her eyes to Willow for a few seconds, but she doesn't say anything.

'Listen out for your drink,' the pink-haired girl says, handing me my receipt.

I nod my head and walk away. Standing at a careful distance from the bar, I watch as Willow receives my order. She smiles. Again. She makes the drink, pouring it into the cup, before looking for the name, then her smile disappears. I focus on her. Her eyes dart towards Libby, then back to the cup.

Oh, so she doesn't like confusing clues either? How ironic.

'Willow?' she says. Her voice quiet, painfully quiet, and right then she is just as she was in the early days. The nervous Willow, the shy Willow, my Willow.

'Wi ... Willow,' she says again, her voice a bit louder.

Fuck. Her voice.

It hurts.

Why did I do this? Why did I go see her? I just feel awful.

I love her.

# Chapter 74

# Willow

I am perched on the bed, whilst Dustin stands awkwardly in the middle of the room over the pub I've been renting for the last month. It's very small, it's very dark, and the light flickers. But it's cheap, and I don't need it to be a palace.

'Sorry,' I mumble. 'There's not really room for any other furniture.'

His eyes move to me, before he sits awkwardly on the bed, next to me. I look at his hand placed on the bed, so near to mine.

Neither of us speak. He looks around the room, silently. Seeing him up close, I realise how different he looks. His eyes are deep, tired, almost glazed over. I've never seen him like this before. His hair is long, slightly greasy, it might be even longer than mine. This isn't the Dustin I remember.

'So you've been staying here then?'

I nod my head. 'Yeah, it was hostels for a bit, until I got the job at the coffee shop,' I say, trying to smile at him.

His mouth twitches, but he stays quiet. I sigh nervously, trying to tuck my hair behind my ears, but it doesn't reach. Dustin watches me.

'So you cut your hair?' he says.

'Oh, yeah,' I say, surprised at the fact he talked again. 'It's grown out a bit now.'

He rubs his bloodshot eyes. 'I've never seen your hair so short.'

'Yeah,' I reply. What sort of reply is that? But what can I say? I felt completely crazed. like I wanted to erase all traces of my old life, all traces of myself, and my long hair felt like a good place to start?

I exhale, trying to get rid of the nervous fluttering in my tummy. I feel like I want to be sick. 'Dustin, where's Zara?' I ask, very quickly, and slightly high pitched.

His jaw tenses, sitting a little bit more upright. 'She's at home with my mum,' he says.

She's safe. She's good. 'So you're back in touch with your mum?'

Dustin frowns, before nodding his head. 'I live back at home now.'

Oh. Wow. I'm shocked. I don't know why because I guess it makes sense, but I fail to hide my surprise. 'Oh, really? That's really nice.'

He frowns further. 'Yes, Willow,' he says. His voice is so cold. 'Is . . . Is Zara OK?'

'Yes.'

And that's it. I don't really know what else to say. I'm trying to be nice. I'm trying to have a conversation, but he doesn't want one. But then why is he here? And let's not ignore the obvious . . . how is he here? 'Dustin,' I say, my voice shaking. I start picking at my nails. I spot him looking down at them briefly, before looking up at me. His face totally blank. Emotionless, almost. It makes me super uncomfortable, it's like looking at a stranger. 'Dustin, I have to say,' I say with a slight nervous laugh, 'it's a bit strange that you're here.'

His mouth tightens even more, his eyebrows lower, and he exhales through his nose. 'Seriously, Willow?' he says between clenched teeth.

'Well yeah, I can't just ignore it, it's strange.'

'It's strange. OK,' he mutters, exhaling heavily. He pinches the bridge of his nose, breathing slowly. 'You're messing with my head, it's not fair.' His voice is shaking now.

I look at him as he stands up, pacing the room. I can feel my nose starting to burn. 'I'm sorry.'

'No,' he says loudly. Breathing heavily, continuing to pace the room. 'You're not sorry. If you were you would stop doing it.'

I stand up. 'Wait – I'm not trying to make you feel worse.'

'No, don't say that, cos you are! I thought you wanted me to come here. I'm glad you are safe, Willow, I'm so relieved about that, but I'm so fucking angry.'

I blink heavily, my lip trembling. 'Dustin, I didn't want to see you.' He shoots me a hurt look. 'I'm not saying I'm not happy to see you,' I add hastily. 'I am, I missed you so much. I just think it's strange that you found me.'

'No, Willow,' he says sternly. He reaches into his pocket, walks up to me, and places something in my hand. 'I don't think it's strange that I'm here, I think it's strange you sent me this. You could have written a letter, you could have called, you could have let someone know you were safe, but instead you send me this, and then tell *me* you don't want to see me.'

I look at the small piece of card in my hand. It's a reward card, from the coffee shop I work at. Someone has written the address on the back.

'I think it's strange you're acting surprised I live at home, when you know full well I've been living there. Do you think I'm stupid?'

What is he talking about?

'OK,' he says, his voice angry, tired. 'You don't want to be in our lives, I get it, but don't keep sending me stuff, it's not fair. It is messing me up, just leave me alone and let me get over you.' He sniffs, wiping his cheek.

'I didn't send this, Dustin.'

'What?'

'I didn't send you this.'

'Are you lying?'

'No!'

'Well then, who sent it?'

'I don't know.'

He is silent for a moment.

'What about your necklace?'

My stomach drops. 'What?'

'I know you sent me your necklace.'

My heart is pounding, I'm scared now. 'I didn't send you my necklace.'

He glares at me, his mouth twisting. 'Well you're not wearing your necklace, and you took it with you.'

'I did, but I lost it. Weeks ago. It fell off when I was walking to work.'

Dustin looks at me, his eyes wide, frightened almost. 'The blanket? Zara's blanket, the one you knitted.'

I look at him, tears now streaming down my face. 'I left that at the flat,' I manage to mumble between my shaking lips.

'Willow, if you're lying, I swear—'

I shake my head. 'I'm not, Dustin. That's the truth.'

'Fucking hell,' he mutters. He looks away, panting heavily. Then he starts walking towards the door.

'Wait, Dustin, don't leave.'

He puts a hand up, his head still lowered. 'I just need to call my mum,' he mutters. 'I promised her I'd let her know when I found you.'

'Please come back!'

His eyes flicker to me, and he slowly nods his head. 'Just give me five, OK?'

'OK.'

As I sit on the bed, I think about what he said. And fear swims through my body. So who was sending my things to him? Why? Has someone been following me? I walk towards the door, lock it, pull across the bolt, and sit back down again.

# Chapter 75

# Dustin

I stand outside the pub and try to force oxygen into my lungs.

'So she's OK?' Mum says from the other end of the line.

'Yeah, I mean, I guess so. If anything she seems quite happy. But then in other ways she hasn't been looking after herself. She's so skinny. I'm confused, Mum.'

'Do you want me to drive and pick you up, it's only about an hour—'

'Mum, the train was fine. But thanks. Is Zara OK?'

'She's as good as gold.'

'Good.'

'You know Willow is welcome to stay with us, you know that, right? If things go OK between you.'

I find myself chuckling. 'Jesus, Mum, how times have changed. Thanks.'

'Love you, sweetheart.'

'Yep. Love you, Mum.'

I hang up, pull my hands through my hair, and hear myself groan angrily. I can't process the emotions going through my head. I see the love of my life standing in front of me, looking a state, and I want to reach out and hug her, kiss her. The mother of my beautiful child, I want to hold onto her and tell her to never leave me again, to never go away. But then I'm so angry, I'm so fucking angry at her. Angry that she left me, and that she seems to have moved on so easily when I'm so broken. I'm angry with myself for being so selfish, for not realising how much she was hurting. And I'm deeply sad for her, but happy she is safe … I try to breathe. I've got too much going on in my head.

I knock on the door. I hear Willow unlock it, unbolt it, and take a chain off. Weird.

When she opens it her eyes are wide. They're so like Zara's. Except she looks ill. Her skin is pale and she looks so tired, a shell of the girl I lived with. 'Shall we talk, properly?'

She looks at me, picking her nails. 'Yeah, that'd be good.'

I look at her, and I breathe heavily; there's been a lot of heavy breathing recently. 'So I met Jake.'

Willows eyes shoot up at me. 'Jake? What?'

I stare at her. Why does she look so confused? Did she not think I'd go digging into everything, clutching at any straws to find out if she was OK? 'Why didn't you tell me about him, Willow?'

Her face crumples. 'I don't know,' she mumbles, her voice quiet. 'I just loved talking to him, I didn't feel like I was moaning with him. He made me feel better.'

I feel a pang of guilt. Did I make her feel like she was moaning?

'You talked to him about things that you couldn't tell me.'

She looks up, nodding. 'I don't know why. I didn't even talk to Georgia about the stuff I was feeling. I know I should have talked to you …'

'Maybe I didn't let you talk to me,' I say, sadly.

I pause. She doesn't deny it, but she also doesn't agree. I sigh. 'I'm so sorry you felt so lonely, Willow.'

She stays silent, her mouth twisting. 'Jake seemed to understand how I felt,' she whispers. 'But he was a single parent, I wasn't.'

'So that was my fault.'

She frowns. 'No, I think it meant there was something wrong with me.'

I chew the corner of my lip. 'I do wish you'd told me about him though, I would have been happy you made a new friend. The thing is, when I found out about him I immediately thought the worst, I thought you guys were a thing, maybe that's why you left.'

Her eyes widen. 'No! Never! I love you, Dustin, it was never like that, until . . . ' She pauses, and I feel instantly sick. Why has she paused? Until what? 'Until one time, he tried to kiss me.'

'When?'

'It was after Gran died. We met up once and I was so devastated, I guess I hugged him, and I just didn't let go, and I said how much he meant to me . . . and I think he misunderstood and . . . '

'Right. He didn't mention that, funnily enough. So that's why you stopped talking to him?'

Willow shrugs. 'I was planning to talk to him eventually, but I was too scared. I was worried I'd led him on. I thought we had a good friendship, and I thought I had ruined it. But honestly, Dustin, I wasn't thinking about him that much. After Gran died, I wasn't thinking at all, really.'

I see her face fall, and her lip start to tremble. I want to reach over and pull her into my chest. Instead I clasp my hands together so they don't do anything stupid. 'Looking back, I

298

could have been there for you more when your gran died, especially now, understanding how you were feeling.'

She looks up at me, her eyes watering. 'She was my best friend, I still don't understand what to do without her.'

I nod my head, and I give in. I hold her hand. 'I'm sorry I wasn't there for you more.'

'You were, Dustin, you had to go back to work. I get that.'

I shake my head. 'No, but you asked me to stay, and I could have. I could have taken holiday. I was just thinking of the holiday we were going to take that summer, our first family holiday, working for our savings. Everything about it was for the future.' I pause, pulling a hand through my hair. 'I think that's where I went wrong – I was so invested in our future. So focused on it. So dedicated to it, that I kind of forgot to focus on you in the present. My present was work, my friends, but you were my future. And I'm so scared I've lost that future now.'

A single tear rolls down Willow's face and she pulls her hand away from mine.

'Have I got it right, Willow?' I ask desperately. 'Is that why you left?'

She shakes her head. 'It wasn't you, Dustin, it was me.'

I roll my eyes. 'Willow, that's such a cliché line and you know it.'

'I'm serious, it was me, it still is me. I couldn't deal with it. I was miserable every day, and it's because I'm a bad mum, it's because I'm ...'

She pauses again. Looking at me, then down towards her hands, that she is aggressively picking again.

'Willow, you were a good mum, a really good mum. Hell, since you left I didn't realise how hard it was, and you aced it!'

She shakes her head. 'No,' she mumbles, before looking up

at me with her now bloodshot wide eyes. 'Dustin, I have to tell you something about my parents.'

'Willow I—'

She breathes in, closing her eyes. 'My parents aren't dead.'

'I know,' I say quietly.

She looks at me, horrified. 'You know? How?'

'Georgia told me.'

For a moment she looks furious. 'When? How long ago?'

'Yesterday. I met up with Jake, and she told me the bits he couldn't tell me. Because you spoke to him a bit about it, didn't you?'

She swallows and nods. 'He asked.'

And there it is again. The difference between me and Jake. I never asked.

'I'm so, so sorry for what you went through, Willow. I wish you had felt able to tell me, and I'm sorry I didn't make you feel like you could.'

'That's not why I'm telling you this. I'm not accusing you. I just need you to understand why I left, why it's better that I did.'

I stare at her.

'I couldn't hack it, Dustin, and everyone could, but me. I was miserable, I was struggling every day, it was like there was weight over me; even though we had so many windows, it always felt dark in the flat.'

Her lip is trembling, and I can see her eyes start to water again. 'Willow—'

'No. I need to speak. After Gran died, I went to see my mum. I had to see her, to know for sure.'

'Know what?'

When she speaks, her voice cracks. 'Whether I was the same as her. And do you know what I realised, Dustin? I was worse. And it was only going to get harder as Zara realised how bad I

300

was. Harder for me and for her. And I couldn't do that to her. I don't want Zara to grow up wondering what she did wrong.'

'But do you not think she will think that, knowing her mum left her?'

Willow sniffs. 'No, because I'm not good to be in her life. Everyone is so happy to see her. Everyone tells me how lucky I am. But I never felt lucky. I never felt happy. What was wrong with me? How twisted is that? I couldn't feel what everyone else was feeling. I'm evil, Dustin.'

'You're not evil, Willow.'

'I am. You know when it clicked? I shouted at her to stop crying. I shouted at my baby to stop crying, because the noise drilled into my head, made me so fucking angry. How bad is that? And then ... I looked in the mirror, and I looked just like my mum. I am just like my mum.'

I hold her hand and lower my head, looking straight into her eyes. 'Willow, if you were like your mother, you wouldn't be getting so upset by it.'

She looks at me, trying so hard not to break down in tears. 'That's not true.'

'It is. Now tell me this: why are you so upset?'

Her lip trembles. 'Because I wanted to do better for her, for both of you.'

I stare at her, trying so hard to keep it together. But it hurts me, it hurts me to see her like this, I just want to hold her, tell her it's all OK, forget it happened. But I can't do that. 'I know you love her, and you miss her.'

Willow nods her head. I turn my head to the microwave, which has a dummy placed next to a coffee cup. 'That's Zara's dummy, isn't it?' Willow's eyes follow mine, and she nods her head. I smile at her. 'Now tell me that's a bad mum.'

She shakes her head, looking dead into my eyes. 'I am

though, Dustin, you don't get it. I had to leave because my head is so messed up. I can't understand it, so how could you? It's toxic.'

I finally give in, I wrap my arms around her and pull her into my chest. She breaks down, and I feel her tears soak my shirt. 'You're not toxic, Willow, you just needed help, and I wasn't there to help you.'

'Dustin, you were there to help me—'

'No, I mean, you probably need professional help, someone to talk to.'

She pauses. 'I tried to look into it, and I also tried to look into forums, but no one has issues like mine. That's what made me freak out, like I am the crazy one.'

I wrap my arms a little closer, kissing the top of her head. 'No matter how rare you think your situation is, there's got to be someone who's been there, someone who's heard it before. I really think you should consider it.'

'Maybe,' she mumbles.

'I wish you had called me, Willow.'

'I know.'

'I wish you gave more information in your letter, or let me know you were safe.'

She doesn't reply, but I think she nods her head.

'Like what were you planning to do, with this coffee shop job? Live above this pub for ever? It makes no sense.'

'I wasn't thinking of the future. I was just trying to distract myself.'

'Well you can't try and distract yourself for ever, it'll catch you up eventually, everything does.'

She nods her head, before looking up at me. Her face is red, eyes puffy. She is sniffling heavily. I so badly want to kiss her, even with the crying face. 'Can we go home?' she says.

Willow didn't even realise that I don't rent the flat in Brighton any more. She didn't even consider what would have happened with it. I had to explain that to her. I also had to explain that I love her, but just because I love her doesn't mean that things can go back to normal. My brain has been screwed. Fully screwed.

I told her she is welcome to come back to my family home for now. I didn't like the thought of her staying in that pub room, despite how safe she said it was. But she wiped her eyes, forced a smile and said she was fine.

So now she is walking me downstairs, to the entrance of the pub, and I feel powerless. I don't how to navigate the situation. A part of me wants her to come with me, another part of me doesn't want to have to deal with any of it.

I know she wants a hug. I want it too, but then I know I won't want to let go. So I turn around and start walking away. I don't know if she is looking at me, I don't really want to turn around to look. It just makes this whole thing harder.

As I'm walking away, I spot him. The guy from the park. The guy that I thought was staring at me and Zara. I recognise him now, with the big beard on his face, the tattoos on his knuckles, the piercings on his ears. The way he looks at me. I wasn't being paranoid. He's a weirdo. A fucking creep. What the hell is he doing here? What the actual hell?

I can feel anger burning through my body. 'What's your problem, mate?' I say, striding towards him. Fists clenched.

His smile fades, and he puts his palms up, calmly. 'I have no problem,' he says, his voice softer than I imagined it to be.

I take a step closer, glaring at him. 'I know who you are. You were back in New Haw, at the park staring at me, and now you're here.'

'Listen—'

'No!' I say, poking him in the chest. 'Why the fuck are you following me?'

'I'm not being—'

'Yes, you are. I thought I was going crazy, but I'm not. You're following me. What's your problem?'

He looks at me, putting a hand on my shoulder. 'Calm down, Dustin, let me explain.'

Sorry.

What?

Did he say my name? I shove his hand off my shoulder, taking an exaggerated step away from him, open-mouthed. 'How do you know my name?'

He doesn't answer me.

'How the fuck do you know my name!' I shout louder.

'Dustin, let me explain—'

'How do you know my name!'

'If you calm down—'

'Dad?'

Our heads both turn, and I see Willow standing by the entrance to the pub, staring at us both. 'Dad!' she shouts again.

'Hey, Angel,' he says, quietly.

'Dad?' I say loudly. Willow turns her head towards me, seeming to remember again I'm still here too. Her face falls. 'Seriously, Willow. I'm done with this.'

She goes to grab onto me, but I pull my arm away. 'Wait, Dustin.'

'So much for your parents being in prison. When did that change? When did you think of telling me this one? So that was another lie up there, right?'

'No, Dustin—'

'I don't want to hear it!' I shout. 'It's too many bloody secrets

304

with you. I had a kid with you, and I don't even know who you are! I literally don't even know the mother of my own kid. Secrets ruin relationships. And you've ruined it.'

She watches me, her bottom lip trembling, but she says nothing, and so I turn away.

# Chapter 76

# Willow

Dad is here.

He is in front of me.

I never really thought I'd experience this again. He couldn't have chosen any worse timing but I can't believe he is here. He looks fatter, yet healthier than how I remember. And now I am struggling to fully process it.

I run up to hug him, but then I realise I'm pushing myself away from him. He holds onto me, but I'm trying to pull away. I'm hitting his chest, pushing, punching, screaming, my eyes are blurry, my head hurts, my heart hurts. Then I eventually collapse into him, sobbing onto his chest.

He walks me into the pub garden as I dry my tears.

He watches me, stroking his beard.

'I hate you.'

He looks at me, nodding his head slightly.

'I hate you,' I repeat.

'I'm sorry, Angel,' he says. Just hearing his voice sends me into tears again. This is too much. This is bloody too much. 'I wasn't planning on you seeing me, if it helps.'

I lift my head, staring at him. 'How does that help?'

'I didn't mean to upset you.'

'No, Dad, if you didn't want to upset me, you wouldn't have been absent from my life three years, that's what upset me.' He goes to touch my arm, but I snatch it away from him. 'And then you choose now to come – how did you even know I was here?'

Dad chews on his nail. 'I've always been looking out for you, sweetheart.'

'Bullshit.'

'No, I have, I've been always checking up, I never erased you from my life, I just erased myself from yours. I lost track of you and your gran for a while, after you moved. But I stayed in Brighton, hoping that one day you'd come back. And you did. Except when you did, you seemed so happy. Happy like I'd never seen you before, not when you were around me.'

'But I needed you. It's been so hard, Dad. With Gran dying and everything.'

'I know, sweetheart, but you didn't need me, I fucked up your life.'

'I *did*.'

'I was watching, you know. I saw you when you met Jake, that day, after your gran died, when he tried to kiss you. I was watching. I was watching when you left. I saw you put the key under the flower pot, and I took it. Then I followed you here. But I knew Dustin needed you, and your little girl too, I knew she needed you. So I sent him those clues.'

My stomach sinks. 'You were sending Dustin things?'

And he tells me. All of it. About how, after he established I had checked into a hotel in Reading, he went back to Brighton. Watched the flat, saw Dustin leave, followed him to New Haw. Saw him turn his bag upside down on the train and realise he was missing the blanket he always saw Zara with. How he had

307

trailed us both for weeks, checking up on us, trying to orchestrate a way to lead Dustin to me. He'd found my necklace on the pavement when he followed me to work. He thought sending it to Dustin would show him how alone I was, how without protection I was, how much I needed him. How he knew Dustin needed to talk to Jake, that Jake was the only one I'd been confiding in. So he sent him those photographs. I listen to him in silence. The whole thing is so bizarre.

I needed a dad in my life. I thought he was dead, it would almost give me more comfort if he was dead, because then I would be able to accept there wasn't anything wrong with me. So he knew about Gran, but left me to deal with it on my own? He could have been a grandad to Zara. Why did he think I'd be better off without him? Couldn't he see anything would have been better than disappearing?

Like I did. Suddenly I am overwhelmed with the realisation of what I have done. The pain I have caused. The damage.

'You need to go after Dustin, sweet,' Dad says quietly. 'You need to face this.'

'He'll probably be nearly at the station by now. I'll never catch him.'

'I'll drive you.'

'What?'

I have never known my dad to drive. But he really is a different guy, apparently. Well you'd hope so, with it being ten years and all. It scares me thinking of it. It's been ten years since he was actually involved in my life, ten whole years. So I get into his car, and he drives me to the station. Dad says he will park, and wait for me. So I step out the car, my stomach lurching. Do I want Dustin to be there? Will it be easier if he's already gone? There's no barriers in this train station, so I go straight onto the platform. And I see him.

308

# Chapter 77

# Dustin

'So she's just been happy-chappy working at a coffee shop while we've been worried sick?' Georgia's voice booms through the phone.

I shake my head, even though she can't see it. 'I don't think she was happy, but yeah, working at a coffee shop. She hasn't told me how long, but she seemed to know what she was doing.'

'So why did she leave? What happened? Has she explained to you?'

I sigh.

'Not really. It's too long to explain right now. I'll text you when I'm home, yeah? Maybe we can go to the pub and talk.'

'Well you better do,' Georgia says, and she carries on talking, but her voice grows quieter as I notice movement in the corner. I turn my head, to see Willow standing at the end of the platform.

I sigh heavily. 'Are you OK, Dustin?' I hear Georgia on the other end of the phone.

'I don't know, Georgia,' I reply, before hanging up.

# Chapter 78

## Willow

As I walk up, he spots me, he doesn't look happy. He shakes his head as he pulls his phone away from his ear. He then grudgingly scoots up on the bench, I think indicating that I can sit down next to him. I do and we are silent for a moment, before he says, practically groaning, 'Why are you doing this to me, Willow?'

'I just wanted to know if you'd call me, whenever you feel ready?' I mumble.

He shoots his head towards me. 'And how do you suppose I do that? You've blocked me.'

'I'll unblock you.'

He clenches his jaw. 'OK.'

'Hey, I want to explain about my dad, cos I totally under—'

'Willow, please, don't bother. You weren't going to tell me until I found out, and it feels it's that way with a lot of things. Which is fine, but mentally I can't.' He pauses, and looks down at the phone in his hand. 'You should give Georgia a call, she is worried about you.'

I nod my head. 'I will.'

He looks at me, his eyes serious. 'You didn't have to cut everyone out.'

My eyes flicker down. 'I know that now.' I start picking at a tiny bit of flimsy skin on my nail. 'The whole thing about the fire and my parents wasn't a lie. They were like that, and they did get arrested.'

Dustin shuffles uncomfortably in his seat. 'I know that, Georgia told me. But when did they get out? How long have you known? I just have so many questions. This whole day has been too much, and I'm tired of it.'

I watch him sadly. He does seem so exhausted and I've done this to him. 'My mum is still in prison, it was only Dad that was let out.'

Dustin shakes his head. 'See? How do you expect me to believe that too?'

'I don't,' I say quietly. 'But I still want to explain everything to you. You don't have to believe it, but I want to say it. It's good for me to say it. I haven't really told anyone this.' I pause, and take a deep breath before continuing. 'Dad was let out for good behaviour and overcrowding, just before we moved to Surrey. That's why we moved. Gran didn't want me to be around him. But when he came out, he surprised me walking home from school. That's when I got the necklace – he gave it to me and said that he couldn't be in my life, but he'd always be there, looking out for me. Like an angel.'

I look at Dustin. His whole body is now positioned towards me, instead of away. He's actually interested in what I'm saying. 'That was just before you met me?'

I nod my head. 'He told me not to tell Gran, and then he left, and I was heartbroken. So I know I might have indicated he was dead, but for all I knew he may as well have been. I made sure to never actually say they died.' I pause, looking down, bringing my hand to where my necklace used to be. I sniff, feeling my nose start to tingle. 'Today was the first time I saw him since he gave me that necklace.'

Dustin watches me, his mouth twitching. 'Don't you think that's weird? I mean, I don't know how I can believe that, Willow. What are the chances he'd be here, at this time? He was in Surrey, in a park staring at me, I swear … Don't you think that is weird?'

I pull my hand through my hair. 'Yes, it is weird. It's really weird. It turns out that even though Dad hasn't been in my life, he's kind of always been checking up on me, on us, from afar. He was there watching the day I left. He saw me put the key under the flower pot, and he took it, thinking he might need it later. And he followed me to Reading to check where I was going. He has spent the last couple of months going between the two of us, apparently. He was following you, trying to find a way to tell you where I was without revealing himself. He's the one who sent those things to you.'

'OK, so he had the key to our apartment. I guess it makes sense that he could have got in there whilst Naomi was out. But what about your necklace? How did he get that?'

'I lost it on the way to work one day, I told you. The clasp was loose, did you notice? I thought someone had nicked it, but I guess he must have been following me and he picked it up.'

Dustin stares at me. I wish I knew what was going through his brain, but his face is blank. 'I don't know how to feel about it.'

I shake my head. 'Neither do I, my head's a mess, I'm very confused and overwhelmed right now. I'm very annoyed at him, but also, I guess … it's good … because you wouldn't have ever come if he hadn't intervened.'

He frowns at me. 'Because you would have never contacted me.'

'I know.'

'And those parcels fucked with my head, Willow.'

'I can imagine.'

He leans back, blowing out his cheeks. I watch him, and I feel my eyes begin to sting, my nose burning. I can feel myself breaking and I'm trying so hard to keep in control. But the weight is getting heavier, and it's pushing on me. I shove my hand in my pocket and stroke the dummy, but it doesn't help. It makes me hurt more, and I hate myself. For what I've done. For ruining the best thing that ever happened to me. What is wrong with me? I want a new brain. I want to be me, but not me. I want to be the me that everyone thought they knew. Not what I am now.

Dustin looks at me, his eyes growing sad. 'Willow, why are you crying?'

I shake my head. 'I'm just sad,' I whisper.

He nods his head. 'I can see that,' he says solemnly. He wipes a tear away from my cheek. 'I'm sorry, I have been very angry, but I shouldn't have yelled at you.'

I shake my head. 'It's not that,' I mumble. 'I can't explain it.'

As I look up to him, his face has grown softer. 'OK,' he says.

Oh no. I hope he doesn't think I'm just trying to get his pity. Trying to make him feel bad by crying. I'm really not. 'Now you are here, I don't want you to go, you know,' I say.

He looks at me, his face almost in pain. 'Willow ...'

'I know.'

He twists his mouth, as if he's really battling the words coming out of it. 'I don't understand what you want. I thought if I could find you it would all become clear. We'd be able to figure it out. But I can see it's not that easy. You're so sad, Willow, and I don't know if I can fix that. And I'm hurting so much, and I don't know if you can fix that either.' He pinches the bridge of his nose. 'I don't know what to do. We're at a crossroads, and I don't know which road to take.'

'Me neither,' I say.

I hear the noise of the train coming. It's his train, it's coming on this platform. This is it now, time to say goodbye. At least it was a better goodbye. I stand up and look down at him as the train stops and the door opens. 'What are you doing?' he says, looking at me.

I look back to the train – yep, it's definitely here – then back to him. 'Your train is here.'

He smiles slightly and taps the seat next to him. I slowly sit back down. 'It's OK, I want to wait till the next one.'

I sit there in silence, just enjoying being next to him, before I find myself carefully resting my head on his shoulder. He puts his arm around me. 'I just want to be in this moment for a little longer,' he says, his breath tickling the back of my neck.

'Me too,' I say, as I close my eyes.

I knew our story wasn't for ever, I knew that, I knew that as soon as I left, but I just want to hold onto the last page for a while more.

# Chapter 79

# Dustin

Four months later

I open the door and see Willow standing in front of me. Whenever I see her now, I seem to pause for a second, my words getting lost in my throat. And then I have to blink, I have to remember where I am, remember time doesn't stand still. I smile, and say, 'Hey.'

She smiles back, her eyes scanning my face, before whispering a small 'Hi.'

Then my attention moves towards the precious little girl in her arms. Zara is getting bigger every time I blink, I swear. It's only been two days since I saw her, but it feels like months. Willow hands her to me, I hold Zara and swing her around. 'Hello, my beautiful girl,' I whisper, nuzzling her neck.

Willow is standing at the door awkwardly.

'You coming in then?'

She still waits to be invited in. Every time. But she does come in.

Every time.

Two months ago we made a plan. Every weekend Willow has Zara, and I have her during the week. I won't lie, at the beginning I was shit scared. What if Willow left again, what if she took Zara with her this time? What would I do then?

But Willow is her mum, and I can't take Zara away from her. So we did it, and Willow took her on the Friday. I was an anxious mess, stressed, pacing, I didn't sleep, barely let my phone out of my sight. Desperately trying to resist the temptation to call her up and check they were both OK. And then Sunday came around, and Willow came back. She came back the Sunday after that too. And the Sunday after that. And we've been doing it every weekend since.

Oh and Zara walks now! She did it, she walks like she's a drunken guy heading home after too many pints at the pub, but she walks. Willow was there when it happened too, which made it all the more perfect.

Mum has baked a shepherd's pie (again) and she's just dishing it out when Willow and I come into the kitchen. I strap Zara into her high chair and Willow takes one of the empty seats next to Elliot. Let's state the obvious: there is always a little bit of awkwardness, forced normality. Mum has been on her best behaviour, and I'm thankful for that at least. I thought she'd be furious at Willow, but she wasn't. Weirdly, I think Mum understands her. It was her idea to start asking Willow to dinner on a Sunday.

'So how is your dad?' Alicia asks, flashing a smile at Willow.

'Yeah, he's good thanks, we're pretty good.'

Willow is now living with her dad in Reading, trying to build a sort of relationship. She is also going to do a course there part-time. Her dad is pretty involved now. It's not the relationship

316

she always grew up dreaming she'd have, because there are missed years and memories and they leave cracks. There is hurt and betrayal in her heart, but there is also her dad in her life. There is another person to love her, and I know he is looking out for her, and for that I'm happy, even if it's hard to not be sad that it's not me. He always drops her off here, and always picks her up. I don't know what he does whilst Willow is eating with us. Heads to a pub maybe, or goes for a walk. I haven't asked. Maybe one day he'll even join us for dinner. I still don't feel we're quite there yet.

After dinner we help Mum clean up, and Willow and I go upstairs to give Zara a bath, together. That was another part of our agreement. A couple of hours each week together as a three. A snapshot of a normal family.

I always find this bit hard. I'm desperate to reach out to hold Willow's hand, something so simple I took for granted. Sometimes I shove my hands in my pocket because I don't know what to do with them. Then we tuck Zara into bed, and my stomach grows uneasy. This always means she is going soon.

I still worry that she won't come back.

'So how was therapy this week?' I whisper once Zara has dropped off. We are sat side by side in the darkness of my bedroom.

She looks at me, her eyes lowering, her awkward smile falling. 'I ... uh ... I didn't end up going.'

I smile at her. 'Hey, Willow, it's cool, it doesn't matter if you miss a session. It's a journey, not a quick fix, you get that, right?'

She looks up at me, nodding her head. 'How is it going for you?'

I chew on the inside of my cheek, suddenly feeling self-conscious. She's never asked me about it before. I didn't even realise she knew I'm going. 'Yeah,' I reply, avoiding her eyes. 'It's going OK, actually.'

She smiles, placing her hand on mine. 'That's good to hear,' she says. And then we just sit there, in silence again. There is always so much I want to ask her. What is her dad's place like? What is he doing for money? Is she going to get a job? How is her university course? She doesn't talk about it. Does she like it? Is she going to stay there for ever? What does she get up to on her weekends with Zara? How is she feeling? Is she happy? Is she sad? Does she miss me like I miss her? Has she considered dating? Me? Other people?

But I never ask her any of these questions. I worry because not asking questions is half of what got us here, but now the relationship is different. I'm not her boyfriend any more. I have to give her the space she needs now. And I have a feeling that when she's ready to answer them, she'll tell me of her own accord. And she knows now, I hope, that I'll listen when she does.

Then we are hugging. I'm not sure who initiated it, but we are leaning forward, arms wrapped around each other, and it feels safe. It feels like a missing piece of a puzzle, it feels right. And I feel myself growing sadder the longer we hug, because it means the hug will end soon, and I really don't want it to. She still smells the same. I used to get annoyed by her hair flicking into my mouth but I don't any more. I used to take her for granted, I used not to appreciate our hugs, and now they are like the greatest gift in the world. I can feel her heavy heart beating against mine.

Then I hear a car horn beep.

Her dad's here.

I don't want to open the door. But I have to, so eventually, after an uncomfortable amount of time standing by the closed door, I open it. Something flashes in Willow's eyes – relief? Or sadness?

Her dad is parked outside our house and he gives a wave through the window. I force a smile, waving back, before turning back to Willow. I sigh. I hate goodbyes. But I can do it. I do it every week because I know it's not a goodbye for ever.

I have to believe Willow won't leave me for ever.

And I think I do believe it.

'Bye, Dustin, see you next Friday.'

I force a smile.

'Yep.'

# Chapter 80

# Willow

There are still times when I feel it's all too much. Living with my dad is fine, but it's not like there's no awkwardness between us sometimes. And after one particularly trying weekend with Zara – when she was constantly grizzly and I just couldn't seem to cheer her up or get her to smile, even for a second – the temptation to walk away from it all again was overwhelming. And when I dropped her off at Dustin's he had looked at me so hopefully that I felt the weight of all his expectation crushing me.

On the drive home from Dustin's I could barely speak to my dad. All I could hear was the voice in my head, the one saying it would never get better. I visualised packing a bag. But my dad must have sensed it, because as we were pulling into the drive he said: 'You know, kid, running away never solves anything. Not when you're running away from yourself.'

But that was months ago now. Since then I've started seeing a therapist. For a while, talking about everything in such detail made it all feel worse. But then, gradually, it got better. I've realised that sometimes things have to get harder before they get better.

Today my therapist said I should write a letter. To bring things round full circle. To understand how far I've come since I left that note for Dustin on our kitchen table. It started with a letter, so end it with a letter.

I take a deep breath, and I start to write.

Dear Dustin ...

# Chapter 81

# Dustin

I always feel weird the day I know I'll be seeing Willow. It feels in a way that it was easier when I didn't see her for an extended amount of time. But I have survived the day. I went to work, came home, and got Zara ready for Willow to collect her. After they leave, Alicia, Elliot and I will cook dinner together and will probably watch an episode of *Stranger Things*. Mum is out with her therapist friend.

Last week I told her I was looking to rent a place with Zara soon and she didn't take it particularly well. Started demanding what was wrong here, didn't I feel comfortable, etc. But eventually she realised that moving out didn't mean I was erasing myself from her life, but that I need to have the space to build my own as well. I can't keep sharing my bedroom with Zara. And I'm going to buy a car soon. I've been learning to drive and my instructor reckons I'm about ready for my test. Turns out I'm a pretty good driver. And it means I'll be able to take Zara to visit Willow in Reading.

Everything is OK.

Life hasn't worked out the way I planned, but I guess that's OK.

I hear the doorbell go, and I gather Zara into my arms and head towards the door.

Willow seems quiet this evening, but not in her usual, anxious way. There's a calmness about her that I don't really recognise. She asks me about my day, gives Zara a huge kiss, and says she'll see me on Sunday.

As I am heading back into the living room, I hear the tap of the post box. I hurry back to the front door and see a letter on the doormat. I pick it up and see it is addressed to me.

Hand delivered, because postmen don't deliver letters at this time. There also is no stamp and no address.

My hand hovers over the doorknob. If I open the door now, I'll catch the person who posted it, they won't have got round the corner yet. My fingers are outstretched, ready to grip, ready to open.

No.

Not any more, Dustin.

I sigh, and let my hands drop.

I pick up the letter, sit on the stairs, take a deep breath, and open it.

Dear Dustin,

I'm really glad you found me at the coffee shop. My life has changed since then. I really thought it was best that I stayed apart from you both, but I realise now that wasn't true for me. I will never be able to make up for the pain I caused you, the trust issues, and anxiety you now have. But I have loved seeing you and Zara again recently, and I'm always counting down the days till we next see each other.

I know there is an elephant in the room, and I always want

323

to talk to you about it, but never manage to get the words out. I haven't fallen out of love with you, I love you. I am very much in love with you. In fact sometimes I wish I didn't love you, so I wouldn't feel sad every time we say our goodbyes. It's not as simple as being in love though. I would love to say I want to get back together, but I don't think it's fair to do that to you again. You already put your life on pause for me when I left.

I need to know what is going on with me, and I need space to do that. Georgia once told me that I have to give all of myself to a relationship, not just hide the pieces I don't want anyone else to see. I think though that I still haven't quite worked out where those pieces are, and how to make them come together. That's going to take some time, so please don't wait for me.

I know you said you felt like we're at a crossroads and we need to choose a road. But I think I'd rather just go straight ahead for now, and not make any turns, in either direction. I know that you might not want that. You're a wonderful guy Dustin, and I know there's someone out there who can make you really happy, so I'd hate to hold you back from that. In fact, I want you to find that person in your life. I think that would make me happy too.

I considered going back to talk to my mum about everything that happened, but I've decided I'm not going to see her any more. Sometimes it's the right thing to say goodbye for good. Sometimes it's not. Sometimes goodbye just means starting again ...

W x

# Acknowledgements

I want to thank my entire family, who have been the most encouraging to me on my writing journey: Henry, Anya, Grace, Ryan – I've done it again, written another book, just like you believed and encouraged, and will always help.

Mum and Dad, you always told me to never give up with my writing, have always been there through my worries and my doubts, as well as sharing how proud you are of me – thank you! Love you!

I want to thank my agency, Bell Lomax Moreton, who represent me, and believed in me; especially Jo, my direct agent, who I can always message with any queries or questions, and who has made this process so much easier for me.

Thank you to Abby, for being the most supportive editor, helping build the foundations of this story, and then Rosanna, who took over halfway and added another beautiful layer to the journey of Willow and Dustin. I was nervous about getting a new editor, but we instantly clicked, and have enjoyed every moment of working with you.

Thank you to Francesca, Brionee, Thalia and Cath, and the

rest of the Little, Brown team for all the work you've done, as well as letting me part of the team again.

I want to thank my friends, who have always had the utmost support for me; a special shout-out to Liam, Joe, Jonny, Anthony, Gee, and Naomi.

Thanks to Karl, who I'm pretty sure is always the first person to pre-order and read my stories.

Thank you to my boyfriend Pete, who makes my head bigger every day; you always boost my confidence, and encourage me to do my best. My partner in crime – thank you!

Additionally, thanks to Pete's mum Kay, who always is spreading the word of my stories and sharing her support.

Thank you to *you* for picking up this book, and choosing to read it – you have made my dream come true.

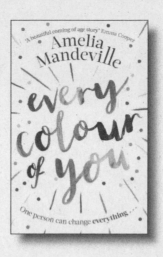

**A book to break your heart and put it back together
again – *Every Colour of You* is the unforgettable
debut novel from Amelia Mandeville.**

Zoe and Tristan couldn't be more different – which is
precisely why, when they meet in a hospital waiting room,
Zoe becomes determined to get to know Tristan more.

But Tristan is struggling with a sadness no one
seems to understand, least of all himself.

Giving up isn't in Zoe's nature, and as the two spend
more time together, it seems like Tristan might be
coming around to seeing the world the way she does.

Until one day when everything changes –
and in trying to put Tristan back together,
Zoe finds herself falling apart . . .

**'An utterly heart-wrenching tale of friendship,
love, happiness, sadness, fun and pure joy'
NetGalley reviewer**